JUMPING OVER EGGSHELLS

Bob Harvey

Jumping Over Eggshells

All rights reserved. No part of this work may be reproduced or stored in an information retrieval system without the express permission of the author.

The right of Bob Harvey to be identified as the author of this work has been asserted by him in accordance with the Copyright, Designs and Patents Act 1988.

© Bob Harvey 2023

ISBN 9798850707866

Revised edition December 2023

This book is a work of fiction. Names, characters, places and incidents are either a product of the author's imagination or employed fictitiously. Any resemblance to actual people, living or dead, events or locales, is entirely coincidental.

Also by Bob Harvey:
How To Make Your Own Video Or Short Film
Falling Through Trapdoors: A Television Adventure
www.amazon.co.uk

To Jane, James and Sarah
for their enduring patience

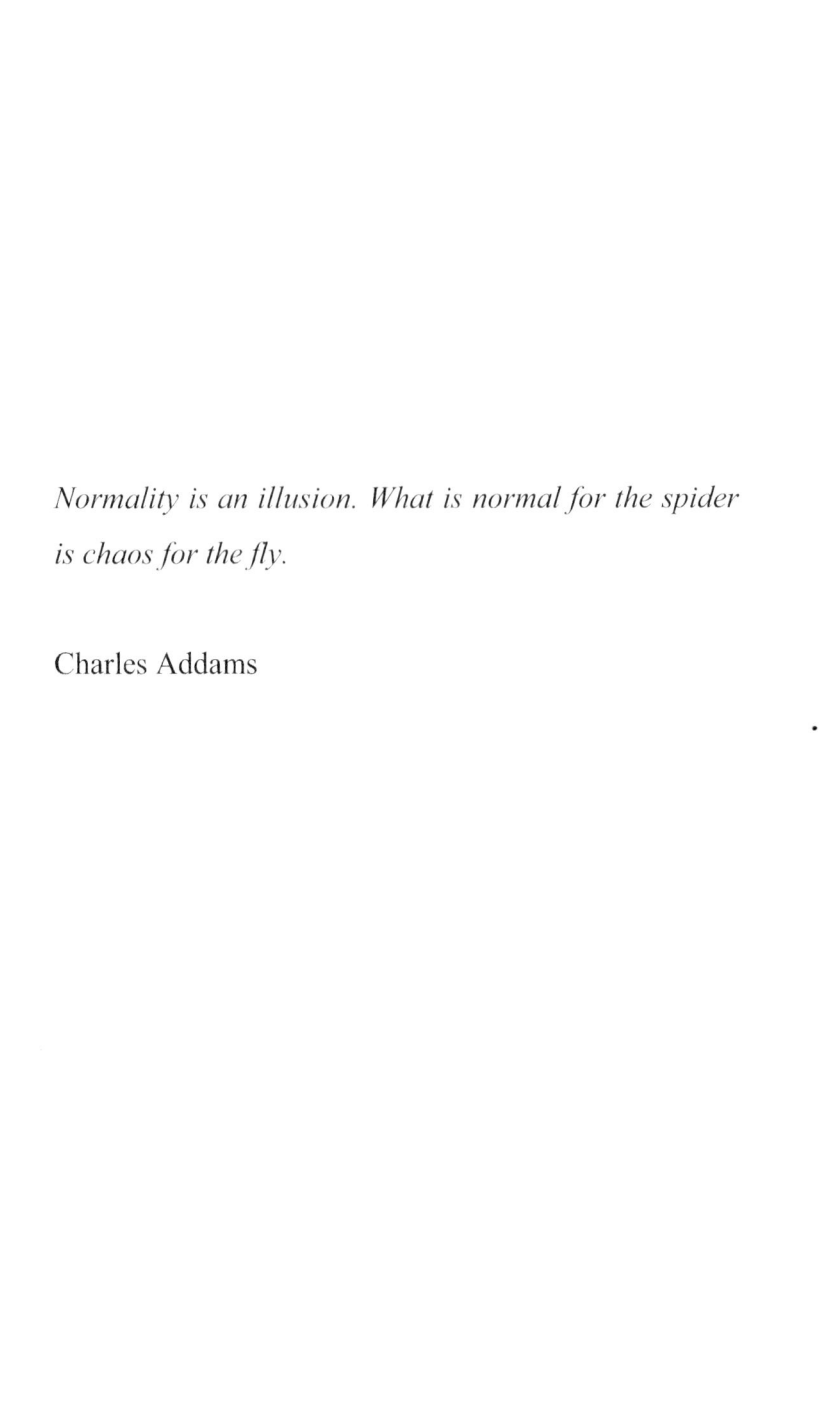

Normality is an illusion. What is normal for the spider is chaos for the fly.

Charles Addams

HOLDING ON

Olly had never experienced pain quite like it. The shock waves surged through him with an intensity that brought tears to his eyes and attacked his nerve ends in one agonising blitz. His hands, wedged between two enormous panes of glass, had become numb and lifeless as if they were no longer attached to his body, the sudden, unanticipated moment of disaster leaving them almost certainly crushed and bloodied beyond repair, his fingers throbbing as a testament to their excruciating confinement.

Only moments before he had roused himself from a particularly pleasant night's sleep and wandered into the bathroom, readying himself for another day of promise and enterprise. His only brief moment of indecision had been whether to wash his hair before shaving or even to bother shaving at all, since there was no requirement for him to present himself at work looking fresh-faced and uninhibited by any trace of stress or worry. Looking a little unkempt might even prove to be advantageous since tension and pressure were the prerequisites for his team as they battled long hours and fast-approaching deadlines.

Having run a finger over the bristles on his chin he decided that looking cool and alert was a more positive message to relay to his crew and accordingly spread a generous helping of shaving foam over his facial area in preparation for the routine assault of steel on skin. Having washed the razor under the hot tap in anticipation of a speedy and efficient tidy-up, he had paused, mindful that the apartment was stuffy and in need of an urgent injection of fresh air and walked promptly through to the living room, where the four-foot-high windows offered an appropriate degree of regeneration.

To access the windows, Olly had to step up onto the adjoining window ledge where he could reach the catch that held the two sash-cord panes in position. It was a manoeuvre he had performed on countless occasions, but this morning the mundane had turned swiftly and unexpectedly into the catastrophic. As he released the catch the sash-cord rope snapped, the downdraught taking his fingers with it and trapping them between the two giant window panes. No matter how much he wriggled and struggled, his hands would not move and he knew there was no hope of an early release unless he could attract the attention of a passer-by and solicit their help. But there was a problem.

The apartment was part of a large Victorian building situated off Queen's Park Road in Brighton, and whilst it was a busy thoroughfare during rush-hour periods, those who walked past at this hour were habitually in a hurry and focused on reaching their chosen destinations, oblivious to everything that was going on around them. Explosions, floods and sinkholes aside, it was unlikely that anything would cause them to break their journey, not least a man wearing pyjamas shouting maniacally at them with his fingers wedged in a sash-cord window and shaving foam on his face. Exhibitionists and fun-seekers were two-a-penny on the streets of Brighton and his plight elicited little response from anyone who might risk being late for an appointment unless it was a matter of life or death.

For Olly Scott, it was of immense concern, no matter how freakish or unnerving it looked from the street but despite several minutes of yelling and pleading, no passers-by risked looking in his direction, let alone give brief consideration to his situation. As the pain grew in intensity it became increasingly clear that he would not last for much longer before passing out. Urgent liberation from the situation was essential if his hands were to be saved, assuming it wasn't too late already, so he had little choice but to keep shouting and imploring pedestrians to stop being so self-absorbed and come to his aid.

As the minutes ticked by he realised that the commuter rush-hour would soon be replaced by the school run. As the shaving foam began dripping down his top and his pyjama bottoms slid down to his ankles, the alarming prospect of him traumatising young children and being arrested for exposure became of more immediate concern. He was, after all, standing naked at a window, on a busy Brighton street, looking every inch a prime candidate for early committal and it was not inconceivable that he was deemed too fearsome to approach, let alone engage in conversation. Those who took a perverted interest owing to more voyeuristic tendencies might, at any moment, start knocking off photographs to distribute indiscriminately on social media, putting an undeserved stain on his unblemished character whilst causing him the ultimate humiliation.

As his vocal cords began to protest at his futile endeavours and the cries became more feeble, Olly tried to take his mind off the mangled digits squeezed into their cavity of horror by analysing what misfortune had led him to be in this bizarre predicament. He had been clumsy for as long as he could remember, even though he had never questioned whether it was hereditary or if his misadventures might simply be attributed to extreme bad luck. Were any of the incidents involving revolving doors, wobbly stepladders, hazardous chemicals and slippery floors just random disasters that could befall anyone, or was it fate, or perhaps some undiagnosed malady that affected 0.5 per cent of the population as might be suggested in the *Daily Mail* ahead of scientific confirmation in *The Lancet* or *The British Journal of Psychiatry*?

Whatever it was, it had become a massive inconvenience and one that was about to ruin his life. Up to this moment, he had always found a way to divert attention and extricate himself from the most compromising of situations, but it seemed his apparent good fortune in side-stepping revelation and jeopardy had finally hit stony ground. As he stood pinned in agony to a window frame that refused to offer any hope of escape, he knew that full, unequivocal disclosure was the inevitable finale to the self-destructive chain of events that had caused so much consternation to everyone who knew him.

SETTLING IN

'He's a regular child, just like any other, so stop fretting, it won't do you any good.'

'It's not that simple. You have no idea. I turned my back for a few seconds and when I looked round he'd run his pedal car over Erica's feet because he wasn't looking where he was going, knocked over the Lego tower she'd been building and crashed into the table, sending my cake mixture sliding to the floor and covering it in goo. Does that sound normal to you?'

'I'm sure he didn't do it on purpose, Helen. He's testing boundaries, that's not unusual in a child of his age.'

'Well he's pushing my bloody boundaries beyond any acceptable limit. You're not here all day having to be on red alert, hardly daring to take your eyes off him, wondering what he's gonna do next. I'm going out of my mind and you seem oblivious to the problem.'

Martin Scott put his hands on his wife's shoulders, aware that she was becoming distraught and desperate to calm her down. 'It's just one episode. I'm sure everything will be different tomorrow and less stressful.'

'Or ten times worse, like Tuesday when he knocked an entire bottle of bubble bath into the tub to the delight of the clockwork duck, which he then removed, resulting in foam being sprayed all over us by a pair of manically flapping wings. I had to wipe Erica down with the bath mat because the towel got soaked. And he thought it was hilarious.'

'Better to have him laughing than crying, he's no different to any child of his age.'

'But he *is* different. The things he does are not normal.'

Martin's face registered instant unease. 'You shouldn't think like that. He's experimenting with his independence, vying for attention, so it's important not to have a sense of humour failure and let him think he's winning any emotional battles.'

Helen turned away, freeing Martin's arms from her shoulders. 'It shouldn't be a battle. He needs to know when he's crossed the line. You try dressing a two-year-old while your four-year-old son is running rampage around the place.'

'I do understand and I wish I could do more to help.'

'Then maybe we should switch roles. You stay here and look after them and I'll go to the office and tap away on a keyboard.'

'You know that isn't a practical alternative.'

'Just for twenty-four hours. Phone in sick, then you can exercise your newly acquired skills as a paediatrician while I exercise my freedom of expression and take a packed lunch to the park for the day.'

He studied her for a moment wondering if she was serious. When he realised she was, he held up his hands to acknowledge that a young and inexperienced father should know better than to doubt the wisdom of a beloved partner who had faced the unique and curious combination of pain and joy that accompanies introducing a newborn to the world.

'He will grow out of it, Helen, we just have to be patient and I'll do what I can to help. Spend more time with him to give you some space and relieve the pressure.'

She appreciated the gesture and although she knew it would not be that easy, felt relieved that they had at least discussed it. Now that Martin was more aware of the problem and how the situation was affecting her, there was a chance that with his full support, Olly would, over time, discard his destructive tendencies and settle into a more acceptable pattern of behaviour.

When the Scotts had moved into the first-floor council house flat in Chelmsford Avenue two years previously, the property had needed extensive decorating and was not particularly inspiring, looking out as it did over a busy road at the front and an extensive array of allotments at the rear. But there were compensations: a well-maintained village green, local shops and schools within walking distance, and an opportunity to grow an abundance of fruit and vegetables which, with soaring food costs, would ease the burden on their finances. They were just starting out, with limited resources, but they had high hopes for the future and were grateful for whatever help came their way and having a roof over their heads was something to be thankful for. Olly's arrival had prompted the move to Chelmsford Avenue two or three years before they felt they were ready to start a family, but Helen and Martin were determined to make the most of the situation.

A new baby brought with it the customary mix of pleasure and anguish, and although Olly was an alert, happy chap, he displayed a tendency to create a trail of mini-mayhem in a variety of disturbing ways. Such as climbing up on a chair at the sink to help dry the washing up, oblivious to the consequences of handling wet crockery when it is slippery and powerless to defy gravity, inevitably ending up in pieces on the kitchen floor. And if he messed around pressing the buttons on the answering machine he would wipe all the messages until Martin realised what had happened and mounted it on a shelf out of his reach.

But whilst Olly's behaviour was exasperating at times, Helen was reassured by the mothers at her playgroup that all toddlers found different ways to express themselves and one day she would look back and have a good laugh at his antics.

By his fifth birthday, Helen had learned to overcome her anxieties for the most part by embracing his clumsiness and laughing it off, since going with the flow was a much better option than allowing insanity to slowly take hold.

October 28. Helen Scott's telephone message to her mother.
We were having a birthday party for Olly today, which had to be cancelled due to him almost setting fire to the sitting room before I'd even had a chance to light the candles on his cake. I'd only gone to the kitchen for a few minutes so that I could ice my Magic Firestation cream sponge creation and sprinkle a handful of hundreds and thousands over it to make sure some of them actually went on the cake and not over the floor, but it was, as usual, mission impossible.

In my absence, Olly had unclipped the fireguard and removed one of the lit kindling sticks. When he heard me coming back into the room he panicked. Faced with the choice of throwing it back into the fire or hiding it under the armchair, he chose the armchair. It took me a moment to find out where the burning smell was coming from and after a brief moment of hysteria, threw the tablecloth over the chair and the water from the flower vase. When I'd doused the flames, the damage was surprisingly widespread considering the short time it had to create a mini fireball.

When two of the mothers turned up with Olly's pals carrying presents they didn't seem in the least surprised that there had been a near disaster and the party was off. They deposited their presents and left with sympathetic gestures and assurances that we would try again when the dust had settled, or more fittingly when the smoke had cleared and our faces could be more easily identified when they weren't covered in black smudges.
When the children had been safely quarantined in the kitchen occupying themselves with colouring books, and Martin bowled in fifteen minutes later, having missed all the fun, his bewilderment could be heard several streets away.

'What the fuck!? How did this happen?'

'We had an incident. Nothing serious.'

'There's a fire engine outside.'

'Yes, Olly was very excited when *that* turned up.'

Helen sat rosy-cheeked on the blackened armchair, with clumps of burnt stuffing scattered around a severely singed rug, waving a glass of Chardonnay, a leg swinging in gay abandon over one of the arms. 'One of the neighbours phoned the fire brigade when they saw smoke billowing from the windows, which I did have the presence of mind to open, in your absence, to avoid asphyxiation. Personally, I didn't think it was necessary because we're all perfectly fine.'

'But you could have been killed! First-degree burns, smoke inhalation, God knows what. There'll be an investigation, police, insurance. And the furniture's ruined.'

'Not all of it. We needed a new armchair anyway. Pour yourself a glass of wine.'

Martin was taken aback by her lack of concern. He walked over to the table where a depleted bottle of Chardonnay stood as an unblemished bystander amidst the scene of charred devastation. He picked it up and regarded her with an exasperation he found difficult to disguise. 'Is this what it's come to, Helen?'

'It's a birthday drink. A recognition of Olly's fifth wonderful year with us on Planet Earth. Don't you think that's a cause for celebration?'

Martin put the bottle back on the table. There was little point in engaging in discord. His family was safe, that was all that mattered, and he felt more than a modicum of guilt that he had not been on hand to share the multi-tasking that inevitably accompanies a child's birthday party. 'I'm sorry, I should have been here, taken the day off.'

Helen laughed. 'You'd need to take the bl`oody year off if you want to help avert our unique tendency for domestic misfortune involving a son who's completely unaware of the consequences of his actions.'

'Then we'll have to do our best to keep him away from anything combustible, electrical, inflatable or sharp. Matches, toasting forks, kitchen knives, plug sockets, exposed wires, or buttons, switches and levers of any kind.'

'Yes! That's the answer!' exclaimed Helen, slopping her wine glass around in a gesture of exaggerated enthusiasm. 'Keep him inside his personal exclusion zone. Order a hundredweight of bubble-wrap to stop him from participating in life and bothering everyone. Why the fuck didn't I think of that?'

'You're upset and not being rational and taking what I'm saying out of context.'

'There is no context, Martin. There's very little we can do to shield him from what the future is going to throw at him. Containment won't solve the problem because he's not inarticulate or stupid, he's very much aware of what's going on around him. He just has more difficulty than most in controlling the unnatural order of things, keeping disaster at bay like thousands of adults attempt to do daily. And one day he'll walk out that door, or over it, or through it, on a personal quest to discover his place in the world, finding his own ways to adjust, because that is what being human is about – adapting to changing situations while accepting that life is generally not fair and understanding the importance of creating mechanisms and attitudes that can help cope with its unpredictability.'

'So what do you suggest we do before he sets off on his big adventure? Give him space to experiment with limited interference on our part? Let him run amock? Destroy the building, maybe the entire street?'

'You know that's not what I meant. He should be able to experiment but we also have to find ways to distract him. Rather than shout at him, or reprimand him, which always has a negative effect, we use misdirection. If he's using a building block to beat a new shape out of a biscuit tin, we tell him what a wonderful job he's done on reshaping the tin, even though the pile of broken biscuits inside may not be as fun to eat as whole ones that depict his favourite cartoon characters, and perhaps he could use that particular skill to crack open a bowl of pistachios that mummy needs for her special ice-cream. Not necessarily using those particular words but as long as he understands that we're not directly condemning his act of misplaced creative intensity but redirecting his energies to something more useful and rewarding. We're just replacing negative vibes with positive ones.'

Martin paused for a moment to take in the potential advantages of playing risky mind games with their son as an alternative to adopting a more disciplined approach. 'I'm prepared to give it a shot. Anything's worth a try if it reduces our anxiety levels.'

'The idea is to help him as much as us, Martin. I don't think anyone outside the family circle becomes particularly stressed by him. Most people probably haven't even noticed he tends to create havoc out of nowhere.'

'Not even the other parents at the school? Neighbours? Milkman? Postman?'

'No, I'm quick to mount a cover-up operation the minute I see the warning signs. Everyone's wrapped up in their own problems to concern themselves with what Olly's doing, so please stop worrying about what anyone else thinks, our son will be the last thing on their minds.

November 6. Adele Chivers, a parent at Olly's school, sending an email to a friend.
Had a terrific time last night, though we were all on edge in case Helen turned up with Olly. Letting him loose with fireworks exploding around us would have reduced my

nerves to shreds apart from putting the other children at risk, which is why we hadn't mentioned we were organising a bonfire party. Having Olly around is hazardous enough at the best of times so although I'm sure he would have enjoyed it, it was a precaution we had to take to avoid another unfortunate incident like last year, which I know we'd all prefer to forget.

November 10. Mr Bukhari, owner of Bukhari's Grocery Store, in a note to his assistant.
Linda, I will be out all morning with the distributors. Mrs Scott usually calls by on a Friday morning to collect her order of bread and croissants accompanied by her son. Can you please make sure the step-up is removed so he cannot reach the counter and, just to be sure, move the sweet jars to the back, in particular the sherbet dabs and jumbo jelly beans. The liquorice strips should be placed well out of reach and it might be an idea to cordon off the cereal packets and replace the Krispie Korns with an OUT OF STOCK label. But keep the broom handy just in case.

Helen's mother, Christine, in a telephone message to her daughter.
Helen, you really shouldn't worry too much about what Mrs Chapman said. Teachers have a habit of dramatising things and if she was aware of Olly's partiality for testing and rearranging anything with moving parts she shouldn't have included him in the puppet workshop tour in the first place, exposing his hypersensitive fingers to rows of wooden arms and legs suspended on strings, surrounded by pots of paint and glue, so frankly I blame her. Olly is an exceptional child with the occasional odd quirks, so stop being paranoid and have a chat with Dr Lowry. I have every confidence he'll offer reassurance and some positive guidance. And give the little monkey a hug from me. Olly, not Dr Lowry.

'You think we should see some kind of educational psychologist? You told me you weren't worried.'

Helen could see that Martin was disturbed by the prospect of seeking outside help, as if they had missed something important, or, worse, it was an admission of failure. 'It's more wanting confirmation that he's a well-adjusted child who needs a high level of motivation to help him find out what makes everything tick. Or not tick. Or would tick if he had an opportunity to pull it apart and put it back together again.'

'In which case, I'd be more interested in what Dr Lowry believes makes *him* tick.'

'So you agree we should arrange an initial consultation? To put our minds at rest?'

'If it makes you feel happier, yes, but we should try and pre-empt some of the areas we've already tried to address, like a lack of concentration that diverts his attention and makes him oblivious to his surroundings, or when he loses interest in a conversation or a particular activity.'

'Because he has a vivid imagination that side-tracks him as opposed to him suffering from some form of mental or physical impediment?'

'That's only how we see it. Lowry can only make an initial assessment on the information we give him and since he'll have limited time to observe Olly in person, it'll be traits in his behaviour that we haven't given close attention to that might provide a clue as to how to go forward.'

Helen's optimism drained from her face as she assessed the implications of Martin's remarks. 'But what if it is something more serious than a lack of concentration? An undiagnosable condition maybe, or something genetic?'

'Do we know anyone in our ancestry who might fit that profile?

'I had an uncle who spent his spare time trying to invent a thyme machine for growing herbs and spices at hyperspeed in his garden shed. The gadget was constantly falling apart and causing injury to him and damage to the shed.'

'There's a difference between being clumsy and eccentric, Helen. Olly's a remarkable individual with a unique personality, so if there is something we're unaware of, or don't understand, the sooner we know what it is the better.

Dr Angus Lowry, speaking into his Dictaphone.
I met with a delightful couple this morning, Mr and Mrs Scott, who had concerns about their son Olly's predilection for attracting physical misfortune and its impact on those around him. We discussed his behaviour at length so that we could eliminate the possible causes and I offered reassurance that clumsiness in one so young is generally not a clinical condition because he is trying to master many new skills at once and the greater the activity, the more likely the chances of accidents.

Most children have a natural tendency to run into objects or other children, although a child who is noticeably clumsier and lags behind in motor skills, may have developmental coordination disorder - dyspraxia - but since Olly has no trouble handling and manipulating objects with surprising dexterity, I told them it was probably safe to cross that off the list.

Degenerative or progressive disorder, such as muscular dystrophy or juvenile arthritis I have also discounted and am more inclined to agree with the Scotts that Olly is a human whirlwind of activity who keeps his mind and body working at maximum intensity, with lapses of concentration that lead to occasional mishaps. My conclusion, therefore, is that Olly is a perfectly healthy child and I see no reason why he should not mature into a normal adult, free of such physical incumbencies, and it's unlikely the Scotts will have very much to worry about.

SAFE DISTANCE

She stood outside the barn listening to the alarming sounds that came from behind the large rickety door. She had been warned by her parents not to venture inside and although curiosity had often got the better of her, she stopped short of stepping into the unknown for fear of what she might find. For these were no ordinary noises emanating from the enormous void that separated her from the familiar world she knew outside in the grounds of Blackberry Farmhouse. Not the usual drilling, banging or sawing she heard coming from the other nearby outbuildings, but a frightening array of grinding and rattling, accompanied by formidable mechanical clanks and powerful electrical crackles. It was a mystery that had terrified yet intrigued her for as long as she could remember but she knew there might be consequences if she attempted to explore the hidden world that beckoned beyond its forbidden boundary.

The other rooms held no such secrets and although she was free to wander around the rest of the seventeenth-century Grade II listed farmhouse with its unique features and maze of corridors, she felt safer staying within the confines of her bedroom, making occasional visits to the sitting room and, of necessity, the kitchen. Her parents, Sylvia and Norman, had tried not to impose too many restrictions on her even though danger lurked in many of the rooms, from unstable floorboards to walls with exposed pipes and wires that needed attention when time and money permitted, the more hazardous of the rooms remaining permanently locked as a precaution.

For six-year-old Emma Appleby, this was home, whatever the drawbacks of living in a remote period property and she was sensible enough to know which areas to avoid and which offered safe passage as she went about the daily business of doing her homework and helping her mother prepare breakfast and lunch. This occasionally involved lending a hand baking cakes and biscuits, despite Sylvia's unorthodox method of producing consumables that looked anything but desirable or even safe to digest. In truth, both parents were possibly the biggest risk to Emma's physical well-being and sanity even though they did their best to protect her; an odd couple who led an unconventional lifestyle, indulging in questionable hobbies and freaky seasonal rituals when they weren't whisking her off in their motor home on a quest to create in her an awareness of the wonders of the outside world.

It was, for the most part, a wasted effort, since Emma had little interest in accompanying them on endless treks over fields and meadows peppered with muddy footpaths and brambles or taking picnics near rippling streams and bluebell woods. All were discounted as being excruciatingly boring and full of potential hazards that only an idiot would expose themselves to.

Emma was a solitary child, preferring her own company to that of other children or adults, no matter how kind or attentive they might be, which was not always the case, since most regarded her as an oddball who lived with her even weirder parents. Emma had accepted for most of her childhood that this was the way things were meant to be. An acceptance that she would spend much of her time in isolation, enduring a routine that held no lifelong ambition until one Christmas, Sylvia, desperate to introduce her to new experiences, took her to the local theatre to see a pantomime. Emma was filled with trepidation until the moment she stepped into the auditorium and was captivated by its ornate columns and beautiful chandeliers and rows of excited children who sat enthralled inside a magical domination inhabited by pirates and a boy who flew out of the sky and into her reinvigorated imagination.

Peter Pan opened Emma's eyes to a realm she had never dreamed possible and discovering more about the theatre became an obsession; a fascination that motivated her to borrow books from the library and trawl the internet to learn as much as she could about how plays were performed. She made mock-up stages from shoe boxes and cereal packets and whilst she was fearful of many of the creatures that lurked within the rafters and along walls of Blackberry Farmhouse – the rats and squirrels and even more detestable spiders – she occasionally appropriated the odd field mouse to play a character part until it lost interest in the strange environment it had been introduced to with its odour of smelly socks and stale cornflakes and scurried off in search of more stimulating pursuits.

Once her curiosity had been aroused by the endless possibilities that life had to offer, Emma became more willing to explore other avenues of interest. Whilst she remained cautious, she knew that one day she would have to face her fears and open the locked doors that ran along the musty corridors and venture into the barn that held so many mysteries, as ominous and forbidding as they were.

TRIAL RUNS

Growing pains. That was something Helen and Martin had talked about constantly when Olly was a child, although it was never clear whether they considered the pain of emotional upset to be of more consequence than physical anguish. Olly had suffered his fair share of both over the years and despite the predictions of numerous experts that he would overcome such temporary misfortune, he continued to be tormented by his inability to conform to society's expectations of what was considered acceptable behaviour long after his childhood days had been left behind.

Moreover, the adult world had presented a fresh set of hurdles for him to clear, intensified, at the age of eighteen by an epic lack of confidence when it came to tackling everyday tasks such as finding work or establishing meaningful relationships with the opposite sex. His inability to foster long-term friendships had only served to amplify an inferiority complex that threatened to wreck his chances of finding any social momentum in an overwhelmingly judgemental grown-up environment.

In the workplace, he was confronted by a cold ensemble of female aloofness that he found relentlessly off-putting, his self-esteem being knocked on a regular basis. He may not have been traditionally handsome in the Bradley Cooper mould, but at six foot two, with light brown wavy hair, an enviable complexion and expressive blue eyes, he was not unattractive, more not having the ability to use his looks to advantage by being outwardly self-assured and assertive. Lacking the necessary conviction to do either, he opted to focus on finding his way in the world without concerning himself with the mysterious whims and motivations of the inscrutable opposite sex.

Easier said than done. His first job was at the local garage, where his father had been taking his car for servicing for several years and had persuaded the owner, Terry, to take on Olly as a junior in the spares department. Here he was tasked with keeping track of replacement parts, ordering them in when stock was low and taking them down to the work area when needed. What moment of insanity had led Terry to agree to employ a lad with limited work experience who knew nothing about cars was never openly discussed, but the assignment lasted a mere six weeks due to Olly discovering an unwanted comic intensity in negotiating the lubricous floor and finding the assortment of gearboxes, batteries and radiators difficult to manoeuvre.

It was a job made all the more precarious by the demoralising presence of Jill the receptionist, whose early flirtations with him degenerated with lightning speed into surly stares from behind her glass partition as she observed, with jaw-dropping regularity, his unique ability to initiate a catalogue of accidents, from smashed tail-lights, oil spillages and rubber tyres rolling around out of control, causing unremitting chaos on the garage forecourt which impacted on the schedules every time the mechanics had to stop and clear up the mess.

Linton's supermarket offered little respite from hazards when he was tasked with transporting perishable goods on trolleys with wheels that had minds of their own, and his efforts to operate a forklift truck at a goods depot, despite a week of intense tuition, led to him being hurriedly escorted from the premises to stem the number of incidents being recorded in the accident workbook from reaching historic proportions.

His two-week trial run as a wine waiter at Boseby's Restaurant merits no further dissertation, as does his three-day stint at the SewToBed garden centre, watering the houseplants and transporting earthenware pots and ornaments around on a rickety trailer. He did, however, have the benefit of experiencing his first sexual encounter with Bronwyn from Plants and Shrubs behind one of the potting sheds one overcast afternoon when the centre was unusually quiet, in contrast to Bronwyn who was exceptionally noisy. Fearful that his future as a nurseryman might be jeopardised by the abandonment of his duties for more carnal pursuits courtesy of the over-zealous and persistent Bronwyn, he requested early release on account of an adverse physical reaction to his daily encounters with the multifarious plant life.

By the age of twenty, Olly had tried a variety of career options and although he managed to steer clear of exposure to heavy machinery, trailers, trucks and hazardous chemicals, he found he had an alarming ability to bodge the simplest of tasks. This included jamming the photo-copiers during his two-week stint at the Kopy Kare print shop, to working as an operative in the TradeTreats store fetching household goods and delivering them to customers who were waiting at selected counters, consistently dropping them en route or mixing them up and having to fill in an endless stream of returns slips. A fellow operative called Azuka found Olly's unintended antics a welcome diversion from the monotonous conveyor belt of domestic appliances that passed before them, her initial affection for him wavering one afternoon during a coffee break when he confessed to the various workplace disasters he had trailed in his wake. She smiled sympathetically, offering reassurance that everyone experienced the fumble factor at times and if he was having such difficulty tackling routine career options, think how much worse it would be if he was an air traffic controller. Olly thought he may have finally met a kindred spirit but, concerned that his ineptitude might reflect on her own abilities, she left the store five days later and he never saw her again.

Growing pains. Do they have an infinite lifespan? Can we ever discard them or do they simply follow us around? Or was the simple truth that in Olly's case they had attached themselves to him, and to him alone, in perpetuity? Was the intense pain he was now suffering with his hands jammed inside a sash-cord window payback for past misdemeanours and if so was there any way on God's perverse, unfathomable earth, such unwelcome notoriety could have been avoided?

    Whatever he tried, Olly had never been unable to put a stop to his escalating catalogue of misfortune;

mishaps that had become accepted as predictable and inevitable and one of his greatest regrets was that so many people had been put to so much trouble in so many ways as far back as he could remember.

UPSTAGED

Mrs Baskins, Headmistress of Packham Junior in an email to her staff.
Despite our best efforts, Olly Scott continues to be a disruptive presence throughout the school, with unpredictable episodes that materialise out of nowhere and are generally the result of him becoming frustrated or bored. We all recognise that he's a lovely chap, extremely bright and creative, but when he loses concentration his behaviour tends to have an unsettling influence on the other pupils - so in his final year and with crucial exams about to take place, we need to find ways to keep him stimulated but not unruly and to help him as much as possible, particularly after today's extremely upsetting incident.

'Where does it hurt the most, Olly?'

Immobilised and looking sorry for himself as he sat on a hospital bed nursing several cuts and bruises, Olly raised his heavily bandaged wrist and winced in response. 'It's not as bad as it was this morning.'

'That's because of the painkillers, Olly,' said Helen as she watched him with her customary concern. 'It's going to ache for a few days and take a couple of weeks to heal but the doctor said it's not too serious so you'll be able to go back to school soon.'

'You were lucky,' said Martin, less sympathetically. 'It could have been a lot worse. What were you thinking? Wasn't operating one remote-controlled plane enough?'

'It's boring flying one when you can have three whizzing about in all directions.'

'Which you managed with disturbing success. One crashed through the gymnasium window, another skimmed through the flower beds decapitating half the daffodils, and the third missed taking you out completely. Mrs Baskins is not best pleased, to put it mildly. She's having to write to every parent apologising for exposing her charges to unauthorised dangerous playground activity and will have to spend an inordinate amount of time filling in forms and explaining what happened to health and safety officials.'

'It would have been alright if one of the levers hadn't stuck. It had a sort of domino effect.'

'Well she's banned all motorised gadgets from being taken onto school property and declared the playground a no-fly zone, so you'll have some apologising to do once you're back on your feet and you can thank your lucky stars you're still in one piece and able to have that opportunity.'

'And don't think you're excused from your studies while you're stuck at home,' added Helen, 'because the school has sent over enough textbooks to keep you occupied while you decide if you want to play catch-up with your pals and pass your exams, or continue to play the fool. It's your choice.'

Olly sheepishly nodded his agreement. The upset he had caused the school was immense and the pain he was feeling throughout his body was enough to warn him that it was time to become a more responsible human being and not allow any unnecessary distractions to put him at a disadvantage with his peers.

Aged twelve he had managed to take control of his clumsiness for the most part through the disciplines of school, particularly his love of history, and a domestic timetable of jobs set by Helen, with occasional lapses that had not proved too calamitous or costly, until his stunt-flying antics backfired spectacularly with far-reaching consequences.

Once he had recovered and returned to school, he found himself excluded from the gymnasium and chemistry lab, along with any activity involving machinery or apparatus generated by either mains electricity, pullies or batteries. As a result, he had to spend most of his time studying alone in his classroom or the library. Olly thought this to be way over the top considering his foray into the complexities of radio transmission was an accident and he had not meant to scare the hundred or so pupils who had been forced to flee in terror as they were being dive-bombed by small-scale F3H-2 Demon fighter jets.

Desperate to free himself from this unjust exile, he scanned the school noticeboards for anything that might be classified as Olly-proof, and came across a request for pupils to take part in the school play. This appealed to him immediately; an activity that offered a creative outlet and a chance to redeem himself. His involvement in drama and the new unexplored disciplines of theatrical performance would, however, due to a complication he could not have seen coming, turn out to be both his salvation and his nemesis in the coming years.

By the time Olly was preparing to leave Packham Junior and transfer to the local high school, Helen and Martin felt a sense of relief that their son seemed to have conquered his unyielding knack for unpredictable misadventure and such erratic behaviour was now the exception rather than the rule.

Martin had proved himself a valuable asset to the IT company he worked for with his exceptional talent for developing security software for large corporations and select foreign governments. This new status allowed the Scotts to leave their rented accommodation in Chelmsford Avenue and buy a three-bedroom house in Havering Road, considered to be a moderately upmarket area. Whilst ground-breaking IT developments made Martin an authority on global security, they also reinforced his general mistrust of the world, compelling him to carefully vet new clients when he was approached to create specialist software, whilst generating a growing suspicion of the information highway, in particular fake news and any form of propaganda that he felt posed a threat to society.

Olly was naturally oblivious to the general scepticism and anguish taking place on the world stage, concentrating instead on his new-found venture in the smaller but exciting world of fictional drama that took place regularly on the school stage. This came courtesy of the deputy head's newly penned masterpiece *The Pirates of Barnacle Island*, which he embarked on in his final year with his good friend Felix, who could tap the William Tell overture on his teeth among his many curious talents in the field of the performing arts.

At auditions, Olly had proved himself more than capable of handling a leading character role and was accordingly given the part of Captain Scar, for which Helen made an impressive pirate tunic, complete with a sash, and a cardboard sword. She also painted a red scar across his cheek, which Olly was particularly proud of. The convincing black beard she made for Felix, who, being a sporty type of muscular build with jet black hair and dark, alert eyes, would have made him a fearsome buccaneer if he had not been given the role of barman at the Barnacle Arms. He had been curiously overlooked for pirate duty to allow one of the girls to execute her acting skulduggery away from the conventional role of housemaid or cook. In the seventeenth century, Felix was assured, many women disguised themselves as men to enable them to sail the seven seas in search of adventure and buried treasure.

Rehearsals proved more of a challenge than either Olly, Felix or Mr Bradshaw – Bradders – the deputy head and creator of this swashbuckling saga had imagined. Some of the children had turned up with knitted parrots because they had seen them perched on the shoulders of pirates in picture books, one arrived with a peg-leg, another with an eye patch. Bradders ruled out the parrots and the peg-leg, the latter mainly for safety reasons, but retained the eye patch as he felt it added a touch of authenticity. On their first get-together, he instructed everyone to take their positions so they could rehearse the first scene of the pirate ship approaching land, with Olly waiting, sword and pistol in hand, ready to launch himself into his ferocious portrayal of Captain Scar.

'Okay, everybody, stand by,' shouted Bradshaw. 'And cue!'

Olly walked to centre stage barking his commands, but his lack of spatial awareness in a small area created general confusion and disarray as he moved about, swishing his cardboard sword with little regard for the safety of his fellow actors as he bumped into the various prop cannons, pulleys, and masts, before falling headlong over a stack of coiled ropes.

Believing, naively, that Olly was finding it difficult to work his thespian magic in such a confined space, Bradshaw suggested he should perhaps make his appearance swinging onto the stage from one of the rope ladders.

Olly looked up at the ladder, which stretched some six feet above his head. 'You want me to swing in from the top of that, Sir?'

'Yes, do you think you can do that, Scott?'

'I'll give it a try, Sir.'

'Good lad, tell me when you're ready.'

Olly looked around at his classmates, who looked on in hushed anticipation. Unphased by their anxious demeanour, he clambered up the ladder in an erratic swaying motion until he reached the top and looked down nervously, realising it was a great deal higher looking down than it was looking up.

The ensuing pandemonium that followed after Olly swung onto the stage, destroying the ship's wheel and two barrels of fake rum, resulted in him being demoted to the role of village baker and spending the duration of the rehearsals handing out paper-maché bread rolls to the ensemble cast. With first rehearsals over for the day, Bradshaw - who took consolation in the fact that it might have been a lot more calamitous if Olly had been wearing one of the eye patches - took him down to his classroom and sat him in a chair opposite the whiteboard.

'Is something wrong, Sir?'

'Nothing to worry about I'm sure, Scott.'

'Only I've never used a rope ladder before, Sir. If you'd have warned me I could have practised.'

Bradshaw gave Olly a sympathetic smile. 'Not your fault, son, I should have used a stunt double. Just look at the whiteboard and tell me what you see when the words and pictures appear.'

For the next few minutes, Bradders asked Olly a series of questions relating to the words and illustrations on the whiteboard, the result being as unexpected to Bradshaw as it was devastating to Olly and no time was wasted in revealing his discovery to Helen and Martin.

Email from Mr Bradshaw, Packham Junior, to Mr and Mrs Scott.
As you know, we held our first rehearsal earlier for the play in the school hall. Whilst Olly has an aptitude for drama, and I applaud his enthusiasm, he will be unable to take his place as a leading character in this year's production due to his being short-sighted, which means he cannot properly focus on his surroundings and would be putting the show at risk if he took to the stage carrying anything other than a tray of fake scones and muffins.
I know this will be a crushing disappointment to you and Olly, especially as he has spent so much time practising his menacing grunts and swordplay skills, but I'm sure you will appreciate that I have limited time in which to meet the deadline for the first performance. It is therefore with deep regret that the role of Captain Scar has been given to another child. In the meantime, may I suggest you take Olly

along to an optician for validation of my findings and remedial action.

The optician, a humourless chap called Mr Maddison, confirmed that Olly was indeed short-sighted and would need to wear glasses, possibly not forever, but certainly for a year or two. It was of no consolation to Olly, who felt immediately deflated. His face would look completely different with two windows of glass straddling his nose, apart from which, characters in a seventeenth-century play would not be wearing a pair of glasses purchased from Romford High Street. It was all very disheartening but his choices were limited so he would have to hope that when the spectacles arrived, it was still Olly Scott who looked back at him in the mirror and not some geek who looked even more nerd-like due to his optimised clarity of vision.

Meantime, he had the thankless task of handing over his pirate uniform to Darren Harper, since it was of no use to him and Olly's mum wouldn't be too hard-pressed in knocking up a suitable, rudimentary apron for the village baker as a replacement. They met to make the exchange in the summer house at the end of the new property, which had been allocated to Olly as a temporary private residence because banks of security cameras were being installed all around the house. Renovation work was also in progress and Martin and Helen thought it best to keep their son a suitable distance from industrial drills, pickaxes and circular saws just to be on the safe side, although he did have access to the kitchen, via the back door, so that he could join them for meals and light refreshments.

It provided an opportunity for Olly to also pass on some of his recently acquired artistic skills to Darren Harper in his new role as Captain Scar. Darren turned out to be a likeable chap embarrassed to be taking over the lead character as much as Olly was distraught at losing it, but Olly gave him all the help he could and wished him well. It was, after all, teamwork that would make the show a success, whatever their designated contributions.

After six weeks of rehearsals, *The Pirates of Barnacle Island* was ready to be presented in the school hall and whilst most of the parents were eager to see their children participate in a colourful theatrical production, Helen and Martin sat through the play on the edge of their seats in anticipation of some calamity involving croissants and Cherry Bakewells, whilst Olly's sister, Erica, could hardly contain her excitement at the prospect of her brother upstaging the entire cast with a moment of unprecedented improvisation that would become legendary in the annals of Packham Junior history.

Such fiascos were averted due to Olly being instructed to observe proceedings from the safety of the bakery doorway with the various goodies superglued onto a wooden tray. After the curtain had come down and the cast had taken their bows, the parents and assorted pirates, drunks, serving wenches, the village grocer and blacksmith gathered in the canteen to partake of cups of tea and biscuits and indulge in congratulatory chatter, drowned out for the most part by the general buzz of excitement.

'Well done, big brother,' said Erica as she sidled up to him with a cheery smile that hid her disappointment at his failure to make her afternoon an unforgettable celebration of chaos and disorder. 'It was….. fun.'

'More fun if I'd had something to do other than standing like a dick holding a tray of fake bread.'

'It did look pretty gross. They might at least have given you an opportunity to defeat the pirates with some poisoned muffins.'

'And made me the villain of the piece? It wasn't a pantomime, Erica.'

'I think you'll find it was, Olly. And you could have been the hero, not the villain - if only someone had recognised your potential.'

'A hero wearing an apron covered in flour and with nothing to say?'

Erica smiled sympathetically. 'Mrs Patterson says you don't necessarily need words to express yourself. Anyway, you'll always be my hero, Olly.'

She turned and walked off to join her pals as Olly observed the animated discussions that *Pirates* had initiated. While the majority of parents were smiling and chatting enthusiastically in groups, his father was in earnest conversation with a parent who was nodding agreeably whilst looking uncomfortable. A few days later Olly discovered an email on Martin's open laptop in the kitchen that shed some light, along with a bucket of cold water, on this incident and he felt the need to share it.

Text message from Olly Scott to Darren Harper.
Hi Darren. Thought you did a great job playing Captain Scar. Real scary. My dad can be scary sometimes too. He's

sent an email to Mrs Baskins complaining about Mr Bradshaw using subtext as a cover for his political views by allowing innocent school kids to act them out. I looked it up. It says subtext is a hidden message in a drama. I don't understand what that means but according to my dad, the pirate invasion is really about foreign countries like Russia attacking other countries and what happens if the natives try to be their friends without putting up a fight. What's he on about? We had a great time swapping bottles of grog for bandanas and singing sea shanties in the tavern while the girls taught the invaders how to crochet woolly jumpers and make Barnacle Stew. My dad says that's sexist, even though the play took place three hundred years ago. Pirates aren't Russian anyway, they're from the Caribbean. I know because I saw the film. None of us can speak Caribbean so it's not true to life anyway, like German officers in the movies speaking English. My dad's over-thinking stuff. It's a school play that's meant to be fun and I'm so embarrassed. Good luck removing the scar, your mum shouldn't have used a Sharpie, you might have it for life. Anyway, we'll be starting new schools next term so we can wipe the slate clean and put all this behind us. To be honest, we could all do with a change of scenery.

NEW CHALLENGES

'I'm serious, Felix, it's time to move on. If we stay in Romford much longer we'll be treading water with no long-term career prospects.'

'So what do you suggest? It wouldn't be any easier finding work abroad. Language barriers, cultural differences, unfamiliar terrain. Doesn't bear thinking about.'

'We don't have to go to those lengths but we could move out of the area, try somewhere new.'

'Like where?'

Olly gave the matter due consideration. 'Cornwall. Or Devon maybe. Somewhere by the sea. Fresh air and a fresh start.'

'To do what? Wheel retired old folk around in bath chairs? Take fishing boats out on stormy seas to catch shoals of mackerel and herring?'

'Brighton. That has a diverse population. Bet we'd find work we'd enjoy and could do together.'

'Like fairground operatives. I've always fancied being one of those,' said Felix with more than a hint of sarcasm. 'Jumping between dodgem cars and florescent carriages rattling around in the dark of the Haunted House, riding the water chutes, clambering up rigging to free roller-coaster cars that have got jammed, taking punters on canoe trips along computerised shark-infested rivers. Fantastic.'

Olly couldn't resist a wry smile. Felix was prone to poking fun, it was the part of his personality that drew people to him because everyone knew his remarks were made with the best of intentions and never meant to be mean. 'Brighton isn't all about fairground attractions, Felix. There are bars and nightclubs and theatres and cinemas and casinos and all kinds of entertainment venues. There's not exactly a surplus of those around here so we'd be no worse off.'

Felix looked thoughtful. Olly was right, there was nowhere quite like it within a twenty-mile radius of where they were now. No premier league football club, no beach volleyball. Romford didn't even have a pier, though it did have a popular greyhound stadium and an excellent amateur dramatics society that Felix had joined and for which he had performed his own plays to fill the void left after his involvement in the school productions. If he were being honest, he was no more fulfilled than Olly, working on the Romford Herald as a junior reporter covering obituaries, store openings and closings, marrow-growing competitions and occasionally interviewing residents who had housing issues, debt problems or were victims of domestic violence, while he tried not to become involved in their personal problems. It provided excellent background material for his plays but did little to raise his spirits when he returned home at night. By applying logic to Olly's suggestion that they would have nothing to lose by moving away, there was always the possibility that opportunities might present themselves that could improve their situation. If there were openings that enabled them to use their imaginations, so much the better and it would be stupid not to at least consider moving to Brighton as an option.

'I'm prepared to give it a go if you are,' Felix conceded, abandoning his cynicism and taking a more encouraging standpoint. 'But there's a lot to think about. And organise. We'll need to find somewhere to stay and be able to pay our way while we're settling in and that won't be easy.'

Olly brightened at Felix's surge of unexpected enthusiasm. 'We could take a trip down to the south coast and suss everything out. Ask around, buy the local papers so we can look for work and accommodation. We'd come away with a suntan if nothing else.'

Helen was not quite so enthusiastic about her son setting off on a journey of discovery in an unfamiliar place that would put him out of sight, out of reach, and potentially out of pocket, since he had not settled into any form of enduring employment after leaving school, and at the age of twenty-five it was unlikely he would find a suitable career path unless he made more of an effort and shed the inhibitions that constantly held him back.

At supper, another reason for his mother's reticence came to light. Erica had decided to move to Edinburgh, which meant she would be away from home for three to four years, leaving the house devoid of its usual buzz of good-humoured chat and customary sharing of the day's events. It came as much as a surprise to Olly.

'Why Edinburgh?' he asked, disappointed that he may not see his sister again for a while.

'I'm taking an interior design course. Everything from the creation of interiors of different scales and timeframes to ways of developing sustainable design practices. It's a fantastic opportunity.'

Olly could see how thrilled she was at the prospect of taking control of her future and pursuing her dream. He could hardly blame her for wanting to satisfy her artistic desires and felt fleetingly envious that he had not fulfilled his own ambition to find a role in the creative arts. 'Then I hope it all works out. It does sound like a great opportunity.'

Erica smiled and jostled his arm affectionately. 'You'll find what you're looking for, Olly. You just have to be patient and make sure you don't let any opportunity pass by that could lead to something bigger. Take a chance now and then, no matter what the risk.'

Olly nodded. It was time he was running out of, not patience, but he appreciated the gesture. 'You're right. Change of location, change of direction.'

'And you can swap notes regularly on Zoom or Facetime,' interjected Martin, adding his personal note of optimism. 'We're paying to set Erica up in Edinburgh so we'll do the same for you in Brighton.'

Olly's face lit up. 'Seriously? My own apartment?'

'For you and Felix,' said Helen. 'A year's rental to help you get started. No point in the two of us even thinking about moving to a bigger house when we'll be left with two empty rooms here.'

'We'll be back on flying visits,' Erica assured her. 'Nobody gets shot of their kids that easily.'

The smiles that followed were a welcome antidote to the undercurrent of melancholy that had dominated the discussion; the realisation that life was about to change for all of them.

For Olly, it meant handing in his notice to the estate agents where he had been working for the past year, showing prospective buyers in and out of the surplus of flats and houses for sale in the area, taking a regular commission that had tied him to a job that he knew would never lead anywhere but which up until now he could not afford to give up. It had not been particularly arduous work and he had met some interesting people with different aspirations and ideas for transforming properties, although he'd been happier showing couples, families and single men around rather than professional, confident women who still made him nervous and brought about lapses of concentration when he was in the vicinity of expensive vases, aquariums or free-standing sculptures. Whilst his work had not elevated him to Employee of the Month status, his efforts had been genuinely appreciated by Gerry Rich of Rich and Brooks Estate Agents, who was quick to praise his contribution.

Email from Gerry Rich to Olly Scott.
Sorry to hear you'll be leaving us for pastures new, Olly, it's been a pleasure having you on board. The staff really enjoyed your stories, especially those involving the radio-controlled fighter jets, the armchair that caught fire and my personal favourite, the pirate who demolished his own ship. Great fun. We enjoyed the embellishments from your deliciously fertile mind and coffee breaks will never be the same. So go forth and, like the hundreds of properties you've been exposed to over the past twelve months, strive to recognise your potential and never be afraid to show your true character. And don't worry about Mr Hardaker's cracked erotic Japanese dancer figurine, or Mrs O'Reilly's shattered Feng Shui Money Tree, they weren't that keen on

them anyway. They were both extremely pleased with the sale of their properties so think no more about it. Bon voyage, Scotty. The agency has benefited immensely from your relatively short time with us and whatever you choose to do next I'm sure it will be a great success. And if you're ever in need of a hot property down on the south coast, Rich and Brooks will always be here to help.

MOVING ON

The FOR SALE sign had been taken away several weeks ago. Now it was simply a matter of walking through the front door, unloading the two suitcases that she had bundled out of the car and appraising the bare walls of her new, unfurnished apartment, imagining how she might bring this vacant space to life with an imprint of her unique personality.

For Emma Appleby, this was a challenge she had been looking forward to for months, despite the daunting task she would face in placing her future in her own hands, without the support of her parents and regular employment that had, until now, guaranteed her a sizeable income.

At the age of twenty-six, Emma had established herself as a respected freelance set designer, taken under the wing of a touring theatre company that had recognised her talents from the moment she left college and introduced her to an exciting vocation that could utilise her imagination in ways she would never have believed possible. Her skill in designing inspired sets that blended seamlessly with the stories whilst being economical in both staging and cost had earned her a reputation that allowed her creative freedom and secured her career for as long as she felt her desire for artistic expression was being fulfilled.

But living out of suitcases in bedsits and hotel rooms and being on the road for energy-sapping days had begun to lose its appeal and even though she remained as passionate as ever about her chosen occupation, she feared there might be a danger of it becoming a treadmill if she did not step off and explore other options. She had been playing it too safe; accepting the accolades and critical acclaim without extending herself rather than experimenting with new ideas, taking a chance on working alongside other talented writers, directors and actors. The weekly routine, for all its merits, had become too familiar, too easy, too comfortable, and she knew it was time to break loose and trust that her talents would take her into more adventurous and possibly ground-breaking territory.

For now, Emma needed to refresh her mind and put creative aspirations on hold while she concentrated on equipping the apartment since she had neither a chair to sit on nor a kettle to make a cup of tea. She had walked through the property after her offer had been accepted but now she could take her time envisaging which colour schemes to employ and what furniture would complement each of the design elements. She had amassed enough in savings to see her through the summer, and even though employing builders and decorators to help bring the dream to reality would be costly, it was important to start the ball rolling with the minimum of delay since an apartment was not a home while it was devoid of colour and the most basic necessities. Or, she mused, of agreeable company. Or any kind of company, since sharing her life experiences with others had never been considered a viable option and she had always been careful to avoid unnecessary associations that might complicate or threaten her situation. It was a task made significantly easier with a schedule that had allowed her to move from job to job, mixing with a variety of artists and technicians, without needing to drop anchor in any particular place for any length of time.

Emma had sometimes mused on the possibility of moving into her first home with someone who would share her life journey rather than spending evenings and weekends dining alone, bereft of the reassuring buzz of good-humoured banter. But she had come to accept that such a scenario was unlikely since she needed to be cautious about who she allowed into her personal space lest her vulnerabilities were exposed and her fractured past became a precarious future. She had always been a loner, afraid to expose her innermost fears and doubts because she was convinced nobody would understand or empathise with her problems. Since long-term relationships had therefore become a slender prospect she resolved to stay focused on protecting her privacy, always wary of unnecessary intrusions. If she was taken off-guard by a seemingly innocuous moment observing her image in a window or a mirror, she saw the person she had always been, rather than the one she had hoped to be: confident and assertive, not afraid to integrate and accept that whatever life throws at you, there is an obligation to embrace it and adapt to the situation accordingly.

But since such reflections can often distort the truth and leave a feeling of emptiness, Emma knew that for the foreseeable future, the walls around her would become her closest ally as she focused on building a new life while taking any opportunity to further develop her skills when a new job came along that might allow her the freedom she had become so desperate for, whatever risks might be involved.

BRIGHTON ROCKS

'You've signed up to be a tour guide? Are you serious?'

'Why shouldn't I be serious?'

'Because you know sod-all about Brighton and even less about how tour guides operate. We've only been down here six weeks.' Felix studied Olly, waiting for his face to crack into a smile to confirm he was only joking. It didn't.

'I know everything there is to know about Brighton. After all, I was born and raised here.'

'No you weren't, you were born in Romford, like me.'

'Not according to my application.'

'You lied? On the application form? They'll check it, Olly, they always do.'

'They won't, and if they did, Mrs Bridlington will come to the rescue.'

'Who the hell is Mrs Bridlington?'

'She lives at number 49, two doors down. Lived there for over fifty years. Told her I'm at number 45 and some employers who are sending me important correspondence have alerted me to the fact that they may have got the addresses mixed up, so if anything arrives on her doormat for Felix Edmonds to let me know immediately.'

'And it's addressed to me because?'

'Because you're a respectable neighbour in full-time employment who can confirm I am who I say I am. A character witness.'

Felix blew out his cheeks in exasperation. 'So you've implicated me in your dishonest scam. We could go to jail.'

'Don't be dramatic. We won't go to jail. They just wanted something to keep on file along with my exemplary references from the garden centre and Rich and Brooks estate agents.'

'But you really thought it was necessary to go to those lengths?'

'It was, yes. I don't have time to muck around. Erica told me I have to take chances occasionally, whatever the outcome, and she's right. I need the kind of work that'll keep me stimulated and help me develop my social skills.'

'Which involves doing what exactly?'

'Well I walk about town showing punters places of interest and explaining the history of the place, and occasionally ride on the open-top tour bus.'

'Those talks are relayed through headphones.'

'Yeah, but if the bus is full, or the comms break down, it's helpful to have someone on hand to answer questions. And I get to wear a stylish blue jacket with a red pocket trim, which happens to match the colours on my new designer glasses.'

'I haven't seen any of the tour guides wearing blue jackets.'

'No, I bought one so I would look official yet friendly and approachable. It's all about branding. And being resourceful.'

'It's about being deceitful.' Felix looked from Olly to the collection of maps and travel brochures strewn across the living room floor. 'So what is this, your stash of intel?'

'Research, yeah. Ask me any question.'

Felix picked up one of the brochures, flicked through it and stopped at a random page. 'Why is The Brighton Pavilion listed as a former royal residence?'

'The Pavilion was built as a seaside retreat in 1787 for George, Prince of Wales, who became Prince Regent in 1811, and King George the Fourth in 1820. The Royal Pavilion and Museums Trust now manage the buildings on behalf of Brighton and Hove City Council.'

Felix flicked to another random page. 'What significant event took place at the Brighton Dome in 1974?'

'Abba won the Eurovision Song Contest on April 6th with a song called *Waterloo*.'

Felix scanned the brochure pages more carefully, keen to catch him out. 'How many light bulbs does it take to light the entire length of the pier?'

'Sixty thousand.'

'When was Sealife built?'

'1869. It's the world's oldest aquarium.'

'How many square feet does the Toy Museum occupy?'

'Four thousand square feet of floor space within four of the early Victorian arches supporting the forecourt of Brighton railway station. Founded in 1991, the museum holds over ten thousand toys and models, including model trains, puppets and construction toys.'

Felix tossed the brochure back on the pile in defeat. 'Now you're just showing off.'

'No, I'm reassuring you that I've done my homework and there's nothing to worry about. I've already taken a mock tour and answered all their questions and I start on Monday. It's only for the summer season anyway.'

There was little more Felix could say. Whether Olly's rash venture, taken without consultation with his closest friend, would see them detained at Her Majesty's pleasure, was dependent on how the paying public responded to the variety of tours conducted by a guide who, up until a couple of months ago, thought Brighton rock was a ragged vertical column of solid mass that could be seen sticking out of the sea at low tide.

As it turned out, Olly's personable approach attracted punters like seagulls to a bag of chips, with a full complement of the trusting following him with animated fervour through the backstreets and historic buildings of Brighton, much to the envy of his competitors. Olly was as surprised as anyone at the popularity of his tours, his only answer to those who were keen to know the secret was that perhaps his jacket, as a symbol of authority and sociability, was a contributing factor.

The proliferation of brightly coloured jackets that swept through Brighton within a matter of weeks was more a testament to Olly Scott's innovation and new-found, if misguided, optimism rather than any astounding psychological findings relative to social behaviour. It did, however, keep him amused and much sought after for the next three months. More importantly, he discovered that because he felt so at ease working in a job that involved discussions relative to history, he was not phased in the company of customers who sought to catch him out with difficult questions, including attractive, assertive women who might otherwise have thrown him off-balance and dented his confidence. It was an element of control he was not used to but which he was happy to make the most of.

Felix, meanwhile, had taken a reporter's job at a local paper following a recommendation from his editor on the Romford Herald. He was still covering the more mundane activities in the area but the addition of sandcastle competitions, street carnivals and celebrity store openings made it more fun. His parents, Sandra and Gerry, had retired to Portofino on the Italian Riviera, having spent their honeymoon and the various holidays that followed in a villa overlooking the port. Sandra spent her time gardening and tending the olive trees whilst Gerry, whose remaining ambition at the age of fifty-eight was, for some unfathomable reason, to be accepted into the Magic Circle, spent his time on social media trying out tricks and illusions that continually came to grief to the consternation and frustration of all who had to endure his doomed routines.

Olly's parents had no such inclination to move out of Essex and thanks to their generosity, Olly and Felix had been able to settle into a spacious ground-floor apartment and vowed to make the move as rewarding as possible. Before long a succession of opportunities opened up that even they had not anticipated, starting with Olly volunteering his services at the TopLite theatre company, a converted barn on the outskirts of the town, initially to help with poster displays, organising children's theatre workshops and helping patrons with disability or anxiety problems to have a more enjoyable experience at the performances.

He had also joined a circus skills course organised by entrepreneur Billy Zando, where he learned to juggle, ride a unicycle and, under the supervision of a professional clown, tumble and pratfall without inflicting injury on himself or anyone else, a practice he found particularly useful given his prodigious inability to steer himself physically through life's meandering path of bothersome stumbling blocks. He stopped short of soaring through the air on a trapeze due to the involvement of complex somersaults; likewise fire-eating and plunging knives into the magician's box of illusions, aware that the assistant handcuffed inside would be susceptible to serious injury. When the circus began setting up for the summer season on the green at Hove, a mile down the coast, Billy offered Olly a temporary job setting the props, clearing up after the performances, and ironing the uniforms, with an occasional opportunity to perform with the clowns. He immediately left his tour guide job to literally join the circus and spent four glorious months having the time of his life, doing what he had hankered to do all those years previously at Chase Hill High.

He bought a second-hand bike because it was quicker and more convenient than walking and threw himself into the role with unrelenting enthusiasm, being rewarded with several mind-blowing sexual encounters with Zelda the Romanian contortionist who had seduced him one night on some bales of straw behind the lion's den, her specific skills offering an eye-opening, and eye-watering, insight into the true meaning of having a flexible friend with benefits. Zelda, a divorcee with a history of tempestuous relationships, presented no threat to his self-esteem and in her company, he felt more at ease than he had with any woman he had ever met. She was ten years older, was warm, tender and thoughtful, and since both acknowledged that their liaison was nothing more than a physical union with neither strings nor any long-term commitment, there was no awkwardness or delusory expectation.

When the time came for Billy Zando's Travelling Circus to dismantle its massive tent and the troupe moved on to a European tour, Olly's involvement at TopLite had come to the attention of its Creative Director, Philippa Chambers, who offered him a full-time post with the front of house staff whilst undertaking training as an Assistant Stage Manager. It was a job opportunity he did not need to think twice about.

Email from Philippa Chambers to all TopLite personnel.
Olly Scott will be joining us on a full-time basis from next week. For the past twelve months Olly has taken on numerous volunteering duties around the theatre and proved himself to be a tremendous asset. He is passionate about the work we do and apart from a natural ability to interact with our customers, performers and stage crews, has cultivated a wide range of creative skills to a level of competence that I'm sure will be of immense benefit to us. He can juggle bowls of fruit and table lamps with the same dexterity as the eclectic range of jobs he undertakes, and his all-round knowledge of backstage disciplines and working practises will help take the strain when we are

working at full tilt. I do hope you will give him every support as he takes on his new role at our wonderful theatre.

Although Olly had found it hard to say goodbye to Zelda, she had awakened in him an appreciation of the opposite sex that gave him the confidence to interact with less reticence in social circles that were not always male-oriented. Apart from being important for his career progression, networking with a diverse range of people with differing views opened up new and challenging avenues of creative expression and the chance to actively experiment with new ideas, for which TopLite provided the perfect setting.

Felix had written a selection of short plays that dealt with difficult subjects, the result of his experiences writing for the newspaper, but his search for a suitable outlet had not, so far, yielded any positive results. Olly persuaded Philippa to give two of his plays a provisional run and whilst they could not be classified as mainstream, the performances resonated with younger audiences who appreciated contemporary stories that were controversial and edgy. Within a few weeks, Born In A Barn Productions, now incorporating plays from up-and-coming writers, had become a regular part of the TopLite programme, with Felix directing to save on costs.

When TopLite's resident stage manager left to join a theatre group in London, Olly took over, successfully supervising a season of plays that utilised the same living-room set, modified during each changeover to give a different ambience, including *Abigail's Party* and *Sleuth*. Feeling the need to be more ambitious, and to confront head-on his past thespian-related disasters with impulsive defiance, Olly suggested the staging of a scaled-down version of *Big Top* as a summer special, with a local troupe providing the music and two of their regular actors playing the principal roles, along with rising star Amelia Barton as the runaway girl. Supporting them would be a select group of artists from Zando's circus, which, by fortuitous coincidence, was due back in Brighton that summer. It promised to be the perfect combination of talent presented in an enterprising format although it almost turned out to be the perfect storm.

A second, smaller barn had been divided into a prop store and rehearsal room, and although the stable yard of the old farm had been transformed into a dressing room block during the renovation work, space was limited when it came to accommodating a ringmaster, four dwarves, a knife thrower, three clowns, a trapeze artist, two acrobats and a selection of imitation circus 'oddities,' including a bearded lady, a human skeleton and a four-legged man. Additional requirements included make-up for each artist and the space to facilitate a collection of additional props which the stagehands were not allowed to touch. Friction was increased by arguments as to who occupied the largest dressing rooms to the point where a large marquee had to be erected at the back of the theatre, with extensive cable runs providing electricity and the installation of portable loos and showers. Add to that the extra work required by the design team, including Betty Knight, the scenic painter and regular prop wrangler, and the costs began to spiral long before opening night, with resident director Adam Stonham tearing his hair out and looking increasingly gaunt with each frenetic day.

The trigger point for his impending nervous breakdown was the antagonism between two of the female acrobats and Amelia, a firecracker of a situation that Adam had handed over to Olly and Hungarian trainer, Miklos, to fix. The actress had been having difficulty getting to grips with the varying techniques of tightrope walking, juggling and balancing on a unicycle, which the professional acrobats found increasingly frustrating since they felt that one of them should be given the leading role due to their experience and proficiency in all of these circus disciplines. They overlooked the fact that Amelia had been given the part after extensive auditions to find a woman in her early twenties who looked eighteen, was strikingly attractive, waif-like in appearance yet fit and strong, with a 'let me at 'em' attitude that enabled her to take on potentially dangerous challenges that would have phased most actors. That, and the fundamental reality that both female circus performers were in their late thirties, with muscular physiques and skills only a seasoned professional could be expected to execute as opposed to a young and inexperienced circus trainee.

On hearing Amelia shouting and dispensing profanities that were entirely inappropriate from a young lady who was meant to be an innocent, virtuous runaway, placid of character and charming by nature, Olly hurried to the stage area to find her swaying precariously on the tightrope with an angry look on her face as she manhandled several large clubs that were spinning out of control and crashing to the floor in protest at being treated with such violent misuse.

'What are you doing?' he called up at her.

'I'm doing what you asked me to do, practising my circus skills.'

'But not all at the same time, Amelia. The script doesn't require you to juggle *and* walk a tightrope when you've only been with the circus for two days.'

'I keep telling her!' shouted Miklos from his seat in the stalls, well away from her perilous presence. 'But she doesn't listen. Bloody woman's determined to wreck the props and break her ankles. She'll be trying it on the unicycle up there if we don't stop her.'

'Oh please don't say that, Miklos,' said Olly in despair. He looked across at the two female acrobats who were sitting a couple of rows further back taking obvious delight in the unfolding saga. 'She wants to prove she can do it as well as anyone but needs to know her limitations - which is what we hired you for, and that's something you cannot do sitting down there.'

'It's safer down here. I'm not going anywhere near her if she insists on being pig-headed and reckless.'

Olly turned and waved Amelia off the tightrope. 'Please, Amelia, I don't have time for this. *We* don't have time for this. You're doing well but you need to stick to the script and take direction or we're going to be in serious shit.'

She gave him her little girl lost look. 'I'm not trying to be difficult, Olly, I just want to achieve perfection.'

Olly was aware of Amelia's ability to initiate her persuasive charm whenever it suited her and although her mere presence always unsettled him, he knew it was important to assert some authority in as diplomatic a manner as possible.

'You're perfect in many ways, Amelia, and have a multitude of admirable qualities, but you're not *meant* to be proficient at any of these skills because the story is about a disadvantaged girl who wants to better herself and discovers the way to achieve that through hard work and discipline, a balancing act in its own right. Becoming an overnight success defeats that objective. You do get that?'

'I do. I just didn't want to let you down.'

'You won't. Just take it one step at a time, listen to Markos, ignore what any of the others think and stay focused without the accompanying drama.'

She kissed him lightly on the cheek and clambered back up to the tightrope as Markos stepped onto the stage. 'A closed set from now on please, Markos. No spectators or any other distractions. We need to get her through this.'

Although Amelia became more adept at her circus skills as opening night drew nearer, the coordination of entrances and exits of the other performers within a limited space proved to be more of a challenge than Olly had expected. The persistent complications threatened to derail the show, with language problems adding to the general chaos. As he staggered through the three weeks of rehearsals, Olly wished that Zelda, who was housebound in Bucharest looking after her father who'd had a stroke, could have been on hand to help with the translations since he had seriously underestimated how much time would be lost communicating with artists from Germany, Czechoslovakia, France and Russia.

Big Top, by some miracle, was a massive hit, boasting full houses at every performance despite the in-fighting and tantrums that took place backstage, drowned out, thankfully, by the music and rapturous applause coming from the auditorium. By the time the final curtain fell on the final night, everyone was exhausted but managed to abandon the hissy fits and screaming matches that had become a regular after-show feature so that celebratory drinks could be enjoyed without recrimination because now was the time to move on and put such discord behind them.

The marquee area had been requisitioned to host the event, with tables decked in white linen tablecloths adorned with flowers and buckets of champagne that fizzed and popped to the general buzz of sycophantic chatter. Olly circulated, glass in hand, to make sure everyone was being looked after, relieved that Philippa was looking composed and smiley after a demanding few weeks, despite the fallouts and the ominous absence of director Adam Stonham.

He was pleased to see that Amelia, looking stunning in a sparkly red dress that someone must have poured from a bottle over her slender frame, had come through relatively unscathed and was deep in conversation with Felix, looking dapper in a dark blue suit and large spotty bow tie that any of the clowns would have been proud to wear.

'Triumph over disaster, a worthy enough excuse to get hammered on any night,' said Olly as he approached them.

'Be honest, it wouldn't have been a success and so much fun without all that tension and unpredictability,' retorted Felix.

'And the perseverance of Amelia, who carried the show magnificently under immense pressure.'

Amelia, in particularly high spirits after several glasses of champagne, smiled wickedly as she looked from Olly to Felix, 'That's right. Olly thinks I'm near to perfection and have a multitude of admirable qualities.'

'Does he now?' replied Felix, aware of the playful direction Amelia was taking the conversation. 'Sounds like a dangerous thing to say to an impressionable young woman.'

'Well, those weren't my exact words,' said Olly, looking from Felix to Amelia. 'I just wanted to boost her confidence, make her feel special so she kept her concentration.'

'So you didn't mean it?' said Amelia in mock disappointment.

'I didn't say that. You are special, that's why we wanted you for the part.'

'Thank you, Olly, you are a gorgeous man.' She flung her arms around him without warning, spilling the champagne over his shirt. 'And I think you're special too. Very special.'

Olly felt his face begin to colour as Amelia refilled her glass. Although in the workplace, even in the presence of attractive women, he had learned to exercise control over his susceptibility to awkward encounters, he felt that tonight Amelia might test his resolve. As her alluring, flirtatious behaviour intensified and the alcohol took hold he decided it was time to leave before she found a way to break through his supposedly impenetrable perspex wall, of which she was veering perilously close.

'Have a good time,' he said, raising his glass, 'you deserve it.'

And with that he was gone, vanishing into the melee before they had a chance to respond or ramp up the teasability factor. After that, Olly took a couple of days off to recuperate and regain his sanity, only to be confronted with an unwelcome memo from Philippa the moment he returned to work.

Memo from Philippa Chambers to all TopLite resident staff. We've now had time to assess the feedback – or more appropriately, repercussions – regarding our production of Big Top. Whilst staging a successful show is always rewarding, it's equally important to ensure that we never over-commit in terms of technical feasibility and budget.

Logistically Big Top was hugely ambitious and although every performance ran with only minor hitches, it was more by luck than judgement, the complications coming close to damaging our long-standing reputation. The kind of creative differences I witnessed during the performances I hope never to see again. They were disruptive and I am now having to deal with the consequences. Adam Stonham, our much-admired director, has walked out, vowing never to return, and Sarah Wyndham, our designer, is taking a six-month break to assess her career options. Felix Edmonds will be stepping into one of the directing roles for the remainder of the season, having proved his exceptional talent with his one-act plays and his articles in the Brighton Recorder which shed some timely and much-needed positivity on the work we do here.

With our remaining budget wobbling at the knees and in need of some innovative thinking to ensure we stay on track, the coming months will pose a formidable challenge. Whilst the theatre will be staging several Comedy Nights for the autumn programme, it is essential we start rehearsals for the winter season as a priority or risk going dark, which would be bad for PR and apply even more pressure to our finances. We must not let that happen.

'Not one to mince her words, is she?'

'No, she isn't, although you seem to have come out of it smelling as fresh as an ocean breeze.'

Felix was quick to counter Olly's understated accusation. 'That's because whenever I see a storm brewing I have the common sense to row safely back to shore, whereas you sail straight into its epicentre.'

'Maybe I do, but Philippa has always encouraged us to take chances and apart from the technical and budget problems it was a success and the theatre's reputation is still intact. It's just a matter of finding a way to use our resources to best advantage.'

'So what do you think she'll do?'

'Not sure, but there are options.'

'Such as?'

Olly took a swig from his beer bottle, placed it back on the coffee table and did his best to look hopeful. 'I'm going to suggest to her that we stage two productions with a small cast and understated set design. *Art* is a possibility. It's a three-hander, funny and compact and has something to say about the fragility of long-term relationships when a friend does something irrational that mystifies the others. It's set in a minimalist living room, with a small white canvas covered in white streaks taking centre stage - a fourth character we won't even have to pay for.'

'She might buy that,' agreed Felix, 'And the other?'

Olly hesitated. '*Shadows Never Still*. It's about a couple trying to check in at a hotel that's deserted during the Christmas holidays. No receptionist, no manager, no kitchen staff. Except it's not one hotel, but several hotels, in different time zones, and the couple are fraudsters being hunted throughout Europe by a detective they murdered ten years previously.'

Felix stared at him, his mouth slightly agape. 'And this is simple and uncomplicated in what way?'

'Well, it's also a three-hander and because the set has an abstract look, the audience knows that nothing they see is for real, which gives us the freedom to play around with minimal design but utilise lighting and sound to maximum effect.'

'In a story involving a ghost who chases a couple around Europe carrying what, an armful of Michelin guides? Or is he multi-lingual?'

Olly sensed he had doubts. 'It's a comedy, Felix, so we can employ artistic license and it would be a first for us because it's never been performed publicly before.'

'I'm not surprised. We'd be better off doing something less ambitious like *Krapp's Last Tape* with one actor sitting in a bunker, or *Buried,* with a single character trapped in a box under the desert, or *Our Town*, which has no sets, no backdrop and only a handful of props. Far less chance of Philippa going into meltdown.'

'They're all possibles, yes, but it's for the Christmas season and TopLite should be developing its reputation for pushing the boat out with relevant but experimental seasonal offerings.'

'You just did that and it almost sunk, along with our long-term employment options. If you want to sell this ghost story to her, you'd better make sure it's a watertight pitch or she'll never let you run with it.'

Over the next few days, Olly mulled over several possible pitches he could make to Philippa to persuade her that *Shadows Never Still* would be a suitable choice for the winter season since it was a ghost story that took place in an atmospheric set, featuring an incompetent detective constantly being outsmarted by a middle-aged couple who always stay one step ahead of the game.

Selling Philippa *Art* as their next presentation was not a problem, with Felix directing in the absence of Adam Stonham, and it gave Olly more time to figure out if it was possible to stage the detective ghost story on limited resources or if he was going to have to conjure up something associated more with the spirit of Christmas than bellowing giants, wannabee mayors, counterfeit cows and screaming witches darting around on broomsticks. The answer came when Olly took an impromptu tour of the backstage area to check that the cables and props had been returned to their respective cubby holes and came across Betty Knight in the storage area sorting out her canvases and paint sprays.

'Over a hundred backdrops and not a single white one among them,' she said as Olly walked up to her. 'I know how Van Gogh might have felt if he was obligated to paint his *Sunflowers* in black and white to save on paint costs, or present a blank canvas and ask everyone to use their imaginations, which apparently is what our next production is about.'

'At least you didn't have to watch the colour drain from Philippa's face when she saw the final *Big Top* budget figures. We have to be resourceful and pragmatic, Betty, we don't have a choice.'

'That was some memo, I must admit.'

'Only to be expected. I did let her down.'

'No you didn't, you stuck your neck out and gave the theatre something memorable. If she wants full houses and adventurous productions she has to expect the occasional blip.'

Olly smiled at her response. A bubbly woman in her early thirties with dreamy eyes and a captivating smile that you could hang your hopes on, Betty always looked on the bright side, gave the benefit of the doubt to everyone, and was always willing to offer help and support whenever it was needed.

While the sun never seemed to set on Betty's world, and despite her good intentions, Olly knew that the theatre could be in trouble if they didn't address the problem with a sense of urgency.

'It was a bit more than a blip, Betty. We're a designer short for the next two shows and one of the plays has already been scheduled for the autumn run but without any creative concepts in place. And the chances of finding someone who isn't booked up are pretty slim.'

'Have you considered Emma Appleby?'

'I don't know Emma Appleby.'

'She tours with rep companies who have limited amounts of set-up time. Has a reputation for creating compact visual scenarios that are inexpensive but effective.'

'Sounds unlikely she'd be available at short notice. Is she on tour now?'

'Don't think so. She bought an apartment near the seafront a few months ago. Word is she's taking time off to supervise renovation and decorating work.'

'She may not be interested if her apartment is a priority.'

'It's the touring she wanted a break from. I'm sure she'll have professional help with plumbing and decorating, so I can ask. We worked together on a show in Manchester a couple of years back and she's very approachable. She's not worked with TopLite before and since it's now on her doorstep she might find it an appealing prospect.'

Olly knew he wasn't in a position to spend time pondering alternatives and although making contact with a set designer without informing Philippa was a gamble, he regarded it more as an informal approach in case it was a non-starter; a meeting with one of Betty's friends to sound her out, that's all it was, no commitment, no guarantees.

'It's a great idea, Betty. Nothing to lose in talking to her. Let me know if she's interested and I'll set up a meeting.'

GIFT HORSE

Olly was familiar with the word angel being associated with backers who invest money in theatre productions, but in the coming weeks, the word was to have a completely different connotation.

The chances of Emma Appleby being free, or even interested in taking on an assignment, were slender at best, so when Betty texted him three days later to suggest the three of them meet at TopLite for a preliminary chat, he was cautiously optimistic. With Philippa attending meetings during the week to discuss sponsorship deals, it meant they could take Emma on an extensive tour without having to explain what she was doing on the premises.

When Olly walked onto the stage and saw her for the first time he was immediately smitten. She was younger than he had expected, probably late twenties, with a disarming smile, eyes bright and alert, and petite features that complemented a beautiful slender body that would wrong-foot the most confident of men. She was, in short, the most gorgeous, captivating woman he had ever met. She extended her hand as Betty introduced him.

'Emma. Betty's told me about the work you've been doing here. It's very impressive.'

He felt his face might betray the sudden ambush on his senses and knew he had to divert attention away from himself in case he floundered before he'd had a chance to outline the game plan. He decided honesty was the best way forward. 'We have a committed team but the summer special took its toll on our resources and we need some fresh ideas and innovative thinking to see us through the winter season.'

She appreciated that he had not overwhelmed her with a combination of sycophantic praise and bullshit. It was a given that she had been asked to talk over the possible choices based on her reputation and the assumption that she might be motivated enough to take on the theatre's forthcoming projects.

Emma walked around the stage area, taking in every aspect of the space around her that would need to be utilised if she were to create effective productions on a limited budget in a confined space. '*Big Top.* Wow. And you staged this in an area this size without any accidents?'

'They were experienced performers so it was more a logistical exercise that fortunately didn't have the added complication of us being trampled underfoot by a troupe of tigers or performing elephants. We just need to prove we have the ability to mount shows that can be successful on a smaller budget without the need for intricate sets filled with spectacle and colour.'

Emma smiled. Olly was arousing her interest without being pushy or appearing needy; just presenting the facts without over-emphasising the challenge. 'So. *Art.* A good choice. Works better in an uncluttered set because of the subject. The humorous text drives the narrative without the need for too many visual distractions. What appeals to me is the option of us utilising the same basic set for both *Art* and *Shadows*.'

'You think that's possible?' Olly was encouraged by her enthusiasm and clear indication that the plays had 'appeal' not just to her but to 'us.'

'Yes, I'm confident we can make it work. I'll read through the scripts and sketch out some computer designs.'

'And you wouldn't have any scheduling problems?'

'Not really. I had planned to take some time off, but I can work from home while the tradespeople do their stuff, and you're only a short drive away when I need to be on site.' She tapped his hand gently by way of reassurance. 'I'd love to work with you. It'll be fun.'

The feel of her hand on his was enough to send his pulse heading off on an unscheduled sprint, her seductive smile completing the demolition of the self-assured persona he had tried hard to convey. 'I'll need to check everything with Philippa our creative director. She'll have the final say.'

'Which won't be a problem,' added Betty quickly. 'Philippa is astute and decisive and recognises good concepts when she sees them. We have the benefit of two exceptional plays that maximise design and budget - and time isn't her most favoured ally.'

'Then we'll do our best to convince her,' said Emma, taking out her cell phone and inspecting her diary. 'I'll make a start over the weekend and have some rough designs to show you by Friday.' She put her phone away and looked at Olly. 'Why don't you and I meet at Grayson's at, say, seven o'clock Friday night?'

Olly looked from Emma to Betty, unclear if the invitation extended to the colleague who had introduced them at such short notice. Betty immediately came to his rescue. 'That's a great idea. You two can get to know each other while you talk shop.'

'Fantastic,' agreed Emma, 'I'll book a table. My treat.'

Olly returned to the apartment two hours later and immediately liberated a bottle of Sauvignon Blanc from the fridge to help reduce his excitement level and generate an interlude of rational appraisal following the meeting. Felix noticed a significant character change the moment he walked into the living room and watched Olly fill his wine glass and drain half of it in one. Unable to detect whether the meeting had gone exceedingly well or particularly badly, Felix cut to the chase. 'Are we celebrating or leaping metaphorically out of windows?'

'I met the most gorgeous woman,' replied Olly, replenishing his glass. 'The kind of woman you'd jump through hoops for.'

'No such creature exists, and with your track record you'd only break your neck trying.'

Olly leaned forward, his calm demeanour giving way to unease. 'That's just it, Felix. I don't know if I can get away with it.'

'Get away with what? You haven't locked her in the prop store until she agrees to sign a contract?'

'Much worse, she's invited me to supper. At Grayson's, Friday night.'

'Sounds a terrifying prospect.'

'But it is, Felix. She's smart and self-assured and I can't afford to screw this up. We have to bring these shows home on schedule and budget and we need her help to do it.'

'So what's the problem?'

'The problem? I have no idea how to make conversation with a woman with that kind of reputation, let alone navigate my way through a maze of creative design concepts. It's a relationship that has to work to everyone's advantage without any degree of risk.'

'You're not arranging a prenup, Olly, it's a business meeting for which she'll set out some ideas and Philippa will handle the negotiations, assuming she likes what you present to her. You just need to be yourself.'

Olly did not look reassured. 'Myself? I'm not even sure who that is since my confidence ebbs and flows depending on who I'm with. I have no idea if the person I think I am is the person I need to be if my evening with Emma Appleby is going to end on the positive note we all hope it will.'

'Jesus, Olly, what do you want, a guide to interpreting social intercourse? Learning to read signals and adapt to other people's thought processes is part of the game everyone plays and you're no different despite what reservations you might have. Just relax and enjoy the evening. She's the one who has to come up with the goods. Let her take the initiative, go with the flow, and everything will go according to plan.'

Olly acknowledged his advice with a nod and a smile but ominous, metaphorical clouds began sweeping across the back of his mind, casting immediate doubt and concern, because he knew full well that when it came to past encounters with the female of the species, things very rarely went to plan.

SHADOWS

In Olly Scott's topsy-turvy world social interaction had never been his strong point, with almost every attempt he had made to strike up friendships coming to grief one way or another for as far back as he could remember.

Life could be unjust and painful, the throbbing in his hands trapped in the window frame now an unassailable testament to his thwarted endeavours and all because he had acquired a reputation as a menace to society because of a basic ineptitude at negotiating life without knocking over the hurdles or crashing into them. Yet he knew he was no different from anyone else once the outer veneer was stripped away to reveal the person who resided in a daily swirl of confusion, uncertainty and vulnerability, but with positive qualities that surely deserved at least some consideration.

If only people could accept one another for what they are and not their expectations of what they should be. As far as Olly was concerned, everyone was a chameleon adapting to different sets of circumstances, modifying their character depending on the company they kept at any given time. Not necessarily with an ulterior motive; not always to compete, or to crave attention, but to nurture friendships, learn from one another, see someone else's perspective and accept their faults whilst appreciating their virtues. Surely that was the common ground everyone should be occupying.

Pain, he accepted, was part of the process of existence, though it did cross his mind that life without his hands would become exceedingly difficult and place a heavy burden on friends and family who would be called upon to assist with the kind of daily chores that up until now he had taken for granted and been relatively undemanding of his time. Similar to a computer program chuntering away in the background sorting out loose ends and fixing minor glitches so that attention could be given to more important issues. Without his hands, his internal software would have to be reset as he faced life, like so many others have to, coping with a disability that would be physical and not just mental and could have a devastating effect on his career as well as his home life. Fumbling about with scripts and props that refused to cooperate would turn his unencumbered routines into a nightmare scenario that would place a question mark on his ability to operate efficiently unless he could quickly learn to adapt.

Which was, he accepted by way of consolation, theoretically more achievable than the pain experienced when friends, or prospective friends, turn their backs on you, or worse, betray you, when you have done nothing to instigate such an upsetting situation and one fated to stick to you, like an indelible ink stain, for the rest of your life.

He knew very little about Emma Appleby other than her reputation as an exceptionally talented stage designer. But after one meeting, he had become besotted by her beauty and intelligence and knew that such an early infatuation might be the forerunner to disappointment and disaster if he was not careful.

He had trod that path many times when hope had been extinguished long before a flame had even been lit, from his early forgettable encounter with Jill the receptionist whose glares still haunted him if he ventured anywhere near a garage forecourt, to Bronwyn from Plants and Shrubs whose fumbling antics and insatiable sexual appetite eclipsed the possibility of them ever experiencing a prolonged and meaningful relationship, to Azuka in the TradeTreats service department who had left in a hurry by the back door to avoid his bungling behaviour having a lasting and irreversible effect on her. And long before that, the mortification of his schooldays with their endless episodes of torment that he had never been able to erase from his memory involving the insensitive girls who had ridiculed him and made him feel so worthless.

Meeting Emma had briefly rekindled the need in him to find true friendship if not something more, but his optimism that their association might prove productive and rewarding was overshadowed by the realisation that in being forced to reassess his journey through the minefield that was his life, he had been transported back to the darkest of days of perpetual embarrassment and loss of dignity from which he thought he had broken free but seemed destined to stay with him whatever his change in circumstances.

It just didn't seem right, or fair, that a person's worst experiences in youthful naivety should be allowed to dictate how their life will unfold, or unravel because they are judged by a single trait of behaviour that has created a false impression of their true selves.

Looking back, were the ordeals of his youth as bad as they seemed or does time distort a person's recollections, exaggerate the experiences, the fears and anxieties, so that all true perspective is lost? Or were those incidents even worse than he imagined despite every effort he had made to wipe them from his memory in order to lessen their impact on his future?

BUMBLE

The single tear trickled down his cheek and onto a cheese and pickle sandwich that had not looked particularly appetising in the first place and was becoming more inedible with each interminable second that passed. As he sat out of sight on the cold step behind the gymnasium staring at his sandwich box, Olly knew he would have to pull himself together before anyone saw him and decided to make his morning even more miserable. A salty wet rim formed around the bottom of his glasses and he took them off to wipe them; those ugly, unwanted facial accessories that were the architect of his humiliation and one that he was having to learn to live with daily.

He had been at Chase Hill High for two years and aged fourteen had been trying his best to cope with an inferiority complex that had come with adopting a new bespectacled persona which in turn had led to a period of readjustment with his vision. This involved walking into a glass door in the corridor and almost breaking his nose, stepping in front of a teacher as he cycled up to the bike shed, causing him to swerve and crash into a wall, buckling his front tyre, and knocking over two piles of books, spilling a corresponding box of lender cards over the library floor, so that the library monitor, Julie Bakewell, had to start over with the categorisation process. With each incident it wasn't simply the embarrassment of his physical ineptness but the inconvenience and annoyance it caused to those around him to the point where he risked becoming the least likeable person in the school, a reputation he was keen to avoid.

This proved to be a formidable challenge since Chase Hill was littered with obstacles that could upset his good intentions without warning, and most of the lessons required a hands-on approach that could not be avoided.

Art classes were the least problematical, with one or two minor spillages with ink and paint which often proved advantageous when creating more abstract offerings, although his art teacher, Mr Sparks - Sparky - showed only minimal interest in his work, spending most of his time sitting at his desk crafting a never-ending collection of origami animals that served no purpose other than to litter the classroom on every available shelf, cupboard and worktop.

Woodwork was not Olly's forte at the best of times, his reputation for creating birdhouses and flower boxes that were out of alignment resulted in assessments that were less than favourable or desirable. Metalwork afforded him a higher rating, but only because of a timely intervention by Felix, who had come to his aid on numerous occasions, most recently when Olly produced a misshapen poker that was too short and twisted to be submitted for approval, switching it for his own, perfectly formed utensil before firing up another one for himself. Felix had also pulled Olly from the river Rom when he slipped and fell in during an ill-advised attempt during a field trip to build a raft out of fallen tree branches, and on another occasion had taken the blame when a firework they lit in Olly's back garden fizzed and flew into Martin's study window, causing an exceptional amount of damage which resulted in both being grounded for the next three weeks with a stack of additional homework to wade through.

History was Olly's favourite lesson, a subject not impeded by the implementation of props and gadgets and one which gave inspiration by way of textbooks and film clips from historical dramas which stimulated his interest in remarkable characters and events that shaped the world. Cookery sessions were the most fun because Olly loved cakes and biscuits and the possibility for serious misadventure using basic ingredients was limited, although not entirely unavoidable. During an afternoon session to bake a Victoria Sponge, he tipped the appropriate amount of flour, eggs, milk, and sugar into the food mixer, with most of the mixture ending on his face the moment he turned the machine on. While most of his fellow pupils sniggered, a more sympathetic girl called Siyanda helped him clear up the mess and replenish the food mixer with a fresh batch of ingredients whilst reassuring Olly that it was a mistake anyone could make and that it was advisable to put the lid on and start at the slow setting before progressing to the faster one. He beamed at Siyanda to show his appreciation for her help in completing his blackberry and cream sponge, hoping this brief encounter might lead to a closer relationship in the coming weeks. She was, after all, an amazingly personable girl, the kind of friend any boy would be privileged to have.

Olly's first lesson in the difficult business of interpreting signals from the female of the species came two days later when he saw Siyanda entering the school gates with Jimmy Layton, the school football captain and all-round superhero, the sparkle in her eyes telling him that she was forbidden territory unless it involved the rudiments of creating baked delights for afternoon tea.

For the most part, he managed to avoid the rougher elements that roamed in and out of the school grounds, namely the bullies who lay in wait to catch him unawares. To them, he was fair game, the idiot who spent his time colliding with anything that wasn't nailed down and tripping over everything that was. While he knew he would probably never be free of the torment, he had hoped that over time they might lose interest and pick on someone else or that one of the teaching staff might realise that he was a moving target and reprimand them. But as the first intolerable year ground slowly on, it became obvious that there would be no easy escape from the persecution, with the rest of the school taking little interest in his predicament or intervening, finding it mildly amusing rather than a cause for concern, with only Felix siding with him if he happened to be on hand to offer support.

His self-worth suffered its most crushing blow one lunchtime when he was queuing for his customary bowl of soup and a sandwich pack in the canteen. Having loaded his tray he turned to take a seat at one of the tables, colliding with Jenny Stanhope and spilling the entire contents of the soup over her skirt. Jenny had been a good friend since their early days at Packham Junior. They had played together, went to birthday parties together, and sat next to each other on the bus taking them to the selected school trips that were deemed safe for Olly to attend. Nothing, it seemed, could stand in the way of their friendship. Until they changed schools, at which point Jenny acquired a new set of friends and involved herself in new challenges that helped her confidence grow while Olly's dipped, denting his self-respect and making him vulnerable to random misfortune, physical assault and emotional upset. Her reaction to the accident was immediate and cutting, yelling at him for being so clumsy and calling him a stupid sod in front of a packed canteen.

And so, on the most miserable day of his life, he sat on the cold step at the back of the gymnasium staring at his soggy sandwich, wishing the ground would swallow him up and save him from having to show his face for any of the afternoon sessions that were bound to impose more misery and cause more damage to his already shattered pride.

'Hey, Olly!'

Olly looked up as Felix walked up to him.

'Been looking for you everywhere. What are you doing back here?'

'Having my lunch without everyone laughing at me.'

Felix smiled and sat next to him. 'You mean the accident with the soup? Hysterical, but they weren't all laughing at you.'

'What do you mean?' asked Olly, confused.

'Jenny Stanhope. Silly cow. Getting too big for her boots. Everyone knows that.'

'But she was my friend, Felix.'

'People change, Olly, have different ideas and goals, mix with the wrong crowd. Think they're smarter than anyone else. You're better off without her.'

Olly closed the lid on the sandwich pack and stuffed it back in his backpack. 'So they weren't all laughing at me?'

'No. You shouldn't be so negative. Worse things can happen. Like if we don't get down to the lab in the next couple of minutes Titmarsh'll have our balls floating around in one of his test tubes.'

It was a gruesome thought and one not far from the realms of possibility, so Olly held out a hand as Felix stood and pulled him up and they made their way back to the playground and along the corridor to Room 16A, where numerous gases, solids, bubbling liquids and Thomas 'Titty' Titmarsh awaited the pleasure of their company in a session that promised to be more informative than sitting around bemoaning the injustices of life. This particular period was made even more interesting by the number of smiles and thumbs-ups Olly received from his classmates as he entered the room, an unexpected reaction that he initially assumed had something to do with the impending afternoon lesson that mercifully focused on water displacement rather than anything that might endanger them by way of electricity, fire, or toxic substances. It gave him the confidence to tackle the experiment with an enthusiasm Mr Titmarsh had not witnessed before and which the teacher found genuinely encouraging.

School report entry by Mr Titmarsh, reference Olly Scott.

Olly has been particularly careful in the lab since the unfortunate incident with the bunsen burner last month which resulted in him inhaling noxious chemical fumes and singing sea shanties but I'm pleased to see him checking the sleeves of his coat to make sure they do not catch fire again, as well as wearing goggles and gloves and standing well back during the experiments.

He had no problem demonstrating how to work out volume and mass when a submerged object displaces a volume of liquid equal to the volume of the object, nor was he phased by mixing sulphuric acid with sugar to illustrate exothermic, dehydration and elimination reactions, but when one of his classmates ignited a mixture of carbon disulfide and nitric oxide in a tube to produce a flame, his reaction to the resulting explosion caused him to jump and drop his third Pyrex glass tube in as many weeks, an indication that Olly has been very much on edge recently. This is a concern whenever he is in a room with hazardous chemicals so maybe he needs to consider taking up an activity like jogging or photography to see if this has a settling effect. He does try his best. It's simply a matter of finding an endeavour for which he has a true talent and can channel his energies.

What had escaped Titmarsh's attention was that when Olly dropped the Pyrex tube, the unkind sniggers that usually accompanied his mishaps had been replaced by a friendlier ripple of laughter that Olly now realised was the result of his earlier spat with Jenny Stanhope due to the accompanying cheers and applause that had rippled around the canteen when he spilt the soup over her. It was the first indication that his sporadic accidents might be providing an entertaining diversion for the other students away from their daily routines of unrelenting study.

A year later the arrival of a new boy, Benny Baxter, dropped a dispiriting spanner in the works when Olly discovered that Baxter, a boxing and jiu-jitsu champion, had a knack for homing in on those he perceived as the weaker elements within the school. As a bespectacled lad who attracted attention for all the wrong reasons, Olly found himself firmly in his crosshairs and for the next few weeks, Baxter tested Olly's reaction to being intimidated, not with actual physical assault, but by the possibility that bodily harm was always an option. He stood in his way when he was trying to walk to lessons and tormented him with callous remarks about his appearance and basic ineptitude. This needless provocation was supported by the usual suspects whose fondness for giving Olly a hard time was boosted by the presence of their new bully-in-chief and their threatening antics were extended to tossing his backpack into the bushes, knocking his textbooks out of his hands into puddles, and confiscating his sandwiches when he was looking for a safe place to sit and eat them.

Olly's means of coping with this new wave of aggression came by way of a fortuitous accident that occurred one February morning when he was making his way to the canteen carrying a large bag of potatoes. Pupils were often asked to take on arbitrary tasks such as folding away tables and chairs after meetings, collecting rubbish around the school grounds, or distributing newly acquired equipment to a chosen destination.

Six students who happened to be on hand when the weekly vegetable delivery was made, found themselves press-ganged into carting bags of onions, potatoes, tomatoes and cabbages across the playground to the canteen where they were quality-assessed and sorted by Marion the school cook. Watching this procession of reluctant volunteers trudge across the frosty school grounds were Benny Baxter and two of his fellow agitators who, on discovering that Olly Scott was among them, repositioned themselves opposite the gardener's shed on a bench where they could wait to ambush him.

A dripping tap outside the shed had created a puddle that overnight had turned into a miniature ice rink. Felix, who headed the convoy, became immediately aware of the treacherous ice patch and stepped around it, not thinking to warn the others. Olly, whose vision was seriously impaired by the bag he was carrying as he struggled to keep it upright and away from his face, followed behind but as he rounded the corner, was distracted by Benny and his mates who waved and yelled at him. He looked over at them but instinctively carried on walking onto the ice patch, where he skidded and pirouetted whilst trying desperately to hold onto the bag, which he dropped as he span in a circle, spilling the potatoes around his discombobulated feet. As they flapped wildly in a vain attempt to gain purchase, he slid backwards and was inelegantly dumped into the gardener's wheelbarrow among a steaming heap of manure fresh from the riding stables.

Jenny Willis, who had been walking behind him, put down her box of tomatoes and hurried over to help pull him out, as Benny and his pals walked up to them, laughing uproariously.

'It's not funny, you moron,' shouted Jenny disapprovingly, 'he's going to smell like crap for the rest of the day thanks to you.'

'He sure is,' said Benny, helping her pull him out, tears streaming down his face, 'but he does get eight points for technical achievement.'

More laughter ensued as Olly brushed himself down, thankful that the incident had not resulted in any bruises, broken bones or concussion, though surprised that Benny Baxter, rather than laying into him with his usual round of insults, had found this unscheduled antic unnervingly amusing. This gave Olly a slither of hope that he might be able to somehow use this unanticipated reaction to his advantage.

In the weeks that followed, he found he could move around the school with less interference from his tormenters and although they kept a watchful eye on him, it seemed more in anticipation of his next impromptu calamity that would provide them with unparalleled mirth and an agreeable distraction from the general monotony of the day. The school in general continued to regard Olly as a harmless figure of fun, although the girls, he noted, were more disposed to giving him sympathetic looks whenever he passed them in the corridor, much like they would a lion cub that had an endearing quality but only if kept at a distance. Jenny Willis, whom he thought would continue to offer moral support after hauling him out of the wheelbarrow and reproaching Baxter, disassociated herself from him in case his predisposition for physical tomfoolery and the need to be constantly rescued became an unwelcome habit.

Despite the lack of understanding and respect from the female contingent, Olly decided it might be to his advantage to capitalise on his newly discovered diversion tactic and play to the gallery since keeping the majority of the pupils entertained appeared to be the answer to making his time at Chase Hill High a great deal less wretched. Comic relief became a currency he indulged in with vigour and executed to perfection, so if a bowl of soup slipped across his tray at lunchtime he would accentuate the movement and manoeuvre the tray to create a moment of mini drama, or if a ball rolled to his feet in the playground, miskick it with an epic lack of skill that was guaranteed to keep his peers amused, particularly if there was the bonus of a spin that would cause his backpack to twist round and knock him off balance. These occasional comedic interludes became his insurance in keeping aggressors off his back whilst ensuring that Felix spent less time having to come to his aid.

A precarious curveball was thrown a few weeks later when a classmate, Millie Clarke, invited him to her birthday party one weekend. Olly had developed a crush on Millie from the moment she arrived at Chase Hill. She was pretty, outgoing, well-liked and always gave him an affectionate, friendly smile, even when he embarrassed himself with typical faltering moments such as walking into tables or knocking over chairs that prompted laughter and derision from her pals. She had even requested him as a Facebook friend, a welcome addition to the two he already had, so this was a perfect opportunity to get to know her even though he didn't stop to question why she had decided to include him in her select birthday group.

'It's a mystery tour, Olly, with lots of surprises and a shit load of fun,' is all she would say. With the chance to spend time with a popular girl who promised lots of surprises and a shit load of fun, how could he possibly refuse?

'My dad's hiring a minivan,' she explained, 'so he can take me and seven of my best mates.'

Olly had never thought of himself as one of Millie's best mates, but being with a group of classmates setting off on a birthday adventure was a golden opportunity to be part of Form B4's inner circle and it seemed an exciting prospect.

When the nominated Saturday arrived and a white minivan stopped outside his house, Olly's excitement was instinctively replaced by apprehension when he saw six of Millie's girlfriends who had previously never bothered to give him the time of day, peering at him from the windows, waving and laughing. As he climbed inside, Millie patted the seat next to hers, inviting him to join her and he willingly obliged, hopeful that his suspicions would prove unfounded.

When the van pulled up fifteen minutes later and everyone disembarked, Olly feared the worst when he realised they were outside the ice rink. 'I can't skate, Millie,' he said, reluctant to enter the arena without knee pads, wristguards, crash helmet and life insurance.

'The others aren't bothered. You're not scared of going on the ice are you, Olly?'

'Scared? No, I don't mind giving it a try.'

A commitment made due to her persuasive provocation, and with more than a degree of reluctance, he followed the others into the building, collected a pair of skates and walked with trepidation down to the edge of the rink. The first couple of minutes didn't prove too disastrous, even though he spent most of it holding on to the barrier as he tried to correct his balance, undeterred by everyone gliding past with varying degrees of proficiency. He was beginning to feel more confident when Millie floated onto the ice in a blue sequined dress with matching gloves and gleaming white boots looking every inch the fairy-tale princess, a vision that unnerved him and sent him scurrying back to the barrier, where he watched her spin and perform a series of loops, flips and spins, to illustrate that she was a natural performer in stark contrast to his floundering incompetence.

His suspicions that he had been deceived were verified by the six school friends who skated past smirking and giggling, followed a few moments later by the heart-stopping sight of Benny Baxter and two of his gang appearing out of nowhere and making a beeline for him with the primary purpose of mocking his ineptitude and goading him into letting go of the barrier to prove he wasn't a wimp, following him wherever his unstable feet took him, laughing and teasing him at every trip, stumble and fall. It was an act of betrayal, an unwarranted payback for facing his fears at the hands of a relentless bully and a girl he adored and in whom he had put his trust.

He sat in silence in the minivan on the way back, refusing to engage in any counterfeit praise they gave him for being such a good sport and making it 'so much more fun', retreating to the sanctuary of his summerhouse as soon as he was dropped off so he could berate himself for being so naive.

When he returned to school on Monday, the looks from many of the pupils told him that word had spread of the weekend birthday outing, confirmed by a selection of Polaroids pinned to the noticeboard showing him sliding over the ice like a graceless gazelle. A sheepish Millie noticeably avoided eye contact, her duplicity evident on her Facebook page, where she had posted more pictures ridiculing him as a blundering oaf who provided partygoers with an endless cavalcade of involuntary entertainment. She had ensnared him in the cruellest possible way and it became the longest day he'd ever had to endure at Chase Hill.

For the next two days, Olly stayed home on the pretext of having a sore throat and the start of a potentially infectious virus, demeaned and depressed and vowing to find another school as soon as possible so that he could start over. But fate intervened in the most unexpected way when messages of support began to pop up in his mailbox and postings from pupils criticising Millie's behaviour appeared on the school's Facebook page. He had intended to delete any association with social media, especially as his only other Friends were Felix and the pizza delivery guy, but as he read through the messages it gave him renewed faith in his fellow students and made him feel more hopeful.

Email from Olly to Felix.

Went to a disastrous birthday party at the weekend. I was set up and it was upsetting but I should have known better. Thought it would be best if I left the school but then I got these invitations to other parties. I know it's because everyone thinks I'm a good laugh, but that's better than being ignored even if I am popular for all the wrong reasons. Even Benny Baxter invited me to a party today. Can you believe that? Not because I'm a mate or anything. He just wants to watch me bumble about so he and his goons can take the piss. That's his nickname for me now. Bumble. I've a good one for him. Wouldn't tell him to his face though. As long as it keeps him amused and not wanting to thump me I'm not complaining. No point going to his stupid party though. I'll tell him I got my foot caught in a drain cover and it's packed in ice so I can't walk. That'll keep everyone laughing without me even having to turn up. Genius. Anyway looks like everyone's out on the field for Sports Day. I didn't get picked for anything, not even the hundred metres, so I've no chance with the skateboarding or abseiling, so I'm in the library researching books on the theatre. Thought I'd put my name down for Bossy Barratt's drama group which is starting up again. Could be more fun if we both joined. It's not the kind of thing Baxter would want to get involved in so we wouldn't have to worry about him and it could be fun. I think we should go for it.

Being an achiever was now foremost in Olly's mind. He was tired of being side-tracked by juvenile schoolgirls and misguided bullies. It was time to reassess what was important so that he did not squander his future, investing his time instead in looking to develop what talents he had to enable him to cope better with everything that life might throw at him. It was the only sensible way he could move forward and fulfil his ambitions, whatever unfamiliar and challenging situations he found himself in.

CURTAIN UP

Olly was pleased to hear that Felix was equally enthusiastic about joining the school drama group. Taking on different personas and participating in fictional role-play away from the conventions of normal school life had tremendous appeal and he and Olly signed up without hesitation. A week later, Byrony Barratt, the drama teacher, summoned the volunteers to her classroom for an introductory chat about her plans for the next school play. Olly saw this as an opportunity to take on acting roles that had been denied him at Packham Junior, believing himself to be a natural performer destined for the thespian life once the shackles of school had been cast aside.

It was a dream that was to be short-lived since Ms Barratt had selected four possible plays for them to perform, none of which, to Olly's dismay, included any contemporary productions, the list being comprised exclusively of period dramas.

'Couldn't we do an Agatha Christie murder mystery, Miss? Or a comedy like *Noises Off?*' he suggested hopefully.

'They're both good ideas, Olly,' said Ms Barratt, surprised to be challenged before the session had even begun, particularly since he had such an interest in history, 'but costume dramas like *The Crucible* and *Twelfth Night* present a challenge to wardrobe and make-up as well as teaching us about historical events and how social and moral attitudes have changed over the years through the portrayal of strong characters.'

'A contemporary play like *Twelve Angry Jurors* has strong characters who are forced to question their morals and values while teaching us about the judicial process, Miss,' countered Olly, 'and since it's an update from *Twelve Angry Men*, it's a good example of changing attitudes within society.'

Byrony stared at Olly for a few seconds, momentarily taken aback and wondering where this resistance to her selection had come from. He had clearly been doing his research. 'Another excellent idea, Olly, and I will make a note to include it in our summer programme. For now, I'm thinking that *Don Quixote* would be a good one to start with.'

Olly looked nonplussed. 'I've never heard of it, Miss.'

'It's said by many to be one of the greatest novels, written by a Spaniard named Miguel de Cervantes, about the adventures of a gentleman from La Mancha who rides a horse and believes himself to be a knight-errant, and his companion Sancho Panza, who recites numerous witty proverbs and rides a donkey.'

'And do either of them wear glasses purchased from Specsavers, Miss?'

Ms Barratt's face reflected her confusion. 'Specsavers? No, the book was published in 1605, Olly. Why would that be relevant?'

'Because I won't be able to take part in the play, Miss. Not with a horse and donkey on the loose.'

'You wouldn't have to actually ride them. They wouldn't be real.'

'I doubt if I would even see them, Miss. I'm short-sighted.'

'It's true, Miss,' added Felix, who had stood as a been a bemused bystander throughout this exchange. 'He's as blind as a bat without his specs.'

'It's not quite that bad,' interjected Olly, correcting Felix's overly enthusiastic contribution, 'but it might be asking for trouble if I didn't wear them.'

'Oh, I see. well, working on a drama doesn't mean you have to be on stage, Olly. There are numerous jobs - important jobs - that need doing by someone who has a keen interest in the theatre. We can talk about some options later if you like.'

Olly could not hide his disappointment. He'd had his heart set on taking to the stage, proving he had genuine performance skills which in turn would boost his confidence and offer new goals far removed from the cack-handed reputation that continually stalked him. Playing a hero in the school play would provide a tangible opportunity to elevate his status to a more respected persona, albeit a phoney one, and although an army of fans wouldn't be clamouring at the stage door for his autograph, a modicum of acceptance as an achiever in at least one sphere of activity would help him establish his credentials and bring some much-needed approval.

Instead, he felt an instant failure, compounded by the catalogue of negative responses he'd had to his numerous applications to join after-school clubs, along with cycle tours, archery sessions and a ski-ing trip to France, none of which should have been a hindrance now he had the advantage of corrective vision. Or maybe it wasn't his glasses that were the root of the problem.

Wondering if his condition might be hereditary, or a medically recognised blip in his physical make-up, he took to the internet to see if there were any remedial procedures he could try, or if he was simply an oddball destined for a life of recurring disillusionment. He spent several days ensconced in the summer house researching the possibilities, the only conclusions being that there was no data to confirm that accident proneness exists as a verifiable syndrome, and that one out of twenty-nine people has a fifty per cent chance or higher of having an accident than everyone else for all kinds of reasons. Olly had no idea how these facts were arrived at, in the same way that astronomers know that the closest star is 25,300,000,000,000 miles away, and the universe is 13.8 billion years old - or 436,117,077,000,000,000 seconds, depending on whether you were counting it now or sometime last week, or next week - or that Usain Bolt could run faster than the combined average traffic speed for the US cities of Boston, New York City and San Francisco. Although the outcome did not offer him the luxury of certainty, there was equally no conclusive evidence that he was a human oddity who would forever carry the burden of being Bumble in both name and disposition, even though it did little to banish his current despondent mood.

Olly's change in behaviour from mounting optimism to one of cheerless isolation had not gone unnoticed by Helen and Martin, who were desperate to know what could have triggered such a swift personality change.

He kept himself to himself, only came back to the house for meals, and refused any form of socialising, even with Felix.

'If he won't talk to us we can't help him,' said Martin in frustration as he looked out of the kitchen window toward the summer house, where Olly had retreated to lick the invisible wounds that had been the catalyst for this disturbing breakdown in communication.

'His chemistry teacher did say he had been on edge recently,' Helen reminded him, 'though he didn't give a reason.'

'Yes, I remember. Jogging or photography, wasn't that what he recommended? Why stop there? Why not give us a full list of options, like stamp collecting, train spotting, and bell-ringing?'

'He was only trying to be helpful. Olly spends a significant amount of time at school interacting with teachers and classmates and being exposed to all kinds of obstacles so they should know better than anyone what the problem is, which could be directly associated with the school. Maybe we should set up a meeting with the headmaster and talk it through.'

Martin was not convinced. 'I don't want to start waving red flags around when there may be a simple solution. We know summer camp isn't an option. Car tyres dangling over rivers, campfires, rock climbing and white-water rafting are the stuff of nightmares for all of us but there must be alternatives.'

'Such as?'

'Well if he's suffering from a lack of confidence, we could suggest he join an activity group not associated with the school where he can network with people in a safe environment and not be stressed. Learn a new skill, like horticulture, or contemporary dance, or be part of a discussion group like a book club, or take up meditation in a community where he might appreciate that other people have alternative beliefs and adopt different cultures.'

'Like Buddhism? You want to pack our son off to a mountain retreat somewhere in the Himalayas so he can meditate with a group of shaven-headed guys sitting in silence eating bowls of fruit and nuts?'

'That's a sweeping assessment of a religion that's maintained its popularity since the sixth century, Helen. You don't have to be a Buddhist to understand its philosophy of leading a life of meaning and value. Buddhism is a *vision* for life, embracing study, friendship and a defined goal of self-fulfilment. Why wouldn't he benefit from that?'

'Because he's a fifteen-year-old boy who isn't ready to press the reset button and explore the deeper meaning and philosophies of his existence when there's every chance he can figure out the direction he needs to go for himself without making him feel his survival rate is severely restricted if he doesn't cultivate plant life, indulge in religious rituals, or wear a pair of genital-hugging tights and take up ballet. We should give him space for a while and see what happens next.'

What happened next came as much of a surprise to Olly as it did to Helen and Martin. Miss Barratt sent a note to Olly asking him to attend a meeting to discuss his role in stage-managing the school play, something Olly had not given any serious consideration to because he was convinced she was merely placating him at their initial get-together when she realised how disappointed he was at not being able to take an active role on the stage. When it became evident she was serious and took the time a few days later to explain the importance of the role in organising and supporting the actors and crew, from rehearsals through to performance, his mojo returned in a surge of enthusiasm that immediately blew away the clouds of dejection and replaced them with a renewed sense of purpose.

Helen and Martin were not quite so enthused since they were still experiencing night tremors from Olly's participation in *The Pirates of Barnacle Island,* wondering how he would cope if he took it up as a career working backstage in upscaled productions among electricity cables, pulleys, trap doors, mechanical props and lighting rigs. They needn't have worried. Passion and commitment can often overcome the seemingly impossible and Olly's focus in the coming weeks saw him avoid numerous mishaps, from sidestepping one of the windmill's sails as it span from its mount and crashed onto the stage, to Quixote's wooden horse careering out of control on its wheels and tumbling into the makeshift orchestra pit, to a key light coming away from its mounting and swinging precariously above his head. It was as if he had become enveloped by an invisible protective bubble that followed him everywhere he went with the prime purpose of keeping him out of harm's way.

Until, that is, he left the school hall and had to engage with the real world again; that unpredictable, unforgiving force of nature that could kick arse if complacency set in and he was not on his guard.

The ever-dependable Felix, was, of course, always on hand to offer encouragement, having taken on the role of sound supervisor, which involved playing in sound effects such as tweety birds, thunderclaps and crowd noises at appropriate moments as indicated in the script. He had encountered a few initial problems, such as activating the sound of galloping hooves when Quixote's horse ambled with mechanical reluctance onto the stage, but these uncoordinated errors were easily corrected and revealed that Felix was just as prone to getting in a muddle as anyone.

Olly recognised the important roles that everyone played in making *Don Quixote* a success. Such was his desire to make the production an unforgettable experience that he learned to overcome any stumbling blocks and managed to alternate between harsh reality and fictional role-play for the duration of the play's three-day run without mixing up the two. The delight on Ms Barratt's face during the final curtain call told him that he had achieved something previously unimaginable.

Miss Byrony Barratt school report entry, reference Olly Scott.
Olly's contribution to this year's school play was outstanding. He not only handled the stage management with measured calm and superb organisational skills but familiarised himself with every aspect of the production, from lighting and sound, to make-up and wardrobe, assisting his fellow students whenever they needed encouragement and motivating them with a maturity beyond his years. I had initially given Olly overall responsibility for communication across the technical and creative teams

because of his disappointment at not being included in the cast but he proved he has a natural aptitude for this unique craft, with an extraordinary ability to resolve issues and make sensible creative suggestions that reveal his genuine love of theatre, a passion that I believe will serve him well in his adult years and give him the confidence to interact successfully both in the workplace and socially.

DANGER ZONE

Grayson's was a new experience, a step up from the usual places Olly frequented for social gatherings, so he decided to check before leaving the apartment that casual wear was acceptable attire for dining out in such a fashionable establishment. Formal shirts and ties had never made as much as a fleeting guest appearance in his wardrobe, their suffocating presence around his neck an impediment to keeping his brain cells alert and tonight, more than ever, he needed to be fully focused.

The restaurant was alive with activity when he arrived at seven on the dot wearing his blue tour guide jacket – the only one he owned – atop a freshly ironed duck blue shirt, and although he felt anxious about being in an environment whose etiquette he was not familiar with, accepted that Felix's advice to go with the flow was fundamentally sound and the best he could hope for.

She looked stunning sat at a corner table in a sequined dress that shimmered in waves over her elegant frame, waving and smiling at him as though they were old friends meeting for a regular get-together in which work chat was a mere adjunct to the more spontaneous act of enjoying each other's company. Which began with Olly apologising for his absence of formal wear and Emma saying it was unnecessary because he looked very smart and appropriately dressed, and weren't coloured jackets quite fashionable around Brighton these days. Olly immediately claimed ownership of their iconic presence due to his previous life as a tour guide, even though his knowledge of the area sat marginally below zero, which Emma found amusing, having been born and raised in Polegate, a few miles along the coast, where her parents still lived.

'You don't necessarily have to be an expert on a given subject,' said Olly defensively. 'It's about branding, creating an image that associates you with whatever it is you're selling, something that makes you stand out from the crowd, makes you distinctive.'

'And does that apply to everything? TopLite, for instance? How would you brand that?'

Olly took a moment to consider. 'Theatre With Edge. As a strap line anyway. Maybe more by reputation than by employing any particular image.'

'You think TopLite is so different?'

'We try to be. The presentations don't usually conform to standard storytelling and we've managed to establish more than a niche following. We have full houses packed with an army of loyal followers most nights.'

Emma looked impressed. 'And did your jacket fulfil its expectations and attract an army of loyal followers?'

She was toying with him but he didn't mind, it was her good-natured way of sounding him out, seeing if he could take a gentle ribbing without being offended, which he was not, nor could ever be by her. 'I did okay until a new lad rocked up wearing a bright yellow jacket and nicked half my customers. I thought blue was symbolic of the sky and sea, whereas to some it may have suggested swirling currents, rip tides and hypothermia. His, on the other hand, evoked sunny days filled with hope and expectation.'

'Oh dear.'

'No, it was fine. I was leaving anyway and it was a lesson learned: there's always someone who'll trump you with more persuasive branding if you take your eye off the ball.'

Although this good-humoured banter set the tone for the kind of stress-free evening Olly had not envisaged but to which he was happy to be a co-contributor, he remained on red alert to pre-empt any possible mishaps, placing his wine glass well out of reach until fortification was necessary and checking that the cutlery was not in a position where the slip of an elbow might send a fork flying over Emma's head and onto an adjacent table, piercing someone's arm. If the waiter warned him the plates were hot he resolved not to touch them under any circumstances and if starters were an agreed option, to avoid selecting the soup at all costs. To that end, his side of the table looked like a military offensive, in which the knives, forks, spoons, side plate and breadbasket had closed ranks to give the gastronomic enemy short thrift if it stepped out of line, his napkin neatly placed on his knees to capture any transgressors if they tried to make a break for it.

Emma put him at ease by relating how interesting her childhood had been living in a coastal setting surrounded by nature, though she side-stepped her preference for limited social intercourse and involvement in communal activities despite her parents' encouragement to be more outgoing. She did give them credit for introducing her to the wonders of theatre production and although they were always well-intentioned, she thought they were as mad as a box of frogs, indulging in madcap pastimes and crazy, unpredictable road trips in their beaten-up motor home. Her creative aptitude, she felt, was probably a legacy of her unconventional upbringing, even though Olly sensed she was not altogether approving of their quirky lifestyle. He, in turn, avoided revealing anything that might have a negative impact, leaving out vast chunks of his childhood experiences, focusing on his early realisation that he also had a passion for theatre, mostly the technical and organisational side, and telling her how much he had enjoyed the past few years and looked forward to pushing boundaries with each new production.

It was an enjoyable exchange of backstories in a jovial atmosphere that dispelled, as the evening wore on, any feelings of foreboding that Olly had and he took the odd moment to appreciate the various animated conversations going on around him that were helping make the evening so pleasurable: the birthday celebrations at the table opposite as a family of varying ages swapped crackers and told jokes; a waiter setting a griddle pan in the middle of a table as two customers selected their steaks; the four young men on a stag night that would most likely end with one of them tied naked to a lamp-post at the end of the pier; the dessert trolley loaded with a mouthwatering selection of chef's specials being wheeled in as three children looked on in excited anticipation, one of them smiling mischievously at Olly as she span her TwizzleWheel on the table in front of her. It was what spending time in relaxed, convivial surroundings was all about and Olly was determined to make the most of every minute, feeling cheated when the arrival of coffee signalled the conclusion of the meal.

'I printed off some initial ideas,' said Emma, placing a selection of drawings on the table as a prelude to shifting the focus from the pleasurable to the obligatory in determining how best to proceed in bringing TopLite's forthcoming productions to fruition within the confines of budget and schedule.

Olly carefully moved his coffee cup to a designated safety zone next to a small flower arrangement and studied the drawings.

'I designed a similar murder mystery in Birmingham three years ago,' she continued. 'The production run was during the spring break so the murder took place at Easter, which meant constructing a set comprising free-standing light grey blocks that could truck and spin effortlessly into different positions and contained small rotating flaps, so we could replace paintings with shelves or cupboards and wall clocks with windows and so on. The props were varying shades of yellow to give a stylised look against the grey walls – a yellow sun outside an open window in Paris which was transformed into a balcony extension when the setting became Vienna, with yellow daffodils if we were in London, and different props, such as Easter decorations and paintings applicable to wherever the action took place. We could utilise the same building blocks, which would be white for both plays, including the floor areas.'

'But the sets would look very different?'

'Yes. The two plays lend themselves to abstract settings for entirely different reasons, which means we can create a distinctive look and atmosphere for each using sound, lighting, smoke effects, dry ice and snow. Shadow-play on the walls would be more effective against the white and the addition of Christmas lights would give a visual transformation from the minimalist look of *Art*, to one that reflects the mood and atmosphere of *Shadows,* while emphasising the jeopardy of the piece. We could do a turnaround inside a week if we combine the technical run with the dress rehearsal.'

'Looks like the perfect solution. Saves us stripping everything back, so we can make nominal modifications between shows.'

'The block concept isn't new but it's convenient and practical for back-to-back shows like this.'

He looked up from the drawings and came straight to the point. 'And you'd be happy to take this on?'

Her lips curled into the same seductive smile that had captivated him during their first meeting, her hand sliding briefly over his to offer reassurance that all would be well if he stayed positive. 'The chance to design two great plays in my home town working with such a dedicated crew? Of course. It's going to be fun.'

She excused herself and went to the counter to pay the bill while Olly leaned back in his chair with a sense of relief and satisfaction. Mission accomplished. Emma had planned their future presentations with a thoroughness that had not only bowled him over but aroused in him a renewed sense of excitement and optimism, on top of which he had sailed through the meeting without drawing unwanted attention to himself. The evening had, without question, been a triumph.

And as the waiter flambéed the Steak Diane, the four men ordered more drinks, the group in party hats began singing Happy Birthday and the children sat poised with their spoons ready to attack their cream-filled dessert selection, the little girl gave her TwizzleWheel an over-zealous flick, which sent it whirling out of control and over the edge of the table.

Instinctively Olly jumped up and made a lunge towards the spinning toy in an effort to catch it, succeeding only in colliding with the waiter who was advancing toward the party table carrying a large decadent sponge birthday cake which oozed a rich pastry cream and succulent strawberry jam, enveloped in fluorescent green marzipan that was soon to end up sliding across the floor and creating unimaginable mayhem.

Olly could only watch in horror as a waitress carrying two bottles of champagne slid along the slimy mess and crashed into the children's table, pulling over the cloth which sent the selection of desserts over the edge as another waiter skidded into the table where the Steak Diane took a sudden unscheduled detour along the tablecloth, setting it alight in a vivid unwanted party piece. And as the manager hurried onto the scene with a fire extinguisher and the children started crying and the four men stood and cheered wildly, Emma returned to her seat with a look of unbridled disbelief and alarm at the scene of culinary carnage that was unfolding in front of her.

'My God! What happened?'

'I think the waiter must have slipped on something,' said Olly with as much cool indifference as he could muster in an effort to deflect any blame.

'We should go,' said Emma, pulling him towards the exit with an immediate sense of unease, 'before it gets out of hand.'

A brisk walk along the promenade put a respectable distance between them and the unprecedented scenes of panic at Grayson's, devoid, thankfully, of the sound of angry footsteps running after them. An accident was an accident after all, even though Olly would be reluctant to admit culpability if it meant blowing his fragile cover and ruining the evening when he had been so close to the finishing line.

'That was quite extraordinary,' said Emma, relieved to be away from the building. 'It's remarkable how such a pleasant, carefree evening could turn so quickly into uncontrolled chaos.'

Olly knew only too well how quickly an innocuous, everyday event could disintegrate into uncontrolled chaos but he wasn't about to offer disclosure or attempt to explain any of the myriad of probability factors. 'Unbelievable,' he replied, looking out to sea and taking in the cool night air with the same nonchalance that he had conjured as they made their way out of the restaurant. 'And such a waste of cake.'

'I should think they'll be more concerned about their reputation,' said Emma. 'Word spreads faster when there are negative vibes rather than positive ones. They should have been more careful.'

'At least TopLite's reputation looks like it'll be in good hands,' he replied, keen to change the subject by applying some timely flattery. She simply smiled in response, happy to take in the pulsating Friday night atmosphere as people jostled around them, intent on making the most of everything a vibrant seaside town had to offer. They walked in silence for a while when suddenly Emma slipped as one of her heels came off. 'Bugger, I only had that replaced last week.'

'Can we get it fixed somewhere?'

'No, it's okay,' she said, sliding both her shoes off, 'I can walk in stockinged feet. My place isn't far from here.'

Olly smiled. Apart from the experience of escaping an unexpected restaurant inferno, very little unsettled her or made her annoyed, a quality he admired among so many others.

When they turned into Portland Place the sound of jovial crowds and sea-on-shingle subsided and she waved her hand in the direction of one of the apartments.

'This is me. Mortgaged to the hilt, but it's my personal space and I count myself lucky to have it. Thanks for a lovely evening, Olly. It was fun and a good use of our time.' She leaned forward, kissed him lightly on the cheek, and then disappeared behind her newly acquired and imposing Regency front door.

Olly stood motionless in the street savouring the moment. Emma was beautiful and smart and although he was becoming more infatuated with each moment he spent in her company, he was thankful she had not invited him in because he was exceptionally bad at reading signals and would have been clueless as to what the expectation would be. He had no desire to put his emotions through the shredder unnecessarily and since the opportunity to test his current confidence levels had not presented itself, he made his way back to the apartment to cast another eye over the illustrations, pleased that at least she was on board professionally. It was, after all, the purpose of their get-together and it was foolish for him to believe their association could be anything more. Olly had allowed himself to be sidetracked on too many occasions in the past, almost every instance leading to varying degrees of distress and regret. Now he was motivated to engage in a worthwhile career; the reason he and Felix had moved to Brighton in the first place and he felt an unswerving commitment to theatre production, without any unwanted distractions that might steer his energies away from the profession for which he felt such a passion and which, like Emma, had started all those years ago, though possibly not with the same sense of positivity.

TESTING THE WATER

'So this detective has been chasing shadows?'

'Yes. The couple thought they had killed him by accident when he caught them red-handed during a robbery in Austria on Christmas Day but their car skidded into a ravine as they were making their getaway, not realising he had survived the shooting.'

Philippa flicked back through the script. 'But he didn't know they had died, which is why he kept looking for them for ten years?'

'Yes,' agreed Olly, 'so the audience believes the couple is real and the detective is a ghost, when in fact it's the other way round.'

Philippa pursed her lips and considered this premise. 'Well he's not much of a fucking detective if he didn't know they were dead, is he?'

'It was a very large ravine,' countered Olly. 'Nobody knew they were dead. The Parsons were just a couple of missing persons whose spirits continued revisiting their favourite hotels each Christmas day, while he kept retracing their steps from his previous pursuits. At each location the couple devises implausible but humorous ways to outsmart a ghost who is, in fact, not a ghost, but a man who is extremely pissed off at being shot at and almost killed.'

'And the fact that each scene is in an entirely different country won't pose a problem?'

'No, the play's surreal storyline is mirrored in the design concept, using Emma's blocks in combination with fast turnaround lighting, props and sound effects to create different moods and atmospheres.'

Philippa looked through the stage designs spread across her desk. 'And Emma's aware we have a limited budget?'

'Yes, which is why she's utilised the same basic set for both plays. I can understand if you're annoyed because I didn't tell you I'd been talking to her. I didn't know if she'd be available or even interested so initially it was just an exploratory chat. I hadn't expected her to lay out her ideas so meticulously.'

'It's not a problem, Olly. I can see why she would want to take it on and I like the idea of staging an eerie ghost story against white and not traditional black. The central theme of revenge ultimately being a waste of energy running alongside the visual humour adds a valuable dimension even if it will get lost on the more vulnerable patrons who'll spend two hours being scared witless.'

'So you'll consider it for the programme?'

'I don't need to. I'll schedule it for the winter season following on from *Art*, and in the absence of an available director, I'll take on this particular challenge myself. We need to arrange a production meeting with Emma and the technical staff as soon as possible. And Felix. He'll need to be kept up to speed on what we're proposing. I'll text you my availability and since you appear to have established a rapport with Ms Appleby, I'll leave it with you to confirm a day and time.'

Coordinating diaries was not the easiest of tasks, with Philippa dipping in and out of sponsorship meetings and Emma having to stay at her apartment to supervise plumbers, decorators and electricians, but design and script adjustments were made via email, with the results forwarded to Olly and Felix to mull over until a face-to-face meeting became a practical option. As the planning process increased in intensity over the following days, Emma suggested that she and Olly meet for drinks so she could 'run some options' past him before making a formal presentation.

'You don't mind doing this do you, Olly? I'd like your opinion before I put this on the table officially.'

Olly was delighted but cautious at the prospect of spending more time with Emma, his enthusiasm tempered by the number of possible mishaps that could trounce him no matter how careful he was. He had experienced a close call at the restaurant even though he reasoned it was an accident that could have happened to anyone. Despite that unexpected blip, he'd had a run of good luck and although it was too soon to say categorically that he was no longer a danger to himself and others, the signs were, in his estimation, fair to good.

Before committing himself to another meeting so soon after sidestepping exposure at Grayson's, he decided it might be prudent to embark on a test run to make sure he really could cope with the demands of daily life no matter how many unseen circumstances might try to foil him. Most importantly, he needed to set out on this experimental tour de force unaided by any form of mechanical apparatus or protective clothing.

Although it was well known that most accidents happen in the home he had, so far, avoided any significant mishaps in the apartment, and TopLite, with its safety procedures in place 24/7, posed no immediate threat, especially with the addition of the illusionary protective bubble that he chose not to question in case it offended the thespian gods who were watching his back. Wandering around a garden centre was a possible starting point, which statistically was not considered a high-risk environment when compared to building sites and nuclear power stations but he was familiar with the potential threats of slippery floors and hazardous chemical products due to his brief period of employment at SewToBed. His only encounter with erratic plant life had been in the form of Bronwyn Evans during their occasional assignations behind the potting shed so on reflection it wasted energy assessing his survival chances in a place from which he had already emerged relatively unscathed.

Bendeck's department store was selected as his first port of call since it was always swarming with shoppers viewing and purchasing a diverse range of products spread over three floors, each containing a miscellaneous assortment of safety hazards, from loose carpeting and items falling from shelves to poor lighting and discarded packaging, to malfunctioning escalators. The toy department seemed a good place to start since small children, whom Dr Lowry once observed had a natural tendency to run into objects and other children, could become a convenient diversion tactic if any accidents occurred while he was moving about, although it was important to give the appearance of a legitimate customer rather than a man with questionable motives who needed reporting to the authorities, questioned, and escorted from the premises. Fifteen minutes of dodging hyperactive kids in toy cars, bouncing around on space hoppers and racing around on scooters produced no calamitous incidents – at least none he could be directly blamed for - so he left carrying an armful of board games and fluffy animals and headed for the Glass and China department, the ultimate test of his ability to claim immunity from the perils of fated catastrophe.

With every step Olly grew in confidence, tempting fate as he passed by the fragile displays, picking up and inspecting a variety of bowls, dishes and glass ornaments - an activity that produced no panic attacks, although Felix may have regarded his stopping off for lunch in the canteen as a reckless manoeuvre since it was packed with fellow patrons walking about with trays loaded with cutlery and hot beverages, unaware of the risks they were exposing themselves to.

But Felix was not with him and might even have regarded the positive outcome of his first test of endurance as a significant achievement as he emerged into the street with his bounty of purchased goods and retreated to the safety of the apartment to take stock and plan his final assault on the precarious world that he was determined to out-manoeuvre.

The Brighton Pier funfair had been left in limbo at the bottom of his list for obvious reasons, jampacked as it was with heavy machinery, water chutes and fast-moving rides, not to mention the vast armies of boisterous fun-seekers who were intent on having a good time in defiance of the dangers that lurked all around them. Olly knew he was more likely to be injured walking or driving to a funfair than being at it, and even though serious roller coaster accidents were reported as only one in one-point-five billion in any given year and he was more likely to be struck by lightning, he decided to err on the side of caution by studying a plan of the amusement park and determining which areas might be wise to avoid during his initial foray into the area.

As it happened, the afternoon turned out to be more fun than he imagined, like a prisoner on day release unburdened by any restrictions on his movements and free to enjoy his time without fear of consequence. Riding uneventfully on the carousel inspired him to progress to the more exciting helter-skelter, followed by the dramatic Wild River log flume, his self-assurance moving up a notch despite being half-drenched, giving him the courage to test both his nerve and resolve on the Galaxia with its sudden lifts and drops, culminating in a more buttock-clenching finale on the erratic Turbo Coaster. Letting go of his inhibitions proved to be both liberating and enjoyable and he wondered why it had taken him so long to appreciate the intrinsic value of self-belief.

Inspired by his journey through the delights and perils of death-defying entertainment, he believed that by grasping the nettle he had made himself impervious to general misfortune. It was simply a matter of considering the potential fallout and devising a plan of action.

Whilst Felix may have had cause to question such optimism and wonder why the apartment had become littered with board games, goldfish and plastic ducks,

Olly remained steadfast in his quest to become impervious to the unpredictable, hoping that a metaphoric ice patch was not waiting to whip his legs from under him and dump him once more in the manure of life.

VOLTE-FACE

Olly watched as Emma opened up her laptop on the small table they occupied in a corner of Chappie's Winebar overlooking the seafront, curious as to why she felt the need to seek his advice before making a presentation to Philippa. 'I'm happy to look them over but I'm sure it's not necessary.'

'Last minute adjustments. Just to be sure. The concept was your idea, after all.'

The final set design for *Art* appeared on the screen, with minimal furniture against basic white as they had agreed. 'It's only one set so what you see is what you get, the background only changing through the timeline when shadow effects are applied on the scenic blocks reflecting Venetian blinds or plants, or there's a glow from an unseen table lamp. What do you think?'

'It's simple but distinctive and the visual representation of props is an inspired use of space. I like it.'

'It's a traditional way of presenting the play, with the advantage that…' she clicked the mouse and a new set of illustrations appeared… 'by moving the blocks around, adapting the lighting and replacing the simulated props with real ones, we create a completely different ambience for *Shadow*.'

Olly nodded his appreciation. The dramatic change utilising basic elements was impressive. 'You have been busy.'

Emma swiped through a succession of scene changes, revealing minimal set adjustments that moved the locations from Austria to Paris, Vienna, Spain, and then London. 'I'm hoping this is what you were expecting. I can add more visual character to each location but then the changeovers themselves would take additional time.'

'No, they're perfect, I wouldn't alter anything. The transitions take place under cover of strategically placed sub-sets and they work well.'

'Excellent. I'm pleased you approve.' She shut down the laptop, pushed it to one side, and signalled to the barman, who walked over clutching a cold bottle of Sauvignon Blanc. 'You're favourite as I recall,' she said as she poured the wine into two glasses and handed one to Olly.

'So. From tour guide to circus performer to stage manager at TopLite and with no formal training I'm presuming. Tell me how that came about.'

Olly felt a moment of panic. Emma had arranged the meet for a work-related chat which by his reckoning had taken all of three minutes, dispensed with by the introduction of a bottle of wine and an unexpected exploration of his background. At Grayson's he had briefly recounted his blue jacket experiences and his time with Billy Zando's circus but avoided details such as losing his virginity to Zelda and an introduction to drama by way of school plays which not only seemed a lame explanation but rekindled experiences he would rather forget.

He chose his words carefully, admitting to no formal training, just a love of theatre that led to him spending a summer with Zane's circus, his voluntary work at TopLite during evenings and weekends, all in his spare time, so when Philippa offered him a trainee opportunity he grabbed it, roped in Felix, who had written a series of plays, and it snowballed from there. He learned on the job, just like lots of people, but beyond that, he had no formal qualifications.

She realised he may have misinterpreted her question and rallied immediately to her defence, saying that experience is everything and reminding him that he stage-managed a successful version of *Big Top* and she wouldn't be asking his opinion if she didn't value it. Sensing his embarrassment at receiving a compliment she shifted focus, telling him that her passion for design and illustration began when she played with makeshift theatres in her bedroom as a child and drew unflattering caricatures of her teachers, which were surprisingly entered into competitions and the winning illustrations pinned up on the school notice boards for everyone to critique and admire. It was a moment of shared humour that had put the evening back on track - until Emma dropped another potential bombshell.

'I've told you about my crazy parents, but I know nothing about yours, so spill the beans, people like us don't usually have conventional upbringings.'

More probing, only now it was about the effects of anomalous upbringings on *people like us*. Did she see the two of them as kindred spirits so early on in their association? Had this turned into a date without any forewarning? Or was he reading too much into it? Best to be cautious and not back-reference Helen and Martin's years of consternation that their son was plagued by epic disasters that required referral to paediatricians and other specialists, not to mention the prospect of him being packed off to a Buddhist retreat to absorb himself in mindfulness. Instead, he could introduce some humour into his response by retelling his mother's oft-told story of the day he almost set their flat on fire and the emergency services had to be called. On the other hand, being categorised as a pyromaniac from such an early age might not be the most promising finale to an evening of possibilities, so he put aside any disclosures about fire engines, radio-controlled fighter jets, accidents with bunsen burners and sulphuric acid and how he almost single-handedly destroyed the set for a school play by swinging down on a rope dressed as a surly pirate.

'My mother was a dab hand at making costumes. Christmas, Halloween, school plays. Mostly for my sister Erica, who's currently in Edinburgh studying interior design.'

Emma looked impressed. 'So creativity runs in the family. What about your father?'

Martin was a less straightforward subject and Olly briefly pondered how to filter his father's fanatical views on society and its shortcomings. 'He's an IT specialist. In security. One of the best I'm told, but it's a career that's given him an overly suspicious view of life in an unpredictably toxic world. He wrote to the headmistress at my school berating one of her staff for using innocent children in a play as a front for sexism and political skulduggery. I was mortified.'

'Drama can conceal all kinds of hidden meanings using innocent faces and innocuous scenarios to convey messages. Was your teacher a political activist?'

'I've no idea. He gave violin recitals and performed at local fairs with a group of Morris dancers waving sticks and handkerchiefs, but when you're thirteen years old you assume that all adults are responsible human beings who lead by example and don't harbour secret ambitions or have peculiar habits. Then you discover a frightening proportion of them are manipulative, deceptive, depraved, controlling, or just plain crackers, which may be excellent material for books and plays but it doesn't give any of us much confidence in that brighter, better future we were promised as youngsters, so maybe I should have listened to my father more often.'

Emma laughed at Olly's unnerving summary of human capability. 'Your father sounds like a man who doesn't take anything at face value and looks beyond the obvious. Whether he was right or not, we need people who are prepared to ask questions and delve deeper into what motivates those we share our space with. I can honestly say, hand on heart, that my parents are true innocents. They have no furtive endeavours or hidden agendas. They block out the destructive elements that exist beyond their front door, taking each day as it comes. Sylvia and Norman embrace all that life has to offer rather than worry about the things they have little or no control over, spending time on their weird and wonderful pursuits, whatever anyone thinks of them, and if they do have secrets not shared, it is for reasons none of us has any right to question.'

Olly picked up his wine glass and held it aloft. 'To innocence and the sanctity of secrets.'

They chinked glasses and after draining her glass, Emma excused herself as Olly pulled out his wallet and handed over his credit card, unaware that the brief coming together of the drinking vessels had caused a crack in the one he was holding and the wine was dripping over the counter and down his trousers. The barman handed over a cloth, apologising profusely for the manufacturing defect in the glass and as Olly wiped his crotch, cursing the manufacturing defect in his brain that had caused the leakage, Emma reappeared wearing a huge grin.

'Oh dear. You were only meant to spill the beans, Olly.'

'Cheap glass,' said Olly, placing the cloth on the counter, knowing it was an even cheaper response to cover his tracks yet again, because his card was marked every time he met up with her and there seemed nothing he could do to stop the inevitable.

'Don't worry, it'll dry in the night air,' she said as they walked back to the street, puzzled as to why he was taking the incident so seriously but aware that a wet crutch was probably not the most desirable way to end the evening.

The walk back to Emma's apartment followed a familiar pattern, with the exception that her goodnight kiss was planted firmly on his lips - albeit briefly - but as before with no follow-up invitation to join her for a nightcap. With a fleeting sense of deja vu, he watched her disappear behind the front door that held its own mysteries, then turned and made his way back home.

The next few weeks saw a buzz of activity as the production team met to discuss the technical requirements for both plays in conjunction with the set designs. Felix and Philippa had both made minor tweaks to each of their stage directions, and lighting and sound offered suggestions that enhanced the choreography and atmosphere, particularly with respect to *Shadows*, after which each department went away to make final preparations until everyone met again on the first rehearsal day for *Art*, along with the actors who walked the set for the first time. It gave Felix a chance to observe Emma at close hand as she worked with him making various tweaks and adjustments to the stage directions and set turnarounds, and he could see why Olly had become so infatuated. She was talented and disciplined, with a refined beauty that would captivate any man and it was immediately evident why Olly was in danger of losing both head and heart whenever he came anywhere near her.

But there was little time to spend evolving a plan of action to help a friend who had struggled over the years to develop close relationships with the opposite sex. The future of TopLite was paramount and that, for the foreseeable future, had to be the focus of everyone's attention. They had a great deal of ground to make up in terms of budget and scheduling, with Felix wheeling in his own stage manager for *Art* since Olly was focused on overseeing *Shadows,* whilst needing to put time aside for reading the script for a play called *One Way Ticket*, which Philippa was keen to produce for the spring run. Since Emma was persuaded, without too much arm-twisting, to stay on through the summer, it meant she and Olly would be spending more time together than either had anticipated. For Olly, this should have been welcome news but he was becoming increasingly troubled by the intensity of his feelings for her and had an urgent need to share his concerns.

Whilst hesitant about bothering her when she had better things to occupy her time, Olly decided he had no option but to ask the one person he felt was best equipped to offer good advice.

Email from Olly Scott to Zelda Dascalu.
Hi Zelda. Sorry to hear about your father. Hope he's making progress and that the situation isn't proving to be too much of a strain on you. You were greatly missed during the summer and although Big Top was a success you probably heard it was not without its problems, which was only to be expected considering its intricate routines, cultural and language barriers and creative differences. The unicyclist collided with the juggler during one performance when they mistimed their entrances, fortunately with no consequences other than a couple of smashed dinner plates, and Crackles the Clown had a mishap when the splatter gun exploded in his face and he accused one of the dwarves of sabotaging it over a disagreement involving a frankfurter and a bag of melons. I don't regret staging Big Top, however, just the knock-on effects that created a few personality clashes and an overspend which almost torpedoed the winter schedules. Thanks to the support of everyone at TopLite we are now in good shape due mainly to the introduction of two new plays and a designer in the form of an angel called Emma Appleby for whom I have the greatest admiration and have grown very fond. We've only been working together for a couple of months and although my feelings for her are intensifying by the day they are also creating confusion because I have no idea if this is adulation, infatuation, or even love, or if it's too soon to know. I'm just a guy whose head rules his heart and is out of his depth, so any advice?

Any tell-tale signs I should watch out for? Your opinion would be welcome.

Having opened up to Zelda he decided it was an opportune moment to send a similar email to Erica in Edinburgh, leaving out the near misses he had experienced on *Big Top* and playing down his fascination with Emma, focusing on the possibility of a 'too soon to jump to conclusions' assessment and enquiring how things were progressing on her design course in the hope that she might read between the lines and offer some sisterly observations to reassure him he was doing the right thing in letting events take their course. She did not. A short text response thanking him for thinking of her, accompanied by a thumbs-up emoji, summed up her overall concern for his predicament, for which he was going to have to sort out any emotional baggage, turbulent or otherwise, for himself.

Zelda, on the other hand, responded after a couple of days with more positive counsel.

Email from Zelda Dascalu to Olly Scott.
My dear Olly, how wonderful to hear from you. I'm flattered you should think a mature trollop like me is an appropriate choice for offering guidance on such a complex matter and that I would be capable of identifying what attracts one person to another for mutual, if fleeting, gratification, or for the long emotive haul. Even love survives terrible trauma or abuse, mental or physical, for reasons none of us can explain. You spend much of your time gazing at a lovely woman, I spend my days looking at a shell of a man who dribbles his tea and spills breakfast cereal down his shirt, which proves that love can take many forms. As for Emma being an angel, remember that angels are not real, only imagined. She, like you, will have flaws and faults that stay

undetected until they rise to the surface, or are discovered, but if you can see beyond her clipped wings and come to terms with the reality, you will have truly found love. I look forward to hearing about your new plays, I'm sure they will be a triumph.

Olly read the email several times, trying to determine whether Zelda was suggesting he should be hopeful or simply accept the inevitable without futile analysis because love came down to a mixture of chemistry, tolerance and forgiveness and was beyond anyone's control unless they were prepared to make sacrifices that demanded the highest level of selflessness and understanding in the face of another person's imperfections. It was the thorny subject of empathy and acceptance that created Olly's greatest dilemma because it was his own inadequacies that concerned him.

'Do you think you might be laying yourself open to disappointment, Olly? Making yourself vulnerable to long-term emotional fallout?'

'Of course. I've never been this close to a woman before. Not someone as exceptional as Emma.'

Felix studied the face sitting next to him, filled with anguish and uncertainty, wondering how he could offer any sensible or valid advice. He was drained emotionally himself, having finished rehearsing for twelve hours in readiness for an impending opening night, not expecting Olly to turn up in an empty auditorium and lay his heart on his sleeve when he had assumed his relationship with Emma was moving on an even keel without the unwelcome burden of intense soul-searching. 'She obviously likes you, inviting you out for meals and drinks when you could just as easily meet here or on the seafront sharing a bag of chips.'

'It doesn't go anywhere though, Felix. The suggestion of something that might extend beyond a professional association always stops at her front door so I never know whether to chance my arm and declare my affection or just accept that she isn't interested in developing our relationship further.'

Felix briefly pondered Olly's dilemma. 'Well you've nothing to lose by letting her know how fond you are of her. It won't alter anything other than to clarify the situation.'

'I've everything to lose. She might walk. Decide it's not possible to work with someone who has feelings for her when they aren't mutual.'

'You think she's been sending out mixed messages? Is that what's bothering you?'

'Partly. But there's another problem. I've had my clumsiness under control for months but since Emma entered my life it's all started up again.'

'It's your imagination, Olly. She makes you nervous because you lack confidence when you're with her. You put her on a pedestal when you should be treating her as an equal. You solved the problem in the past by being upfront and not hiding it.'

'I can't take that chance, Felix, risk frightening her off because she realises the guy who can organise complex theatre productions involving scores of technicians and performers is a ham-fisted jerk who can't coordinate or control basic physical movement when he's let loose in public.'

'So deceiving her is a better option?'

Olly considered the implication. 'No. Because I have feelings for her I have to take a step back otherwise I would be living a lie and I doubt she would ever forgive me. Losing her companionship is one thing, but I would never want to lose her respect.'

BELIEF

'I didn't say it would be *wrong* to deceive her.'

'Well you inferred it, Felix, and I'm not disagreeing.'

'Then look upon it more like concealing a temporary problem.'

'One that I've had since I was four years old.'

'Everyone has accidents when they're kids, it's part of growing up.'

'So maybe I never grew up, just gained a height advantage.'

'Emma sees you as a grown-up, Olly. What she doesn't see, and doesn't *need* to see at the moment, is a lack of belief in yourself when you're with her, but there are ways around that.'

'You think?'

'Of course. We just need to talk them through.'

Olly was intrigued. His co-conspirator in all things relating to matters of harmless deception was already plotting a course out of the impasse. 'So how exactly do I find a way to spend time with her when I ought to keep my distance?'

'It's a simple strategy, Olly. You don't go anywhere with her that's potentially littered with hazards, like boating lakes, swimming pools, nightclubs, moto-cross, firework displays, theme parks, antique shops, bowling alleys, clay-pigeon shoots and a whole bunch of others I haven't even thought of.'

Olly looked momentarily crestfallen. 'Jesus, Felix, developing a relationship is meant to be *fun*.'

'Then use your imagination and look at the possibilities. Picnics, coach trips, the cinema, quiz nights, music recitals, even cosy evenings in with a takeaway watching the telly. It's not all about being extravagant and going out to fancy restaurants. I'll help whenever I can so you can build your confidence until you're ready to fly solo.'

It made sense, of course. No need to push the boundaries until the time was right. And no need to panic. Not yet. It was just a matter of control. Play it cool and don't become too anxious.

Olly's first opportunity into this new initiative presented itself during the turnaround for *Shadows* a few weeks later, after *Art* had completed a successful ten-day run and everyone was feeling more buoyant about the new schedules. Emma, he noticed, was never phased by any of the customary glitches that demanded attention: lighting changes that needed tweaking, timing on shadow play requiring adjustment and set changeovers that could be achieved faster and more efficiently. She took it all in her stride, directing operations from a seat in the stalls without once stepping onto the stage, preferring to video the activity on her cell phone for later analysis.

'No need to get in the way,' she had said as a sound and logical reason for allowing the blocks to be trundled about and spun into position while the props were being wrangled into place. 'Getting under everyone's feet just slows down the process.' Olly admired her attitude, it not only made sense but was a reflection of her trust in the lighting technicians and stage crew to make the necessary adjustments unhindered by constant interference from the designer. Both Olly and Emma had been unusually busy during the run-up to the technical rehearsals but as everything fell into place, the problems faded away and a sense of calm replaced the frenzy as life settled into a sense of normality.

'We should get away from all this for a few hours,' Emma suggested as they were about to take a break from the technical run-throughs to allow Philippa to prepare for blocking with the actors on the stage now that Emma's ground plans had been finalised.

'Not a bad idea,' agreed Olly, frantically contemplating which of Felix's options he should consider.

'You've not taken me on your secret tour of the town,' she said, inadvertently coming to his rescue.

'No, I haven't.' It was the one leisure pursuit with which he had always felt safe; an activity that had never phased him, even in the company of mischievous customers who tried to catch him out with a barrage of awkward questions.

'Okay. Let's do it tomorrow. You're not due back on set until Wednesday, so no excuses.'

Olly had no intention of making excuses. He had been playing it cool as he and Felix had agreed, and it was Emma who had suggested that they should take time to chill out. It was the perfect opportunity to rekindle their association outside of the work environment and give him a chance to determine in which direction it might go.

When Emma arrived promptly outside the Brighton Marina at two-thirty as agreed, Olly was waiting with two brightly coloured bicycles gleaming in the sunlight, one with a basket attached, inside which he had placed a picnic wrapped in foil.

'Coffee and cake,' he said with a broad smile, 'our afternoon indulgence.'

'Brilliant,' agreed Emma, 'let's work up an appetite.'

They pushed off together, Emma following Olly's lead as he took her along some of the bike-friendly paths, past the more customary sights of Brunswick Square, Preston Manor with its secret garden, and the Fishing Quarter, occasionally going off-track to explore lesser-known locations: the smugglers' tunnels beneath the Old Ship Hotel, Quadrophenia Alley, and the Booth Museum, filled with a million objects relating to the natural world. Olly opted to give the Victorian Sewers a miss, taking her instead to Madeira Drive to admire the flint grotto, with its magical collection of sculptures decorated in shells from the beach.

After a brief stop off at the Beach Club, a permanent pop-up style beachfront village, they propped up the bicycles and unwrapped their picnic treat to spend a leisurely half-hour talking and laughing and generally enjoying each other's company before rounding off the tour with a visit to the Duke of York's Picturehouse, the oldest operating cinema in Britain. Emma admitted to being a regular visitor here, prompting an invitation for them to come back one evening together when a suitable film was being screened. Their final destination, the Mechanical Memories Museum, reminded them of summer days spent at various holiday venues as children when life was less complicated and a world of possibilities stretched beyond the horizon.

'My childhood was filled with mixed memories,' said Emma, as they headed back to the Marina. 'But I found the perfect career, so I can honestly say I haven't much to complain about.'

'Me neither,' agreed Olly, 'except I tended to fall into my career path by accident. Or maybe it was fate, or incredibly good fortune, I'm not sure, but I'm not questioning how it happened.' He dismissed any notion of elaborating to her on how he literally fell, stumbled, collided and crashed into his career, content to accept that everything seemed to balance out in the end and there was little point being analytical when you had employment, a beautiful woman by your side, the breeze blowing across your face, and the chances of finding romantic fulfilment potentially within your grasp. He was tempted to ask her if she felt anything was missing from her idyllic lifestyle but decided it was a conversation that put him at risk of stepping over an invisible line into forbidden territory. Relationships, children, joint mortgages, pension funds and life assurance were all subjects for another day, possibly in a different time zone, or maybe never. Certainly not for now. Not if he wanted their friendship to develop into something more significant.

'So. What next?' she asked.

'Next?'

'Yes, what are your plans for, say, the next five years?'

'Haven't given it much thought to be honest. I'm quite happy at TopLite and I've no plans to leave Brighton.'

He knew the expectation was that he would ask what her plans were, but he was afraid she might reel off a list of prearranged projects and trips to far-flung corners of the world that would eliminate him from the equation. 'And you?' he heard himself say, hoping she didn't notice the hesitancy in his voice.

'A West End musical possibly. I'd love to design a full-on production with spectacular visual effects, rotating sets, banks of flickering lights and quick-fire costume changes played out in front of a full-scale orchestra.' She waved her arm in the air in a theatrical gesture of triumphant anticipation. 'The adrenaline charge would be amazing. Music, colour, unremitting moments of magic and wonder…'

A small dog ran between them as Emma's hand came back down to grip the handlebar but the front wheel wobbled and she left the pavement and went into the road, causing a car to skid around her. Olly took hold of the handlebar bringing her bike to an immediate stop.

'Shit, sorry, Olly, didn't see it.'

'It should have been on a lead. Are you all right?'

'I'm fine. Shouldn't get so carried away.'

They pushed off again, the realisation that she could have come to harm reinforcing his feelings for her whilst accentuating his fear that Emma had her mind fixed firmly on advancing her career in a direction, and with a passion, he had not envisaged,

'TopLite can put on something spectacular. *Big Top* proved it's possible to stage a musical despite the teething problems.'

She gave him a sideways glance and noticed a tinge of despondency in his eyes. 'Sounds like you wouldn't want me to leave and take on new challenges.'

'No, no, I'm not saying that,' he replied in momentary panic. 'You should do that, yes, of course you should, you have an amazing talent and you deserve to be offered bigger shows.'

'But you'd miss me?'

'Of course I'd miss you. I've enjoyed your company, it's been special.'

'And I've enjoyed our afternoon together. It was lovely, thank you, Olly.'

Ten minutes later they arrived back at the Marina, where they dismounted and Emma checked her watch. 'Perfect timing. I'm having supper with an old friend later. Gives me plenty of time to make myself look presentable.'

'You always look presentable. I mean, you *do* look presentable,' he said, wishing instantly he could fold the words back on his tongue. 'Not so much in a blizzard maybe, or a thunderstorm, or if you'd fallen head-first into a bog,' he added in the hope of covering his eagerness to compliment her with light banter.

'No, I wouldn't be appropriately dressed if we were standing in a thunderstorm,' she agreed, 'and it would be stupid of me to be out in a blizzard dressed in a T-shirt and shorts.'

Olly smiled. 'What I meant was, I've grown quite close to you over the past few weeks and you've made everything seem so much more… interesting.'

She leaned forward and kissed him on the cheek, a recognition of their friendship as opposed to an acknowledgement of something that might hold more promise.

'I know what you meant. See you soon,' were her parting words as she turned and strode off along the promenade, leaving him holding the two bicycles and wondering if he had just put a spoke in his own wheel by revealing his feelings too soon. He never could read the signs, even if they were staring him in the face.

The first technical rehearsal with the actors took place the next morning in earnest but with the noticeable absence of Emma, who had not turned up due to a 'domestic' situation.

'So how are we supposed to do a technical without her?' asked Olly after Philippa had given him the news.

'You've run through the changeovers with Emma several times so we'll step through them slowly so the actors can familiarise themselves with the lighting and set changes and adjust their timings. You should always trust your team, Olly. We'll be fine.'

She was right. All he had to do was steer everyone through the mechanics that the stage crew, lighting and sound had been rehearsing for several days under Emma's guidance, hardly missing a beat during any of the changeovers. At this stage, it was accepted that the team would be capable of exercising their professional skills if a technician, designer or actor had to be replaced. The actors had understudies and Betty was on hand with the ground plans she had been meticulously working to and knew the schedule and timings inside out.

'That's the advantage of precision rehearsals,' Betty reassured Olly, 'everything should fall into place like clockwork.'

'I know,' he agreed, 'it's just not the same. Emma has a calming influence, never panics, knows what she's doing and it's inspiring having her around.'

Betty smiled. 'You don't need to explain, I know how fond you are of her, I see it in your eyes every time you look at her. But we're more than ready, so stop worrying. She'll be back.'

Olly, of course, couldn't stop worrying. Was Emma's domestic incident merely an excuse? Was she ill? Was she keeping her distance because he had declared his hand too soon and scared her off? That was unlikely. She was dedicated to the production and wouldn't miss a rehearsal so close to opening night without good reason, so two days later he decided to take a chance and call on her to check she was all right in case he could do anything to help.

There was a single lamp shining in the window of her apartment in Portland Place when he arrived a little after seven, but when he received no response after ringing the doorbell, it was evident she was not at home and there was little point hanging around risking the neighbours thinking he was a degenerate stalker or casing the property for nefarious purposes. He made his way back to the seafront, accepting that he had no right to be snooping around, intruding on her life in this way. Whatever her reason for her not turning up at the theatre, it had nothing to do with him and he just had to suck it up.

Portland Place led to the promenade where Olly stood for a while watching families having fun at the Jungle Rumble golf attraction with its palm trees, boulders and plunging waterfalls, wondering if it was a venue that might feature on Felix's safe list, before discounting it as an idea that was literally full of holes. He turned his attention instead to spending some time at the Yellowave Beach Café next door, since it was a pleasant evening and there was no rush to get back to the apartment. But as he walked down the steps he saw her sitting at one of the tables chatting and laughing with someone he did not recognise: a tall, blonde man with a ruggedly handsome face that exuded unrelenting charm. It was no chance meeting. The body language, smiley faces and touching of hands suggested there was history between them, a history in which Olly played no part. He turned around and made his way back to the promenade, his stomach turning somersaults, his breathing out of kilter with legs that could not escape from the scene fast enough. He kept walking without looking back, hoping she had not seen him, wishing he had not called on her uninvited, a decision motivated by a fixation that he knew would only lead to disappointment.

Emma Appleby had a life in which he was not a leading man, and he needed to face that sobering reality before he made himself look foolish. Her cool demeanour after their bike ride was confirmation that while she enjoyed his company it was not a long-term commitment and never had been. It was a business arrangement, advantageous to both of them, and Olly had to console himself with the simple truth that advancing his career by meeting her was something he should be grateful for.

SURPRISE INTERVENTIONS

On returning to the apartment, Olly sensed his motivation and enthusiasm for future projects had dipped, his concentration levels compromised when he attempted a read-through of the script for *One Way Ticket*, which Philippa was keen to talk to him about later that evening. Whilst her ability to switch focus between projects was impressive, Olly found her energy levels difficult to match, particularly as he wasn't currently in the mood for analysing a play that presented challenges he had not had time to properly consider. But like a large unstoppable boulder rolling towards him, she rang at precisely nine o'clock and resistance was futile.

'So, what do you think?'

'It's an interesting piece but I'm not sure it's right for the spring run.'

'Why so?'

Olly hesitated, hoping not to offend her. 'It's complicated, contrived and lacks credibility.'

'It's a farce, Olly. It's meant to be contrived and over the top. We just paper over the cracks as we always do.'

'But the action jumps between two locations involving three sets, assuming we don't include an interior train, with a businesswoman who oversees an office in London and one in Glasgow, dallying with a lover in each, neither of whom knows about the other. Will the audience buy the implausibility of that situation?'

Philippa was baffled as to why he felt so uncomfortable with the premise. 'It's not that far-fetched. Conflict and deceit in matters of the heart drive the majority of stories, or is it a woman manipulating two men that you find lacks credibility?'

He hesitated again, aware of the trapdoor. 'It's more their naivety that bothers me. David in London doesn't question that April always stays at different hotels in Glasgow, while it doesn't occur to Duncan in Glasgow that she has never invited him to her house in Twickenham, a house she shares, as the audience is aware, with David. I don't think either men or women are that trustworthy, or so lacking in suspicion.'

'But if you look beyond the plausibility of the situation, it's a funny scenario with some interesting turning points. You can argue that Duncan finding a receipt with April's address on it and deciding to give her an impromptu visit is a contrivance, but it's not outside the realms of possibility and provides a moment of tension when April has no other option than to whisk him off to her parents' house in Hampstead to avoid being found out.'

'Yes, but putting aside the visual humour associated with a mother who has trouble adjusting her hearing aid and a father who can't even nail two bits of wood together to save his life yet is building a pergola in the back garden, neither of them has conveniently never met David, who happens to live with their daughter only fifteen miles away, with only a photograph they have of him as a point of reference.'

'Which creates a humorous moment of confusion when April turns up with Duncan, who looks nothing like David.'

'Yes, but her mother's deaf, not blind, and neither of them is stupid.'

'You just have to park your disbelief and go with April's explanation, fragile though it is, that it's the beard and baseball hat that's misleading them.'

'Just like her mother's misunderstanding that David is a baritone and not a barrister?' enquired Olly, wondering if the logic of his reasoning would merit consideration at any point.

'I understand where you're coming from, Olly, but farce is an exaggerated version of life, and the more absurd the better.'

'But whose life? These people are caricatures.'

'Nevertheless, they mirror life's complexities and how we, as real people, can dig very deep holes for ourselves.'

'But is it a hole we all want to jump down?'

'I don't see why not. It's the depth of the deception that provides tension and humour, whether you think it's overly fabricated or not. Duncan and David may be naïve but they're very likeable characters.'

'And easily led,' countered Olly. 'When April's mother asks Duncan to stay the night, April has to phone David with the lame excuse that she's staying at her parents so she can help her father build his pergola, the unlikely upshot being that David drives to Hampstead the next day to lend a hand only minutes after Duncan has left to catch a train back to Glasgow.'

'Leading to a very dramatic but amusing situation when the two men unwittingly cross paths.'

Olly realised he was on a hiding to nothing. He gave it one last shot. 'So David turns up at the parents' house looking exactly like his photograph, only that doesn't click with the mother who thinks he's a builder who's come to help construct the pergola. Added to which, David is a conman who's even more incompetent than April's father, having had a series of jobs as a gardener, plumber, plasterer and bricklayer, while Duncan is a barrister and not a baritone, which ultimately leads to the denouement that April is pregnant but we have no idea by which one, leading us all to wonder about the long-term ramifications.'

'Exactly. Art imitates life and we paper over the cracks. Read it again, you'll get to love it for all its faults. See you down our other rabbit hole tomorrow.'

With the discussion terminated for the time being and with no alternatives lined up for the summer schedules, Olly retired to bed to read through the script again, resolved to applying a more positive mindset in the hope that he might look upon the possibilities more favourably. His difficulty in aligning his best intentions with greater positivity was interrupted by a message that pinged up on his cell phone from Helen.

Email from Helen Scott to Olly.
Hello Olly. It's me, sending you an email, not by choice I hasten to add. I don't approve of this absurd way of communicating, especially with my own son, but I know how busy you are (you're probably working right now when you should be taking time out) and I hate the idea of bothering you with my innate sense of timing, because I'd much rather talk to you on the phone. I do have one, I'm holding it now, and there's another one plugged into the wall. Never mind, it will be more special when we see you again, perhaps at the opening night of one of your plays, assuming I can drag

your father away from making the entire world a safer place. As if.

Erica tells me you have a girlfriend, or a friend who happens to be a girl, the definition being a little vague due to your own confusion regarding the status of the relationship. Chemistry decides everything in the end, not that chemistry was ever your strong point considering the trouble you had mixing elements that didn't invariably blow up in your face, but stay positive and don't let your heart rule if you feel for a single moment that your friendship with Emma is not going where you had hoped. Just enjoy her company because every relationship is a learning process that takes time to find its level and that is what will ultimately determine the outcome because, in the end, all experience is good experience, even if it doesn't seem so at the time.

Anyway, lots of love

M

The missive did little to lighten Olly's mood, only to add guilt to his general feelings of disappointment with the way things were panning out. His mother was upset that he had not been in touch and she had every right to be. He had been too absorbed in his problems, professional and domestic, to spare her the time she deserved and he vowed to make amends as soon as possible. Not now, of course. Tonight he had to finish reading the script because Philippa might catch him off-guard by interrogating him about the play's dubious subtext regarding the dangers of digging holes, and there was a final technical rehearsal for *Shadows* first thing in the morning. He sent Helen a brief reply to let her know he was still alive and eating properly, though avoiding the lesser commendable statistic that involved takeaways since his culinary skills were often impeded when in the vicinity of hot plates, kitchen knives, grinders, mixers and juicers. He did, however, confirm that, yes, he had been spending quality time with a female acquaintance of whom he was very fond and he would invite her down to see one of the plays once the current ghost story, a genre that was not her preferred choice, was put to bed, with a promise to phone her at the next opportunity.

He then took an executive decision to ditch reading the script and take his chances on being cross-examined, allowing the folder to slide to the floor as he switched off the light and went to sleep.

In the morning he ambled down to the kitchen with droopy eyes and dishevelled hair, to discover a perfectly formed, blonde-haired female dressed in skimpy shorts and a T-shirt, rummaging around in the fridge. As she turned, milk bottle in hand, he let out an involuntary gasp.

'Amelia! What the hell?'

'Charming. Do you greet all your guests this way, Olly?'

'No…sorry… I… I wasn't… I wasn't expecting to find…'

He certainly wasn't. Bacon and eggs and a bowl of cornflakes being eagerly consumed by Felix, perhaps, but not Amelia Barton, star of *Big Top*, ornamenting his kitchen wearing next to nothing other than the wickedly mischievous grin she transmitted wherever her angelic form chose to descend in surroundings normally reserved for mere mortals. Disoriented, he tightened the strap on his dressing gown and sat on one of the stools by the island, fumbling for words to express his consternation that his morning privacy had been disrupted without warning.

'Big surprise, huh? Bet you didn't think I'd pop back up so soon?'

'No, I didn't. I thought you were still travelling with the circus.'

'Jesus, Olly, I don't *work* for the fucking circus. I'm an actor, not a trapeze artist.'

Oh, if only the words that slid from her lips matched the refined beauty of her exquisite countenance, but then if they did, she would not be the same lovable Amelia Barton, whose very presence had unsettled him to the point where he hardly dare lay hands on anything within reach that might spin, fall, tumble, or cause unprecedented damage to any of the kitchen surfaces. 'No, of course, sorry… an actor, and an excellent one, which was why we booked you.' He fiddled with the handle of a nearby coffee cup, aware that he was fast losing his ability to retain any vestige of control while she was hovering within melting distance.

'Are you okay, Olly? You look confused.'

'Not at all, it takes me a while to wake up first thing. Late night solving work problems.'

'Okay, coffee then. Where do you keep it?'

'Keep it. Right, I'll get it.'

He went to one of the cupboards and pulled out a large bag of coffee beans which he attempted to open as she stood waiting in patient anticipation. 'So have you been busy, Amelia? In demand I should think, even more so now you can tightrope walk and crack a whip.'

She smiled at his feeble attempt to make conversation as he struggled to open the coffee bag, first with his hands, then with his teeth. 'Curiously there's not been much demand for the former, though I've no doubt my whip-cracking abilities will serve me well at some point in my role as a fearsome dominatrix dolling out punishment to those naughty boys who need to be tamed.'

The coffee bag suddenly split open and the beans shot out, spraying the work surface and the island and rolling all over the floor.

'Christ, Olly, what's *wrong* with you?' she cried, side-stepping the cascade of beans that had cut short her vivid depiction of a woman with sadomasochistic leanings attired in mask, cape and shiny high-heeled shoes who was now towering over a nervous wreck crawling along the floor scooping up the debris with his bare hands.

'He's accident-prone,' observed Felix as he entered the kitchen and knelt down to help Olly clear up the mess. 'With an extensive repertoire you would not believe.'

Amelia grabbed a dustpan and brush and joined them. 'Wow! Accident-prone. I didn't know that, Olly. Does it hurt?'

'It's not a disease,' replied Olly, a little aggrieved. 'And I wasn't dropped on my head as a baby. It's just something that creeps up on me now and then.'

'Around attractive, independent women mostly,' added Felix, hardly able to conceal his amusement at Olly's bizarre exchange with his bewildered house guest. 'A fact only known by a select few, of which you are now one. Welcome to the Olly Preservation Society.'

Amelia tipped her collection of soiled beans into the rubbish bin. 'But I don't understand. We worked together for weeks in a congested stage area surrounded by electricity cables, lights, jugglers, fire-eaters, unicyclists, knife throwers and all that shit, and you didn't have a single fucking accident.'

Olly stood and despatched a second cluster of dusty beans into the bin. 'I know. It doesn't make any sense, but I don't have problems when I'm working inside the theatre .'

'Then maybe you should move into TopLite permanently. It would save on heating costs.'

'It's an option, Amelia. Not a very practical one since Philippa would probably object and it would limit what sparse social interaction I already have and prevent me from taking part in those day-to-day essentials that are part of the fabric of life, like shopping, going to the launderette and walking barefoot along the beach but, yes, it is an option, and I'll bear it in mind.'

Felix opened the cupboard and pulled out another bag of coffee beans. 'And a brilliant idea for a play. A man doomed to live inside a theatre trapped by his physical limitations, the living room set being a visual metaphor for his unwanted confinement, an inmate who is unable to function the moment he walks out of the exit doors into an unpredictable world.'

A depressed Olly sat back down on the stool and watched as Felix opened the bag with the minimum of fuss, poured the contents into the coffee machine and set it in motion. All he wanted when he woke up was to have a quiet, leisurely breakfast, uncompromised by contaminated beans, a friend who seemed to delight in taking the piss and a wannabe dominatrix.

'So what happened about building my confidence until I can fly solo?' he asked as Amelia distributed cups on the island and filled a milk jug.

'You'll be fine,' said Felix, 'you have to expect a little turbulence now and then. I should have warned you that Amelia's staying over.'

'Yes, it would have been useful. So what is it with you two? Are you an item?'

Amelia smiled and looked at Felix. 'Too early to say, we've only been going out for a few weeks so it's a sort of dress rehearsal, trying not to fluff our lines before we've got to know each other.'

'I doubt if anyone's ever word perfect in a relationship,' commented Olly with more than a hint of scepticism. 'Something invariably happens to upset the narrative.'

Felix sat on a stool opposite, his suspicions aroused. 'That doesn't sound good. What's going on? You did meet up with Emma?'

'Yes, and we had a good time.'

'But?'

'There's no but. I took her to a lot of places she pretended she didn't know about or had never seen and then we went home.'

'That was it? You didn't arrange to see her again?'

Olly thought it best not to mention he had seen her again, only with another man. 'I don't think she's looking for anything beyond friendship so there didn't seem to be much point.'

Amelia poured coffee into Olly's cup and slid it over to him. 'What makes you think she's not serious, Olly? Has she said so?'

'No, but I get mixed signals that I know I'm going to misinterpret because I always do.'

'Mixed signals? Surely not. That would be dishonest, inappropriate and completely unacceptable.'

Olly detected a twinkle in her eye and sensed she was moving the mischief up a notch. 'You see? I can't even interpret what *you're* talking about.'

'I'm talking about the games we play, Olly, the ritual of testing the water to see if a romantic liaison has real merit, true depth: the apple you have to chance taking a bite out of, the dangling of a carrot that you either take without question or leave for someone else to filch when your back's turned. In the early stages of a relationship you can't afford to lose control or to take everything at face value.'

He thought maybe he should go back to bed and start over because neither of them was being much help in unscrambling his troubled thoughts, simply adding to his confusion and discomfort, with Amelia reducing his quest for love to the incongruous role of apples and carrots. He remembered how Millie Clarke had misled him into thinking she was a friend when she was setting him up for a fall that had damaged his self-esteem.

'I don't have time to play games, Amelia. We have our final tech rehearsal for *Shadows* tomorrow and Philippa's already out of the traps making plans for a new spring play I need to get my head around, so a working relationship with Emma has to take priority over anything else because I can't risk screwing with my career. Or hers.'

Amelia shrugged her shoulders. 'If you think you can work that closely with Emma without your emotions sidetracking you then you're kidding yourself. You'll need to stay detached or find a way to clear the air and establish what her feelings are for you so you know where you stand before it gets more complicated.'

'Invite her to supper,' suggested Felix. 'Here at the apartment. With the four of us so there's no pressure. We can help with the cooking to keep any disasters to a minimum.'

'Then you can see if it's just a working relationship she wants,' added Amelia.

Olly was not convinced. 'I appreciate you guys want to help, but it's too risky. More accidents happen in the home than anywhere, so if there's a way for me to seriously damage my chances it's by inviting her here. I'm not ready for that yet and it's a safe bet that she isn't either, so thanks for the offer, but I'd prefer to keep it from becoming part of my unenviable portfolio until I'm more equipped to deal with the consequences.'

KNIFE EDGE

The technical rehearsals for *Shadows Never Still* were imbued with the same mixture of excitement and terror that perpetrates all final rehearsals, because no matter how much effort and commitment is poured into a production there remains the niggling reality that success is never guaranteed, particularly if the piece is both new and experimental.

Thankfully Emma had returned to the fold to cast her critical eye over the transitions and Olly made a point of keeping all conversations with her to a minimum and on a strictly professional basis without reference to any social endeavours, or to query why she had missed the first rehearsal day. She, as always, stayed focused on perfecting every aspect of the design and its associated choreography of actors, staging and lighting, not noticeably phased by Olly's sudden indifference to the friendship that they had both been actively fostering. If Emma inquired, matter-of-factly, if he had any plans for the evening, he would respond with a ready-made excuse for not being available, even for a swift after-work drink, ever mindful of Amelia's caution that his emotions would get in the way if he did not find a way to maintain distance between their social and professional activities.

At the end of an intense week where everything finally fell into place and the crew was ready and primed for the preview performance the following Monday, Olly took the opportunity to corner Betty in the prop store to find out if she knew what Emma's plans were now that *Shadows* was more or less operating on auto-pilot.

'She hasn't committed to anything as far as I know, Olly. Philippa sent her a script for a new play to look over but I don't know if she's read it, or any of the details.'

'It's a story about how we dig holes, though not in the literal sense.'

Betty looked confused. 'I thought it had something to do with trains.'

'Well there is a train in it, but it's more to do with how there's no going back when you misjudge the consequences of deceiving people, in this case, a woman misleading two gullible men.'

'A story for our times then. I thought it was meant to be a comedy.'

'A farce, and one that could bite us in the arse if we don't get the logistics and timings right.'

'Sounds like you have reservations.'

'Maybe not the best choice of words, Betty, but yes, I have reservations.'

'Then you should discuss it with Emma, she might see it differently, as a woman as well as a technician. She'll have some ideas if you think there might be problems. You know she loves a challenge.'

'She does.' Olly hesitated for the briefest of moments, long enough for Betty to realise it wasn't just the new play that was troubling him. 'But it's a challenge that might persuade her to look for other options. Is she considering anything else?'

'Not seriously. A Scandinavian director, Finn Pedersen, came over a week ago to try and persuade her to design a new play he's producing in Stockholm but I don't think she'll go for it.'

'Finn Pedersen?'

'Yes, we've worked with him before, but his approach is a bit off-the-wall, and it's not always easy to understand his stage directions or his intentions. Apart from which, Emma's perfectly happy here.'

'And is he still in Brighton, Finn Pedersen?'

'No, he stayed with me for a couple of days then flew back to Sweden when he realised Emma wasn't going to commit.'

'He stayed with you?'

'Not in the way you're thinking, I'm not his type. Long-term friends with the only benefit of one of them being in possession of a comfortable spare room and the kind of culinary skills that, coupled with an extensive wine selection, are guaranteed to keep a man captive in the dining room with a limited capacity to function when the time comes for him to stagger into the bedroom and collapse onto freshly laundered sheets.'

Olly doubted if such a man existed, but Betty seemed confident enough that she could manipulate the male of the species if she felt so inclined, not dissimilar to Alice the intrepid train commuter, with well-practised tactics at the drop of a hat. 'We don't stand a chance do we, Betty? Centuries of male dominance – assuming you make the mistake of discounting the influence of Queen Boadicea, Joan of Arc, Emily Pankhurst, Betty Friedan and Meghan Markle - and now we're being picked off one by one.

If it was a man deceiving two women the audience would be willing his character to get his comeuppance. Don't you have even a modicum of sympathy?'

'Not for a second. You still have your occasional uses and for that you should be thankful.'

Perhaps she was right, maybe *One Way Ticket* was a story for our times.

The weekend brought with it a welcome respite from the last-minute tweaks that were needed on the play, giving Olly a chance to phone Helen after she had left a message on his answer machine asking if he would be home for Christmas. Olly had never been particularly fond of Christmas. The very mention of the word rekindled memories of children's parties where rowdy games came to inevitable grief when disagreements arose during pass-the-parcel or musical chairs and the participants' anger was taken out on the jelly and ice-cream in shambolic skirmishes that usually resulted in him taking the blame simply for being present at such wanton acts of vandalism. Even in his late teens, he had dreaded the yearly round of Yuletide merry-making, with its noisy get-togethers in pubs and friends' houses. High spirits and low self-control always led to intoxicated couples paring off to fornicate in cupboards, bathrooms and bedrooms, leaving Olly to amuse himself, devoid of company, in the worrying presence of tables littered with glasses and half-empty wine bottles, after which he would have to negotiate the sprawling revellers who had passed out on the floor to make his exit back to his familiar less degenerate world more hazardous than was desirable.

'Olly! How lovely to hear from you! You got my message?'

'I did, yes, and no, I haven't decided about Christmas yet. We have an opening night and three more performances of the play before we take a break and I'd need to be back on Tuesday.'

'Well that's four days. We'd be disappointed not to see you. But if you can't you can't.' Helen was practised at sounding nonchalant while ramping up the guilt factor.

'I'll do my best but I can't afford to get stuck in Romford.'

'Nobody can afford to get stuck in Romford, Olly. Not when Lanzarote is such a tempting alternative, but for the moment it's the best we can offer.'

He smiled at the absurdity of the remark. Sunburn was never a tempting alternative, or having sand permeate his cracks and crannies, or getting lost at sea on a paddle board, and she had no idea of the consequences if he didn't make it back to Brighton in time for curtain up. But why should she? He was her loving son who she hardly saw because he was too busy being successful to visit, even at Christmas, which to her was more important than the possibility that his return train might be cancelled or they could be snowed in.

They concluded the conversation with Helen informing him that Erica would be home for the holidays and was looking forward to seeing him and wouldn't it be lovely for them all to be together like they used to after enjoying some home-cooked food. Meals that would be better for him than his usual takeaways was, he had to admit, tempting in itself, even though the journey back to his home town by train over a bank holiday in the absence of a car was likely to negate anything that could be considered remotely advantageous.

He spent the afternoon checking out Finn Pedersen, the photograph on his website confirming it was the same attractive blonde-haired man he had seen with Emma at the beach café. The rehearsal photographs of his numerous plays, however, were of less appeal, the sets being blank canvases with the actors either chained half-naked to sections of the scenic flats, or walking sideways up and down them, with living props such as hedgehogs and tortoises ambling unsupervised around the stage. Finn was clearly a disturbed human being, with an artistic flame that should have been extinguished years ago, not left to rekindle itself in the presence of mainly unsuspecting audiences. It was difficult to see what kind of design elements Emma, or anyone else, could bring to these unsettling experimental works, though Olly conceded that art in all its forms should be entitled to free expression, even if it did appear to him half-baked and meaningless.

It did not alter the fact that Emma might find Finn's work had creative merit and be tempted to share in his distorted vision of the world. She and Betty had, after all, worked with him before, most likely on early plays that were the catalyst for his later foray into the bizarre and the surreal, possibly productions that had the potential to upset established conventions and change the landscape of creative interpretation. Or they could be one-trick wonders destined for theatrical obscurity. He might not be able to keep Emma at

TopLite if she was keen to spread her wings, but he would not want to see her waste her talents on niche productions that attracted minimal audiences, with few, if any, long-term advantages.

It was, however, noticeable that her affections toward him had cooled recently, suggesting she may not envisage any long-term association beyond basic friendship, in which case it would be best if she did move on so he did not have to torment himself having daily contact with a woman he adored but whose feelings were not reciprocated. If Emma had no serious intentions it was important he did not become obsessed with running an emotional gauntlet that would put his long-term ambitions on the line and so felt inclined to accept that they had both been testing the water for long enough.

Shadows Never Still had its own gauntlet to run by way of the critical assessment dished out by those sections of the media that could make or break a show before it had a chance to establish its credentials, but despite that gamble, the first-night preview also allowed Philippa to evaluate the merits of the production based on audience reaction. Knowing where laughs were or were not forthcoming often generated script modifications and in the case of a ghost story, the adjustment of certain visual effects and timing of lines required to increase the tension. For the duration of the performance, Emma stood in the wings observing every transition, every lighting change and each sound insertion with apprehension, giving Olly approving looks and smiles as each of the scene changes moved like clockwork through the two hours of the performance. In the most unexpected way it created a sense of camaraderie that the intensity of the preceding weeks had not allowed for and Olly sensed it may have established a revival of the bond that he had put in doubt.

As if by confirmation, Emma gave him a passionate embrace after the final curtain call, kissing him on the cheek as tears of relief streamed down her face. He had not witnessed such an outpouring of emotion from her before and wondered if her characteristically controlled demeanour had been concealing a level of stress that had been building and led her to send out negative signals. If that was the case he wished he had been more alert to her situation rather than taking it personally, since the most experienced professionals could suffer moments of insecurity, especially when their work was under scrutiny by the media and the public.

The after-show shindig gave everyone an opportunity, as was customary, to let their hair down and discuss the merits, or criticisms of the production, depending on the amount of alcohol they had consumed. Olly had not seen Emma since their brief moment of physical contact at the end of the performance, but as the party became less animated and the revellers began to disperse, she emerged from the dwindling crowd looking as gorgeous as ever as she approached him with a radiant smile that gave no hint of what was on her mind.

'You've been avoiding me, Mister Scott.'

It was not the opening line he had anticipated but he did his best to look composed and alert. 'It's been a busy time, finalising the show, reading new scripts, guests coming to stay.'

'You've had guests?'

'Well, one guest. Amelia Barton, the lead in our *Big Top* production. She and Felix are trying each other out for size apparently, doing their best not to fluff their lines before they get to know each other.'

'Sounds sensible. Everyone should have a trial run before they commit to something more serious. Is she staying long?'

'No, she has a read-through in London on Christmas Eve and Felix is going with her for moral support, not that she needs it. Amelia can hold her own whatever the situation and whoever she's with. She's feisty, independent and outspoken, but I like her because she doesn't tolerate bullshit and she's obviously fond of Felix.'

'And what about us? Are we okay? I haven't upset you have I, Olly?'

Of course you've upset me. I thought we were a team, Emma. I believed what we had was so much more than friendship, but you've created confusion and distrust and I don't know where I stand, what you want from me, or where we're going and it's obvious you've been keeping something from me that must be so damaging you'll never feel able to share it with me.

'No, you haven't upset me, we've had a lot of fun and I've enjoyed your company.' He paused briefly to consider if he might be about to torpedo this unpredicted revival in their association but opted to take the chance. 'I was planning to invite you to supper at the apartment once the show was underway. Amelia's keen to meet you so it seemed like a good opportunity for us all to get together before she heads back to London.'

He had not intended to make the invitation at that moment, or any moment, but it occurred to him that if Emma thought he was not interested in taking their friendship to another level she might decide to take up Finn Pedersen's offer, or try her hand at designing a musical with rotating sets, flickering lights and quick-fire costume changes. Whilst he acknowledged that was a selfish reaction, he did not want to risk that happening. Keeping his distance seemed to have created some favourable vibes and brought them closer, so maybe the time had come to clear the air before it all evaporated and the opportunity was lost. It was, for Olly, a moment that offered a glimmer of hope after weeks of uncertainty.

'I'd love to, it's a wonderful idea, let me know when you want to arrange it. And Olly…' She smiled and kissed him. 'Well done, the show wouldn't have worked so well without your guiding hand. You've been amazing.'

On that congratulatory note, she turned and vanished into the night, returning to the part of her life he had never been invited to share, the mysterious world she inhabited with its invisible boundary he had not been permitted to cross and seemed destined never to penetrate unless she lowered her guard and let him in. Not that he had been altogether open and honest with her, concealing his embarrassing secret for fear it might frighten her away before tolerance and understanding could play their part in ensuring that he and Emma would be together no matter what. As a wise woman once told him, if you can come to terms with the reality when flaws and faults in a relationship are discovered, you will have found true love. It was advice that should have given Olly a determination to move forward without the distraction of minor imperfections coming between them, rather than be burdened with further anxiety and his usual sense of foreboding.

Three days after the invitation had been extended, Olly waited at the apartment in a state of nervous anticipation for the imminent arrival of Emma, despite Felix and Amelia assuring him that everything was under control and that nothing had been left to chance. Felix would be on hand to help when needed and Amelia would cook her celebrated baked salmon-with-lemon-butter-sauce, with Olly accorded the honour of taking the credit for organising this gastronomic delight, whilst standing well back from the oven and work surfaces to avoid contact with anything sharp, hot, or flammable. Amelia had reminded him that he was the host and it was essential he made a good impression by assuming the role of head chef without giving Emma cause to suspect he had a natural gift for manufacturing chaos out of nowhere.

Since Olly was unable to engage in the chivalrous act of picking Emma up at her home, due to not having a car or a driving licence because he had failed his test twelve times after bringing two experienced instructors to the verge of tears with his ineptitude, felt such deceptive behaviour in taking credit for the meal would be an acceptable compromise if everyone emerged unscathed from the evening soiree.

Amelia had already prepared most of the ingredients for the meal, with the salmon cooking slowly in the oven, and the peppers and tomatoes starting to sizzle under the grill. The water for the peas was in the pan and the potatoes and carrots were sitting on the island waiting to be sliced and then sauteed.

'I leave the lemon butter sauce until the last minute, after the salmon and the peppers have been seared,' she explained to Olly, who was observing with interest from the sidelines. 'Then a few minutes before serving, I melt the butter, add the garlic, white wine, lemon juice and parsley and pour it over straight away.'

Olly looked from the island to the oven, intrigued by Amelia's ability to multi-task with everything grilling, baking and boiling in impressive culinary rhythm. 'I'm not sure I could have coped making the meal if you hadn't volunteered, not with so much to keep an eye on.'

'I'm a dab hand at juggling, don't forget, Olly. It's just down to manual dexterity and timing.'

It was true, he had seen her juggle, even with dinner plates, though not with hot meals on them.

A ring at the doorbell announced Emma's arrival and Olly welcomed her with a restrained but friendly hug, introduced her to Amelia, and then took her through to the dining room where Felix had finished laying out the serviettes and was lighting the candles. The pleasantries complete, Olly excused himself and returned to the kitchen, leaving Felix to entertain

Emma while final preparations were made for the meal.

'Could you put some ice in the glasses please, Olly?' asked Amelia, her concentration now firmly on coordinating the various elements as she moved speedily between oven and grill, removing the salmon and the tray of peppers and placing them on the island.

Olly took the ice tray from the freezer and placed it beside the glasses that were lined up next to the wine and the Sicilian lemonade as Amelia removed the blowtorch from a drawer and fired it up, ready to sear the fish and vegetables. Finding difficulty removing the ice cubes, Olly bashed the tray on the edge of the work surface as Amelia made her way back to the island, causing them to shoot out in a cascade, spilling onto the floor and taking her feet from under her. As she crashed to the floor, Olly ran over in a panic, took the blowtorch and tossed it onto the island where it ignited a tea towel. Amelia staggered up, grabbed the flaming tea towel and took it to the sink, dowsing it immediately in cold water. Realising that the wine had not been added to the butter that was melting in the pan, she grabbed the bottle and poured it in, stirring madly before it boiled over. 'Shit - the potatoes!' she cried, remembering they still needed slicing before being sauteed.

'It's okay, I've got it,' said Olly as he picked up the knife and sliced into one of the potatoes.

'Olly, no –'

Too late. As Olly attempted a second slice, he made a deep incision in one of his fingers, resulting in a stream of blood oozing out and covering his hand. As it dripped down the side of the island, he fainted and slid to the floor as Amelia turned off the hob, removed the pan and dashed over to administer what first aid she could, tearing off a strip of kitchen roll and wrapping it around his finger. She held his hand up above his head, realising that she needed help.

'Felix, could I borrow you for a moment please?' she shouted, trying to sound as composed as possible.

Felix appeared behind the island seconds later, skidding on the ice cubes and looking suitably horrified at the sight of Olly lying unconscious on the floor with Amelia doing her best to prop him up.

'Water! Fetch some water, Felix!'

Felix raced to the sink and returned with a glass of water as Amelia slapped Olly in the face. 'Olly! Wake up! For God's sake, wake up!'

With no response, she took the glass of water and threw it over Olly's face, which produced a low, stupefied groan.

'What happened?' asked Felix, trying to adjust to this weird turn of events.

'Silly sod cut his finger.'

'Do we need to call an ambulance?'

'Ambulance? No, he's cut his finger not sliced off his hand. He'll be okay. A plaster would be useful though.'

As Felix walked over to one of the drawers and pulled out a pack of plasters, Olly murmured and attempted to move his arm.

'Keep it upright, Olly, you need to reduce the flow of blood.'

Sensing the concern in Amelia's voice Olly kept his hand above his head and took some deep breaths as he slowly came to. 'Sorry, Amelia, I was only trying to help.'

'It's okay, just stay still for a minute and you'll be fine.' She took one of the plasters from Felix and applied it to the gash.

'I'll fix the drinks,' said Felix, hastily transferring a couple of ice cubes that had been slowly melting on the work surface to a tall glass and filling it with the lemonade.

'Is everything okay?'

Emma appeared at the kitchen door, sensing that there may have been a minor setback.

Felix immediately picked up the glass and walked over to her. 'Ice cubes. They decided to do a runner over the floor. Not a problem.'

'Can I do anything to help?'

'No, no,' said Amelia as her head popped up above the island and she dropped a handful of ice cubes onto the surface. 'My fault. Have it sorted in a jiffy.'

'Okay.' Emma took the lemonade and looked around. 'Where's Olly? Is he okay?'

'Olly? Yes, he's fine, he had to take a call from Philippa, you know how it is. I'm sure he won't be long.'

Emma nodded, she knew exactly how it was. Philippa was omnipresent even when she was nowhere in sight and since they had a production meeting with her the following day to discuss the new play, it was inevitable she would be making last-minute checks. This excuse gave Olly time to pull himself together and try to see the evening through without further mishap and as Felix led Emma back to the dining room, Amelia looked into Olly's face to make sure he was fully recovered.

'Can you stand up, Olly?'

'I think so.'

She helped him up and brought him a glass of water, which he downed in one as he stood by the island supporting himself before taking a step forward to make sure his legs were still in coordination with his brain.

'Okay, let's do this.'

Felix was relieved to see Olly and Amelia enter the dining room a few moments later carrying starter plates of wild mushroom pate with toast and salad. Having taken his seat next to Emma, Olly went through his customary routine of sliding the wine glass as far from him as possible and keeping his hands away from the cutlery until it was needed.

'So what did she want, Philippa? Fussing about the new play?'

Olly took a brief sip of his wine as he gathered his thoughts, hoping to sound convincing without giving Emma cause to ask awkward questions. 'She just wanted to check I'd made time to read it through a few times. As if once wasn't enough.'

Emma laughed. 'It's certainly a one-off, though I can't say I'm looking forward to explaining the game plan to the technical crew.'

'They like surprises. Very little phases them.'

Emma turned to Amelia. 'Olly tells me you're keeping busy too, Amelia. A read-through in London this week.'

'Yes, a television drama with a director who came to see *Big Top* one night, an opportunity I owe to Olly for making the bold, yet immensely sensible decision, to cast me as the runaway.'

'I didn't know that. Did you two meet at the circus skills school?'

'No, I didn't have any formal training, he just had blind faith that I could do it, a decision that's changed the course of my career despite a few nightmares he had about me juggling on a unicycle, six feet from the ground on a tightrope while a manic Hungarian trainer screamed at me from the stalls. Olly was very patient and understanding and that's what got everyone through.'

As Emma smiled admiringly at the revelation, Olly sank a few inches in his chair hoping that, between them, Amelia and Felix were not about to overdo the adulation and promotional banter and alert her suspicions as to the purpose of the meal. 'I couldn't have done any of it without Felix, he's always been my reliable wingman,' he said to divert the spotlight.

'Of course, you two were at school together,' said Emma. 'Felix, you must have some tales to tell about Olly. Did he always have a love of drama? Make up scene-stealing vignettes to act out in front of teachers and parents?'

Felix cautiously considered his response. Olly had been persistently creating his own dramas, taking starring roles and scene-stealing throughout his entire life, mostly unintentionally and often at great personal expense. But that was not for tonight, or any night, because Olly the cool-headed protagonist performing on the stage of life was how he was to be presented at this moment and not the blundering oaf from their far-off schooldays.

'He's always had a passion for theatre, yes. Roped me in on our first school production of *Don Quixote,* which is what sparked my interest.'

Olly felt a ripple of relief that Felix had skipped over *Barnacle Island* and on to more agreeable experiences. 'Being short-sighted I couldn't take a performing role, which is how I discovered my interest in the technical. A quirk of fate but from that I now have my extended, highly talented, theatrical family, to whom I am very much indebted. It's been great fun, despite the questionable involvement of an inept detective being outsmarted by two dead people and the antics of Crackles the Clown and a splatter gun.'

Felix raised his glass. 'To Crackles the Clown!'

'Crackles the Clown!' responded the others, including a bemused Emma who was only too willing to engage in this presumably harmless ritual of piss-taking even though she had no idea who, or what, they were referring to.

A few moments later, Amelia and Felix returned to the kitchen to fetch the salmon dish which, remarkably, had survived its recent traumatic experience and looked every bit as appetising as it was on the palate soon after it had made its welcome appearance at the dining room table. Olly, wisely, left the others to dish out the vegetables and the drinks, content to keep his hands out of harm's way under the table until called upon to participate in the meal that he had so commendably cooked without lifting a finger, apart from the one that was still throbbing beneath its sticking plaster.

'So are you guys spending Christmas in London?' Emma asked Felix, aware that they were setting off in a couple of days.

'Yes, we're booked in at the Grosvenor for three days. Haven't been in the city for the festivities in years. Then on to Manchester to spend New Year with friends. And you?'

'Polegate. With my wacky parents who indulge their obsession for the seasonal tradition by plastering the house and garden with singing elves, dancing reindeer and an obscene collection of flashing coloured lights.'

Olly made a mental note to avoid accepting an invitation to Emma's parents' illuminated house of horror until at least the spring, should such an unlikely invitation be forthcoming.

'What about you, Olly?' asked Emma, aware that he had been sitting quietly without contributing much to the conversation.

'Me? Haven't decided. My parents are keen for me to go back home but travelling over the holidays doesn't appeal, apart from the problem of having to travel back.'

'You don't want to be rattling around here with everyone partying all over the place. You know what Brighton's like.'

He did. Partying and having a good time had become part of Brighton's DNA, and the thought of wandering the streets watching everybody revelling while he collected his takeaways to eat alone had limited appeal. 'It's a good point, I'll think about it.'

He detected a concern in her eyes which he hoped wasn't pity, because that might take her one step closer to considering inviting him to Sylvia and Norman's for the holidays, and that was certain to throw up more than a few complications.

'Christmas is over before you know it anyway,' he said, steering the conversation away from the image of Tiny Tim left to eat gruel and sing carols alone by the fireside. 'By April we'll be staging the new play and then planning the summer run.'

Emma brightened. 'Yes, a new play's always something to look forward to, whatever its shortcomings. What are your plans for the spring, Felix?'

'Another series of one-act dramas for Born In A Barn introducing new writers and actors I hope. They're good fillers when TopLite doesn't have matinee performances scheduled. The future of theatre on our doorstep.'

'So, we'll all be working together again, how fantastic. To new beginnings.'

They chinked glasses in appreciation of the sentiment. 'New beginnings.'

Just after ten, Emma announced that, with reluctance, she had to return home to complete her notes for the morning meeting and thanked everyone for an enjoyable evening. Olly walked her to the door, wondering if completing her notes was an excuse for such an early departure since it was unlikely a person who had built a reputation on meticulous organisation would have left final preparations so late in the day.

'Olly, thank you, you have some lovely friends.' She hugged him, drew back, hesitated briefly, and then kissed him gently on the lips.

Due to Olly's inability to read signals with any degree of accuracy, he discounted any notion of asking her to stay, opting instead to maintain an air of friendly detachment so that he wouldn't be tempted to say, or do, anything he might regret. 'Drive safely. See you tomorrow.'

She nodded and smiled, a brief look of puzzlement crossing her face as if she was taken off-guard by his body language and parting words.

Olly was equally wrong-footed when he saw her hesitation. Did she want him to ask her to stay? Without a written request he wasn't prepared to risk embarrassing himself by taking such a rash initiative.

'Yes. See you tomorrow.'

As she drove away, Olly closed the door and returned to the dining room, where Felix and Amelia were finishing the last of the wine and giving him hopeful looks.

'That seemed to go well,' said Amelia, as if the early disaster featuring bubbling liquids, an unguarded flame-thrower, a blooded work surface and an unconscious man were of no consequence.

'Yes,' he said, accepting a welcome refill in his glass. 'Thank you, I really appreciate everything.'

But as he sat and listened to them outline their plans for the holidays, Olly took a moment to reflect that the evening, overall, had been a disaster, not simply because of his uncoordinated attempt to slice a potato, but the ridiculous compromise of him having to endure the evening's pleasantries on high alert, not daring to move unless it was essential because in Emma's presence, away from the vicinity of the theatre, he was still unable to exert any meaningful control over his thoughts and movements, bringing him to the conclusion that any possibility of a long-term relationship was now, finally, without doubt, out of the question.

WRONG TRACK

'Let's go over it again but without applying any conventional logic to the story. Maybe talk more about the sets themselves.'

Philippa watched as Olly and Emma flipped back through their *One Way Ticket* scripts, wondering what methodology she could apply to enthuse them and get them on board with her ideas.

'I don't see a problem with employing four sets,' said Emma, making a rough sketch on her notepad. 'The interior Glasgow flat could be built up a level at the rear of the stage and stay in situ throughout, being lit only for the scenes between April and Duncan.'

She sketched a sofa and chair directly beneath the Glasgow set, positioned to the left. 'On the stage itself, we can construct the living room of the Twickenham house, including a sliding outside wall, complete with a window and a front door that we can trundle in when April leaves and finds Duncan on the doorstep.'

'So we see both Duncan and David on the set together but with a dividing wall between them so they're unaware of each other. I like it,' beamed Philippa.

'So when April takes Duncan to her parents, we revolve the Twickenham set to reveal the kitchen of her parents' house in Hampstead, while at the same time lighting the right-hand side of the stage where we see the garden set, including the half-built pergola.'

'What about the interior train?' asked Olly. 'There's not much room to squeeze a physical set in unless we light a single train window seat.'

'It's an option,' agreed Emma, studying the breakdown. 'It risks becoming unnecessarily repetitive but it does allow us to throw the rest of the stage into darkness during the set changes.'

'If we needed to,' said Philippa, pleased to see that they were both taking an enthusiastic interest in the staging at least. 'Audiences don't have a problem watching set changes happening in front of them but train scenes do offer the audience an insight into April's complacency as she journeys between the two men, blissfully unaware that the game she's playing is about to go off the rails.'

'We only need to include a couple of selected scenes once we've established she's travelling on a train,' suggested Emma, scanning through the breakdown and counting the number of allocated train carriage sections, marking up possibles for deletion. 'After that, maybe we capitalise on that knowledge for comic effect by amplifying the sound and using a lighting effect without needing to see the set again.'

'As if we were fast-forwarding through a movie. It is a farce after all,' agreed Olly.

'Precisely. It's a farce,' said Philippa, taking the opportunity to validate, not for the first time, the play's lack of conventional logic. 'Nothing is for real either in the interplay between the characters, or the staging. We can do what we like - within the scope of what's achievable, but it's an opportunity to push the boundaries and surprise the audience with a creative distortion of time and space using a range of techniques.'

'I get that,' said Olly, 'but why does David have to be so spectacularly incompetent when April's father assumes that role and it's unlikely that a sophisticated, intelligent businesswoman like April would choose to live with a conman who's been unable to hold down permanent jobs because he's so inept at all of them and destroys everything he touches?'

'Including setting fire to a kitchen sub-set, which is an additional complication involving fire officers and additional Health and Safety inspections and risks putting the actor in danger,' added Emma, visibly irritated at the inclusion of a scene that would be difficult to stage without the flames being genuine.

'It's only a small fire,' argued Philippa, not convinced that Emma was making a serious objection, 'but we can drop it if it bothers you. I just thought it would add to the comedy value and strengthen April's affection for David.'

'How does setting the kitchen alight achieve that?' asked Olly expressing equal concern that a fire on set was something they could do without whilst wondering if Philippa might feel so affectionate towards her own partner if he burnt down their kitchen.

'Because if you love someone you acknowledge they have faults, just like you,' responded Philippa. 'David may not be the most competent of partners but he isn't conning April, he's incredibly fond of her and she knows that.'

Olly recalled Zelda's remark about true love being the acceptance of a partner's flaws, although he was sure there had to be limits beyond which someone's behaviour did become unacceptable. 'She *is* conning David though, by having an affair, so maybe she's not so committed to him after all.'

'Or maybe she just enjoys the sex,' added Emma taking a more pragmatic view. 'She is two-timing both of them, which suggests love may not be a relevant factor. Unless she does love one of them, or both at the same time.'

'You two need to lighten up,' commented Philippa in a burst of frustration. 'It's irrelevant whether she loves them or just enjoys the sex. The audience wants to know if April is going to get away with it or be found out. Anticipation, tension, humour. Those are the elements that drive the play, with a polarised cast ranging from a smart, manipulative woman, to a clever but naïve barrister, to a bungling, accident-prone builder.'

'Not forgetting an over-ambitious father who lacks basic domestic skills and a mother who misinterprets virtually every piece of information that's relayed to her,' said Emma with a scepticism she found hard to conceal, while Olly shuddered at the thought of stage-managing a clone of himself stumbling around the TopLite stage to gales of laughter.

Philippa stared at them, trying to decipher if there was an underlying problem she was unaware of since they had been avoiding close contact with each other, not at ease with either themselves or the play. 'Look, I know these characters have exaggerated faults and mannerisms and, no, they're not typical of the complex protagonists whose subtext we prefer to explore, but sometimes the narrative works better when the audience can see the characters for what they are, even though the other players can't. It adds to the anticipation and humour - so when David starts hammering in nails, we know what's going to happen next, even though the father doesn't. When Duncan admires April's mother's cut glass, the audience isn't surprised when she takes him to the garden shed and hands him the mower so he can cut the grass. The more we get to know the characters, the more we can build the anticipation.'

'And nobody will question the stereotyping of modern, self-assured woman, gullible, incompetent man and dotty mother?' asked Olly.

'No, because that's the expectation - crude characterisation in ludicrously improbable situations. The real credibility comes with our ability to produce the play with an understanding of comic timing involving the placement of actors, the delivery of lines and set turnarounds. These are disciplines we all need to get to grips with because we're creating a unique representation of traditional farce. What will appear to be theatrical mayhem has to be well-choreographed comedic confusion.'

Olly had to admit that Philippa had given serious thought as to how they needed to approach the staging of *One Way Ticket* and short of wheeling in Finn Pedersen to apply his unique brand of theatrical mayhem, the three of them were left with the task of orchestrating sets, actors, lights and sound in an entertaining two hours that had the potential to break new ground. Whatever his reservations it was likely Olly would learn more about precision comic timing than any other play they would produce over the next twelve months and that in itself was a challenge he could not afford to take lightly.

'So, what do we think?'

'It doesn't matter what we think, Olly, Philippa's made an executive decision and since we haven't been issued with a return ticket, we need to apply some positive thinking.'

They had left the theatre after another half hour of analysing the complexities of the play, during which the possibility of them creating well-choreographed confusion had become increasingly attractive, even if strewn with potential hazards. It was, at the end of the day, Philippa who would be taking on the major responsibility as director and it was only fair they should give her the benefit of the doubt.

'You will still do it, though?' he asked, hoping she wasn't having second thoughts.

'Of course. She has good instincts and she has supported your weird ideas.'

'What weird ideas?'

'Well let's see. Cars plunging down ravines? A detective chasing shadows? Freaky clowns with splatter guns? And they're only the ones I know about.'

Olly winced. 'I admit she has been generous and supported most of my lunatic ideas, so yes, I owe her. But you don't. You're not obliged to stay when your reputation can guarantee you a steady flow of work.'

They stopped as they came to Emma's car and she opened the door. 'There aren't any guarantees in our business. One error of judgement and I'd be fighting to re-establish my credibility because a thousand accomplished designers are waiting to step in and shove me into the orchestra pit without a second thought. You just have to weigh up the risks against your confidence in achieving the most effective result.'

'Then we'll apply positive thinking because pulling you out of the trombone section would not be a desirable outcome.'

'Good, so we should stop analysing why it might not work and start considering how it *can* work. Look upon it as an opportunity for us to extend our range and gain more experience while we figure out how to fix any problems. I'll draw up some initial stage plans and send them on. Are you heading back now?'

'No, best I stay here. It's our last performance before the break, then I'm off to spend a few days with my parents before coming back and pulling up the drawbridge to repel unwanted festive invaders.'

'Well party-pooping aside, I'm pleased you've decided to go and see them, they'll be excited to see you. What made you change your mind?

'Partly the thought of kicking my heels if I stayed in Brighton over Christmas and because Amelia offered me a lift to London with her and Felix, so I only need to make a half-hour train journey from Liverpool Steet.'

'Then I won't see you until after Christmas. Maybe we could meet up when you get back?'

'Sure. I'll give you a call.'

She hugged him and slid into the driving seat, perturbed by his apparent lack of enthusiasm for a get-together. His words were positive but the delivery was hesitant, with a lack of conviction which disturbed her because committing to a future at TopLite would be less appealing if their initial enthusiasm for projects and the stimulating chemistry between them was beginning to fade.

HOME TRUTHS

Olly had not been back to Romford for over two years. Not because he felt the need to maintain distance between himself and memories that were best forgotten but for no better reason than the pressures of work and the need to stay in Brighton so he could establish a firm foothold in his future at TopLite.

While it was unlikely that much had changed during that time, as he stepped out of the train station and into South Street, he felt a sudden compulsion to embark on a brief exploration of the town to see if there had been any significant transformations while he had been away. He noted that he could still catch the bus to Havering from the same pick-up point and the shops had undergone minimal modification. A coffee could still be enjoyed at Costa, or lunch at The Moon and Stars, and as he stood looking at the jackets and trousers on display in Next, he mused on the fact that a shop front was one of the few acceptable vantage points where anyone could stand and stare for any length of time through a window without being detained by the authorities.

Having purchased a caramel custard doughnut from Greggs to sustain him until Helen plied him with her customary selection of savoury specialities, he chanced to stop at Hunt and Chatsworth estate agents and on peering in through the window, came across a sight that sent a brief shiver down his spine. Seated at the rear of the room and very much alone was Benny Baxter staring forlornly at a computer screen. Olly had not seen Baxter since they had left school yet here he was, still in Romford and still sporting the same surly face and curled lip he remembered so well.

His instinct was to flee the scene in case he was spotted and given *the treatment* he had all those years ago, but as he studied Baxter's world-weary features he realised that this was not the same person who had tormented him so unremittingly when they were at Chase Hill High. His eyes no longer had the mischievous glint that used to spell instant trouble and he was carrying a great deal more weight and correspondingly an inability to chase and close down his prey before going in for the kill, his entire demeanour suggestive of someone for whom the passage of time had not been kind.

Strangely, Olly did not feel in any way pleased to see that life's lottery had not secured Benny a more favourable situation. He had no idea if he was the manager or an employee who had been left to guard the fort on his own the day before Christmas Eve and his seemingly unhappy disposition may have been the kind of temporary blip that everyone suffers from time to time caused by illness, family tragedy, or a bad relationship. Or because potential buyers were leaving towns and cities in their droves and heading for rural areas, with few looking to buy property in the more congested towns and cities. Which is why Hunt and Chatworth had incorporated a Holiday Hotspot sales section displaying seductive summer retreats in Spain and Italy to diversify the business while it rode the slump. With global warming on the increase, however, Olly thought Benny might take a moment to console himself with the probability that coastal erosion would eventually bring those customers who had relocated to the coast flocking back before their houses toppled into the sea.

Whatever it was that had brought about this change in personality in a former adversary Olly felt more sad than vengeful and, aware of how bruising life can be for so many, chose not to walk through the door and reacquaint himself but to move on and be thankful that his personal prospects were, for the moment, filled with promise.

To save time he aborted the idea of catching the bus and jumped in a cab to take him to the family reunion in Havering, making a brief detour to the playground of his youth, Packham Junior, where his remote-controlled fighter jets had once sent scores of screaming children scrambling for safety, then on to Chase Hill, where he had skidded across the ice patch and landed in a pile of horse manure to the delight of some onlookers and the despair of others. The visits had been prompted in no small measure by his close encounter with Benny Baxter, the buildings looking equally neglected and worn, with offensive graffiti daubed over the walls, a leaving present no doubt from some aggrieved pupils, not dissimilar to another school he had heard about that had its entire art department set on fire at around the same time.

Chase Hill was a desolate, depressing sight, devoid as it was of any activity; no laughing children, no ball games or playground fights and no sporting pursuits on the playing field, much of which had been sold off to developers for a housing estate. A sign of the times, no doubt. He remembered his grandfather telling him that one of the supermarkets in the area had once been the home of the Rex Cinema, which closed over sixty years ago after a showing of *Blood of the Vampire*, and Romford Football Club had been sold off forty years previously, leaving the town with neither a professional team nor a pitch to play on.

Only recently the skating rink had been demolished, but he had no desire to visit the site of his most embarrassing and mortifying experience at the hands of Millie Clarke. Millie had emailed him the week before they left school telling him how much she had enjoyed *Don Quixote* and to say how sorry she was to have upset him at the ice rink and maybe they could get together sometime and have a coffee. Olly had not bothered to reply. When he walked out of the school gates for the last time, more than two years had passed since that fateful afternoon and she'd had plenty of opportunity to contact him and save face but had elected not to. Or to declare her guilt publicly even though she had made the photographs of his humiliation available for everyone to see on social media. Nor had she taken to the streets in her dad's hired minibus with a megaphone to apologise, or read a declaration of regret during morning assembly that would have indicated true remorse.

Maybe it was churlish of him not to respond but perhaps some things are unforgivable and Millie wasn't alone in her quest to demean him; many of her friends had been guilty of openly laughing at him even though they never dared to tell him to his face why they considered it necessary to make his life so intolerable with their relentless teasing and tormenting.

Emma would never treat him that way; demean him and try to destroy his self-worth. There was much he did not know about her, events in her past she might consider imprudent to lay bare, but whatever confidences Emma preferred to keep to herself until she knew him better, there would be a valid reason because her fondness for him was obvious and she had shown the utmost respect throughout their association. The problem was not with her but his lack of belief that they would be able to build a trusting relationship once she discovered that he had misled her and for that he had no answer.

As the cab pulled up outside the Scott household, Olly was pleased to see Erica's car parked in the driveway and an over-indulgent but well-choreographed display of Christmas lights hanging from trees, bushes and window ledges.

He was, as expected, welcomed with the tightest of hugs from Helen, which served to intensify his guilt but gave him the satisfaction of knowing he had made the right decision in coming home even if it was primarily to avoid festive isolation on the south coast. Erica beamed proudly as he entered the hallway and even Martin dispensed with his customary handshake to give him a bear hug that literally squeezed the breath from him.

The greetings over, Helen picked up Olly's bag and he followed her to the bedroom he had occupied before moving out to the summer house. 'We locked it up for the winter since it wasn't being used,' she explained, 'but since the building work's finished the house is no longer accorded Danger Zone status, so you can relax and just enjoy being at home with us.'

Olly found his mother's optimism gratifying even if he remained wary of any area she designated as a safety zone. He resolved to stay away from anything electrical or sharp, or had moving parts, until he was more confident of being let loose on the premises, turning his attention instead to the room which had, in his youth, offered temporary escape from a tormenting world. Little had changed. Captain Scar's tunic which he never wore remained defiantly limp in the wardrobe, his cardboard sword from the pirate play and the Chase Hill High school photograph still occupied their place on the chest of drawers where the miniature fighter jets were proudly displayed alongside them, with posters of Miley Cirus and The Script pinned to the walls even though the sunlight had drained them of much of their colour. They evoked many good memories despite the frustrations and unfavourable external influences and he was pleased to be able to share his special retreat with them once more.

'So tell us all the news,' Helen asked as they sat down to their evening meal.

Where to start? Perhaps with all the positive stuff. 'Our theatre programme's going well. We've had mainly full houses even though the current play is largely experimental.'

'What, no seasonal stereotypes?' enquired Erica. 'Boys flying through open windows? No obnoxious siblings showing off their knickers to vulgar innuendo?

No underprivileged street urchins rubbing lamps and clambering up beanstalks?'

'No, we decided to go with the element of surprise rather than tradition. A ghost story with a twist. It's proved very popular.'

'Good for you,' said Helen, handing him a bowl of potato salad to ensure his plate was amply stacked. 'And what of Felix?'

'Felix has been a real trouper. His plays have given new writers and performers the chance to display their talents. And he has a girlfriend.'

'Oh good,' said Helen, her eyes alive with expectation. 'Is it serious?'

'I think so. Early days so we'll have to see. Amelia starred in our circus special.'

'Oh yes,' remarked Helen, 'the one I didn't get to see because you thought it would all go tits-up and that might embarrass me.'

'I'm not sure he used those exact words, Helen,' interjected Martin. 'The lad wanted you to be proud of him. Not let you down.'

Olly was taken off-guard by his mother's surprising proclamation of suppressed annoyance. 'It was a make or break career moment for me, staging something as complicated and riddled with risk, what with fire-eaters and knife-throwers and performers coming to blows backstage. We came close to disaster more than once and went so far over budget we had to trim our ambitions for the next two plays or my career could have disappeared in a puff of smoke.'

Helen looked appropriately contrite. 'Yes, I'm sorry, Olly, I know I shouldn't judge from a distance when you've been under so much pressure. Just let us know when you'd like us to come down. Maybe in the spring?'

Olly took the plate of sliced chicken being offered by Erica, pausing for a moment to consider how he might suggest that a play about a woman indiscriminately shagging two men who lived three hundred and fifty miles apart was more about the dangers of deception than the joys and benefits of female emancipation. Even though his father might not be so bothered about reckless fornication, he would doubtless relish the opportunity to hold court during the after-show get-together to discuss gender discrimination and the prohibitive cost of train fares that impact mainly on the working classes.

'Yes, you should both come down in the spring and see the new production, you'll enjoy it,' he said, abandoning all hope of persuading them otherwise. The pitfalls of deception, however, loomed large with Erica's next question.

'And how are things with Emma? Are you still seeing each other?'

'We're good friends, but I wouldn't consider us an item.'

'Oh. You seemed so keen. I thought she was the one.'

'She might be or she might not. It's difficult when you work alongside someone. Conflict of interest, confused emotions and so on.'

Helen looked reproachfully at Erica. 'Olly didn't come home to be interrogated on his love life. There's no need for them to commit until they feel ready. It's sensible not to rush into things. More chickpeas, Olly?'

Olly declined the offer, thankful that Helen had intervened, content to steer the conversation away from unresolved relationships to the more relevant subjects of the unacceptable number of planned housing developments in the Havering area and the apparent advantages and delights of living in the inspirational city of Edinburgh. Helen repeated her promise to visit Brighton and to meet Emma, which Olly acknowledged as a well-intentioned gesture but most unlikely since she and Martin rarely ventured much beyond the confines of the home counties, which was just as well since his relationship with Emma was at best lukewarm and frustratingly inconsistent.

After supper, Olly took time out for a breath of evening air so he could gather his thoughts on being back home and how much information it would be wise to divulge about his life in Brighton, particularly regarding Emma. As little as possible, he concluded, although Erica had other ideas.

'So, big brother,' she said as she joined him and handed him a conciliatory glass of wine. 'Sorry if you thought I was prying. You sounded troubled in your email and I didn't know how to respond so I figured you'd sort it out since you thought it might be best to let things take their course.'

'I had hoped you might offer some advice. From a woman's perspective.'

'I'm hardly in a position to offer advice, Olly, I've had two failed romantic attachments since I moved to Edinburgh but I couldn't tell you why. You and Emma working together shouldn't necessarily be a problem, or is something else bothering you?'

Olly took a sip of his wine as they sat together on the patio bench. 'She's so secretive. Tells me everything yet reveals nothing. I've never been inside her apartment let alone the secretive corners of her mind.'

'And are you being completely honest with her?'

'I'm doing my best to keep everything in check until I feel it's safe to open up to her. Problem is, I'm all fingers and thumbs when we're together. Can't seem to control my physical incapabilities outside of the workplace. It's a problem I've never been able to solve, but I don't expect you to fully understand.'

'Really? I'm the little girl whose head you spilt milk and custard over on a regular basis and whose dolls you ran over with your tricycle in the middle of tea parties, to name but two incidents out of an extensive, somewhat disturbing, back catalogue. Fortunately, I matured into a reasonably adjusted and balanced human being, so I don't hold it against you.'

'That's the problem. Everyone around me seems to turn into sophisticated adults with the ability to handle themselves in emotional and physical situations and I stay trapped in a bumbling time warp. No woman would want to be with a man like that.'

'But it's a part of who you are, Olly. Trying to hide the problem from someone you care about will not end well because the truth has to come out sometime. Love can survive most obstacles but not if you pretend to be someone you're not.'

Zelda and Erica had much in common when it came to proclamations about love being able to survive the worst aspects of human behaviour, a coming to terms with reality, something everyone can find themselves out of their depth with at times.

'Is that what I'm doing? Pretending to be someone I'm not?'

Erica could see he was panicked. 'No. Emma must know you're a decent, honest guy with honourable intentions. That's the *real* you. There just happens to be another side that she's unaware of, though how you've managed to keep it from her is a bloody miracle in itself. You're a man of the theatre so you know how easy it is to slip behind a mask and assume another persona. The question is whether you should, or need to. Or face up to what you see as a problem and be Olly Scott for *all* his faults whatever the consequences because being you is nothing to be ashamed of. You're familiar with the speech by Polonius about being true to yourself, so if even you're not sure about taking my advice you might at least listen to Shakespeare.'

Olly emptied his glass. 'For a girl who held impromptu tea parties with stuffed toys and had custard spilt on her head, you make a lot of sense, even if it is hard to know how to fix the problem without putting everything at risk. Being back here has reminded me that my affiliation with accidents started in this town, in these schools, inside the places we lived, and has followed me around everywhere.'

'Then you have to lock all that away in a box, put the lid on, and bury it deep in your imagination because you can't live in the past, or blame the past for a condition that's a part of you.'

'A condition I've lived with all my life and can't seem to shrug off, whatever I do.'

'Then you have to accept who you are, Olly, and look to a future that might give you a fighting chance of overcoming your fears and coming to terms with the hand you've been dealt for better or worse. There is no other way.'

ANOTHER WAY

There was ample time to reflect on Erica's words as Olly made the two-hour journey back to Brighton in the company of excited families on extended holidays and party revellers who were hell-bent on keeping the festive spirit alive until they succumbed to exhaustion and the realisation that escape from everyday reality had a fixed time limit.

Had he been trying to make his escape from a past that had bedevilled him since he was a child? A past where he was constantly the victim and never the victor? A past that had prevented him from removing the shackles of persecution because he had not been strong enough to release them and move on? Once a blundering idiot, always a blundering idiot, the mantle he believed he had inherited at birth and which he had allowed to define him.

Fear of the bully, he realised, was unnecessary baggage he had been dragging around for too long. Until he had chanced upon the forlorn sight of Benny Baxter sitting alone and drained of the mental and physical resources he once had to inflict the kind of torment that Olly believed would stay with him forever because he had not had the sense to disown it - or lock it away in a box as Erica suggested.

Benny Baxter was no longer a threat, confined as he was to a work environment that sold dreams of a better life in the sun to hundreds of customers while not gifting him the same privilege because he had spent so much time on destructive pursuits rather than applying himself to a learning process that might have offered a variety of prospects. Millie Clarke's Facebook page had long since been removed, along with her apologetic email. The skating rink was no more, Chase Hill had become a collection of unloved buildings in need of refurbishment, and before saying his goodbyes to the family, he had removed the school photograph, the model fighter jets, Captain Scar's sword and the wall posters and hidden them away in the bedroom cupboard in the hope that positive action would generate a more positive mindset.

On his first evening back there was no time to ponder further on how things might pan out since *Shadows* was back in performance mode and actors and crew were arriving at the theatre extra early for run-throughs and checks on lighting and sound playback. Whilst many may have wished for a longer spell away to enjoy the festivities, Olly was pleased to have the distraction, with Felix being away over New Year and little else to keep him occupied other than marking up initial stage prompts and cues for the upcoming spring production of *One Way Ticket*.

With only one matinee performance during that week, time dragged more slowly than he had anticipated, the revelling crowds along the seafront re-energising their boisterous enthusiasm in the run-up to New Year's Eve which was now only twenty-four hours away. It was an event guaranteed to bring with it an excess of every known human indulgence along with some unfathomable new ones destined to navigate everyone through the traditional minefield of obligatory happiness and mind-numbing celebration.

Spending time drinking with strangers and risking accidents in crowded bars and clubs surrounded by bottles, glasses, the joyfully inebriated and lines of mischievous merry-makers held no appeal, so Olly opened a bottle of Pinot Noir and settled down to an evening of inebriated indulgence in the company of numerous soaps and game shows that drifted meaninglessly through his sub-conscience. He realised, after emptying three glass-fulls, that he had not prepared for the shops being closed for another extended holiday so he made his way cautiously to the kitchen and rummaged through the cupboards and refrigerator, both yielding little that he would be prepared to eat without first testing for bacterial content.

Resigned to leaving the apartment despite his condition, he walked to the mini-mart, bought some groceries and a copy of the *Radio Times* and checked which takeaways would be open for a party of one on the evening when the theatre would be dark again and madness would sweep over the town to last long and noisily into the early hours.

Having staggered back to his apartment weighed down by the box of groceries and a carrier bag containing a supply of beers and wine, he discovered, to his dismay, that he was locked out because he had mislaid his keys and hadn't the faintest idea where he last saw them. As he fumbled about in the dark, his cold hands rummaging despondently through his jacket, he dropped the box of groceries, smashing a box of eggs and splitting a carton of milk, the mixture leaking around his feet in a gooey mess before spilling into the gutter.

'Woah! Need some help?'

Olly turned to see a well-dressed man, whom he guessed to be in his early forties, standing a few feet away, watching him with a measure of concern and curiosity.

'Lost my keys. No idea where. Any number of a dozen shops. In the street even. As if I needed this.' Olly stepped back, instantly squashing a meat pie and a cod fillet underfoot as he unsteadily surveyed his demolished food stock.

The man leaned forward, picked up the empty carton and the broken egg shells, placed them to one side, and picked up what remained of the box. 'I'm at number forty-three. We could phone some of the places you've been and see if anyone's handed them in.'

'It's okay, I don't want to put you to any trouble. I have my mobile.'

'And five very numb fingers holding it. I'd be quite happy to make a coffee to help you thaw out so we can make some calls - unless you'd prefer to stand on your doorstep in the freezing cold trying to tap into a cell phone.'

Upsetting a neighbour he had never met who was only trying to be helpful was not in keeping with the spirit of the season, so Olly put down the carrier bag and extended his hand. 'Sorry. Olly Scott. I'd very much appreciate the use of your phone.'

'Chris Okoro. No problem. Can you manage? It's just a few steps away.'

'I'm fine, lead the way.'

The antique furniture and expensive oil paintings that adorned the hallway of Number forty-three revealed Chris Okoro to be a man of good taste as well as being incredibly well-heeled and as Olly entered the spacious, spotlessly clean living room with its open-plan kitchen looking out over a neatly kept lawn and flower border, it was evident no expense was spared in daily visitations from housekeepers and gardeners. While Chris brewed some coffee, Olly took a moment to survey the room, noting that although there were only two photographs propped up on the sideboard, none featured a wife, partner, or children. The desk in the corner, with its open laptop and piles of paperwork sitting alongside, was indicative of a man who spent most of his waking hours working, verified by the rows of shelves crammed with weighty volumes that even the most avid of readers would find intimidating each time they passed them.

'I'm assuming you're okay with coffee,' said Chris, handing over a steaming cup as Olly sank into one of the plush leather armchairs.

Olly nodded and took a tentative sip to make sure he still had feeling in his lips even if his legs might, without warning, temporarily abandon any possibility of transporting him, without risk of incident, from one place to another. 'So how long have you lived here, Chris?'

Chris stood at the island and placed a plastic replacement box alongside Olly's soggy cardboard grocery container. 'Four years, give or take. Forty years since we moved to the UK. I was five years old when my parents decided to uproot us and leave Nigeria for good.'

'Sounds like a big step. For someone so young.'

Chris started transferring the groceries to the plastic box to save them from decomposing sooner than was necessary. 'It was frightening for all of us because we'd had a good life back home. I wasn't old enough to understand at the time but my father had a successful construction business and we were comparatively wealthy, but politics got in the way, there were problems with developers and disagreements with some of his business partners, so he sold his shares and decided to start afresh. Looking back, it was probably for the best.'

Olly looked around the room. 'I don't think anyone would argue with that. Can I ask what you do?'

'Corporate law. Spend most of my time with my head buried in paperwork and arguing time-wasting legalities but it's a career I never saw the five-year-old me achieving.'

'Because you felt disadvantaged?'

'Yes. Not because I was the only black pupil but the one who wore a brand new uniform and had rich parents. I suffered discrimination daily and it's something that either defeats you or drives you on.'

'I can understand that. I was bullied persistently at both my schools. Couldn't wait to get out.'

'Being gay probably didn't help. Kids can be unkind when they don't know better.'

'I'm not gay, Chris.'

'Oh, I just heard that two guys had moved into number forty-five.'

'Felix is an old school friend. We share the same interests, including a mutual admiration for the opposite sex. He's on holiday with his girlfriend now. I wasn't bullied because I was gay, I was just clumsy.'

Chris regarded him for a moment as if attempting to get his head around this disclosure. 'You were bullied because you were clumsy? You mean, like, dropping things?'

It sounded an insignificant, almost paltry reason for being discriminated against the way Chris said it, laced with a dash of incredulity as it was, and Olly felt almost embarrassed to cite it as a substantial reason for his years of torment. 'It may not sound serious,' he said defensively, 'but it was on a scale bigger than you might imagine.'

Chris did not look convinced. 'I don't think any individual, whatever their colour, gender or disability would necessarily agree with you, Olly, unless they kept bumping into walls or falling off their wheelchairs. You have the advantage of being able to peel away past violations and outgrow the problem. Others are encumbered with who they are throughout their lives, even in our modern, supposedly more educated and understanding world.'

Olly took another sip of the coffee in the hope that it might help him regain the power of reasoned argument before his new-found friend and neighbour embarked on a cross-examination that would render any claims for unjust treatment unsustainable and without merit. 'I appreciate that discrimination is prevalent everywhere and it affects many of my friends and colleagues who are disadvantaged because they're not regarded as normal.' He thought of his team of dwarves and those who historically had been employed in circus troupes because of their physical deformity. 'They cope incredibly well and find ways to overcome their impairments. Theatre folk are generally resourceful, finding ways to try new ideas and overcome the seemingly impossible.'

Chris smiled as he finished repacking the groceries. 'And how about you? Have you overcome the seemingly impossible?'

'I think so. I recently revisited my home town where it all began. They say never go back but I'm glad I did, it made me realise how stupid it all was and how it has little relevance today. It's opened a door that's remained shut for most of my life.'

'Some doors can be opened if you try hard enough.' Chris jingled Olly's front door keys and threw them over to him.

'You found them.'

'In with the carrots.'

'The carrots. Of course they were. First place I should have looked,' said Olly, taking the keys appreciatively. 'And I've put you to all this trouble.'

'It's no trouble, we should get to know our neighbours. We all need help at one time or another - and it's always good to chat.'

Olly nodded his agreement. It *was* good to chat. Bottling things up was never a long-term solution to resolving issues and Chris's opinions had not only been invaluable but life-affirming. Olly had been more fortunate than most and had much to be thankful for, so it was folly to waste any more time being negative when there were so many choices available.

He was, however, keen to know more about Chris Okoro, how he overcame prejudice and became a successful lawyer, why he appeared to be a loner when he cared about people and society generally, and although having money would have been advantageous in warding off some of the obstacles, true success can only be achieved with passion and commitment and there was little doubt that Chris had that by the bucketful.

But that was for another day, so he took his leave, armed with the plastic box containing the remains of his food supply and made his way gingerly back down the street, being careful not to skid, skate, slide, or undertake any other manoeuvre that might alert another concerned neighbour to his predicament, compelling them to take him under their wing and invite him for a New Years' day dinner since it wasn't right for him to be left on his own at this time of year because he had been abandoned by his gay partner. It was a thought that prompted Olly to message Felix to tell him about the charitable neighbour who had rescued him from spending a freezing night on his doorstep and renewed his faith in the goodness of humanity.

The following morning, Olly focused on working through a selection of new design concepts that Emma had emailed to him, trying his best to put her to the back of his mind and contemplating whether to embark on an experimental sortie so he might assess his new positivity. He debated if the relinquishing of the past might be achieved at one of the local restaurants, alone and unchaperoned, an initiative immediately dismissed as an act of folly that carried undeniable risk, particularly on New Year's Eve.

At eight o'clock on this last day of a predominantly rewarding year, he turned on the television, resigned to spending the evening in the company of an endless carnival of pre-recorded entertainment that was soon speedily relegated to second place in the Hugely Disappointing category when he discovered that all the local takeaways were anticipating a two to three-hour wait. So he opened a bag of crisps and took a bottle of wine from the fridge so he could at least enjoy the evening in good spirits with himself; a man on the cusp of warding off his past demons, a resolution that was put to the test sooner than expected when the doorbell rang and Emma stood on the doorstep holding two carrier bags, a folder, and a bottle of champagne.

'I know the card said by invitation only but it's always more fun to gate-crash a party.'

'There is no party, you must have the wrong address.'

'Right address, wrong attitude. Nobody should celebrate on their own when they can spread the joy with a friend.' She held up the carrier bags and Olly sniffed the air approvingly.

'Peking duck with noodles. How did you know?'

'The *Wok Ahoy* menu's pinned on your noticeboard. I didn't see you standing in the queue that snaked around the building, so I took a punt.'

'Then I was seriously mistaken, you do have the right address. Come through to the dining room, Madam.'

Emma breezed past and took a seat at the table while Olly fetched her a glass and opened the champagne with a mixture of elation and confusion, taken off-guard as he was by her impromptu appearance. Not sure how best to handle the situation he elected to let providence take over. He emptied the contents of the cartons onto two plates and transported them through to the dining room, relieved to make it to his seat carrying their celebratory evening dinner, plus cutlery, without mishap. The omens were better than good, so it was just a matter of remaining positive.

'Lucky I was in,' he said as he sat opposite her and poured the champagne.

'Lucky I knew you would be,' she retorted as she watched the bubbles fizz in the glass.

'I might have popped out for an ice cream. Or a Mars Bar.'

'And leave the apartment open to rampaging festive invaders? I don't think so.'

'At least you came alone and armed with reinforcements. I'm pleased you did, I've missed you.' The words slipped from his lips without too much thought being applied but he didn't regret it. He had missed her.

'You said you'd give me a call.'

'I wasn't sure you were serious. Thought you might have better things to do than sitting eating a Chinese takeaway on New Year's Eve with a party pooper.'

'I can't think of anywhere else I'd rather be. No music playing at three hundred decibels, no skidding around on beer-soaked floors or side-stepping vomiting pleasure seekers. I can do that any time, but tonight's unique. Tonight we're marking a year in which we both achieved new goals and made new friends and that's something special, don't you think?'

Olly was transfixed. Was this a declaration of intent or was the champagne working its magic earlier than might be reasonably expected? *Who cared? Go with the flow. Take a chance and to hell with the risk.* 'I do, yes,' he said as he held up his glass. 'To ...'

'Do *not* say Crackles. Whoever he is, and wherever he is, I do not, tonight, give a rat's arse. This evening is about us.'

The evening meal dispensed with, they moved to the sitting room and took up residence on the sofa in a cosy, intimate scenario that Olly could only have previously fantasised about. A bottle of wine swiftly replaced the depleted champagne and as Emma slipped off her shoes, with her inhibitions melting away, Olly decided it was time to cast aside his apprehensions and take the initiative.

'I did mean to call you. I *wanted* to call you but I didn't want you to think I was being possessive of your time.'

'It's been shared time between us, Olly, enjoyable and productive and I wanted to ask you what you thought of the new designs. You have seen them?'

'The designs, yes, they're brilliant, innovative and ground-breaking. Everything I'd expect from you.'

She burst out laughing. 'Olly, you're hilarious. They're a visual representation of a dysfunctional train set that's devoid of trains, or train lines, or compartments, just a static visual metaphor utilising light and sound, a creative vehicle to accommodate a bunch of losers who've been shunted into the sidings or found themselves on the wrong tracks and have no idea where the brakes are or how to apply them.'

Olly regarded her open-mouthed for a few moments, wondering what other revelations might be pouring forth now she was free of the restraints of sober deliberation and keen to reveal her innermost feelings.

'I didn't realise you were so train-averse.'

'You spent half of Christmas travelling on them, what do *you* think?'

'I think they're a perfectly acceptable form of transport if the train companies stick to a timetable that's not rooted in the nineteenth century and get me to my destination on time and hassle-free.'

'Wishful thinking aside, this play isn't about trains, it's about people getting older and losing their marbles and others who take advantage of each other and engage in unacceptable and dangerous deceit, for which audiences who are neither free of nature's torments, nor virtuous when it comes to social intercourse, are encouraged to find it all so incredibly amusing.'

Emma grabbed another bottle of wine, whipped off the screwtop and poured herself a hefty portion, downing half of it in one as Olly processed her biting criticism of a play that was intended to be a lightweight comedy, not a catalyst for two people becoming intoxicated with discontent on the eve of a promising, re-energised friendship, despite her alluding to the pitfalls of dishonesty.

As Emma's glass swayed in her hand and her head drifted closer to Olly's, he ventured to address the elephant in the room that carried on its back a smiling Zelda signalling encouragement for him to either take control of his immediate destiny or waste the moment.

'Emma, why are you here?'

'You know why I'm here.' She looked him directly in the eye, the alcohol adding a seductive, watery charm to her beautiful features. Not eliciting an immediate response, she leaned forward, put her hand gently on his cheek and kissed him long and slowly, relegating the conversation to a prolonged silence that became a moment of truth that encapsulated every unspoken word, every restrained passion and every undemonstrative declaration of affection.

As she drew back to gauge his reaction he found himself lost for words, not daring to believe that the unimaginable had just happened.

'I love you, Olly Scott. Have you not realised that?'

'No. I wasn't sure *how* you felt, you've been giving me so many mixed messages.'

'Did you think we'd have spent so much time together if I didn't have feelings for you? I'd hoped you'd realise I was serious without me having to send a memo or plaster it on a billboard outside the Brighton Centre.'

He considered mentioning that she was extraordinarily unpredictable and secretive, had a habit of disappearing for days on end and had never invited him into her apartment, but decided this was not the moment to introduce negative vibes into a pivotal moment of mutual desire.

'I'm glad you've told me, text and Facebook free, with everything out in the open.'

'Which is how it should be. I'll only text you when I dump you.'

He looked unsure about the remark for a second until she laughed and gave him another passionate kiss.

He gripped her tightly as she was about to draw back, not wanting to let her go. 'I'm sorry I didn't tell you how *I* felt. It would have avoided any misunderstandings.'

'Well we're here now, so what are your plans?'

'Plans? Not sure. I ought to give Philippa a call, I haven't seen her since the break.'

'I meant, are you planning to throw me out on the street so I have to walk home in the cold and the dark without any appropriate clothing?'

Since it was apparent she was incapable of stringing a sentence together with her usual degree of coherence, her little car parked outside would be extremely wary, if not perplexed, by her sitting behind the wheel and driving it through streets rammed with bibulous partygoers.

'Well it's not that far, and it's not that cold, and since you can't drive it seems you don't have much choice.'

She pulled away and gave him a reproachful look. 'You want me to walk home?'

'Of course not. Not when there are cosier ways to spend the night with someone you care about.'

'Then you'd better stop talking and show me.'

Olly didn't remember much about the transition from sofa to bed, only that he must have floated there, but however it happened it was a night he would not forget; a long, intense night of passion that was as amazing as it was unexpected.

In the morning, as the sun spread its warm glow into the room, he stared at her warm body curled up under the duvet, desperate to hold on to the moment until he was able to accept that it was real and not his imagination writing a narrative that was devoid of credibility.

When she stirred, opened her eyes and smiled at him he felt contentment wash over him, his emotions under control for the first time in a very long time and he had an urgent need to tell her how he felt.

'Did you really queue for two hours to buy me a Peking duck with noodles?'

'Don't be ridiculous. I drove to Hove and waited fifteen minutes at The Crispy Dragon, otherwise you would have had to settle for that Mars Bar.'

Their passion and good humour reignited, he whacked her playfully with his pillow and then lay gazing at her soft face which was glowing with a contentment that reassured him all was well. 'I'm glad you came to see me and I'm sorry if I misread the situation. My antenna has a tendency to overlook the positive signals, even the obvious ones.'

'That's not good, Olly, you've no reason to let negative influences into your life when you have so much to be confident about.'

'Was I that irrational?'

'More confused, although there was a moment when I thought you were going to invite Philippa over, which would have made the evening interesting, though not as much fun.'

'And unnecessarily complicated, though it's a safe bet she'd be too busy studying your designs and making mock-up sets to find time to upstage us.'

'Then we shouldn't spoil her fun if she's not spoiling ours – which means putting TopLite out of our minds for at least a day and making the most of the good weather.'

'Agreed.' Olly slipped out of the bed and drew back the curtains, allowing the light to flood into the room. 'And since it's like a summer's day, I can't think of a better way to start the new year than a walk in the park.'

'I'm bloody freezing.'

'You'll soon thaw out,' Olly assured her as he draped an arm around her shoulders. 'Centrally heated apartments can be deceptive.'

'Yes, but erect nipples never lie. Or fingers and toes that have lost all feeling. At least the wildlife has had the common sense to hibernate.'

The morning frost crackled underfoot as they walked around Queens Park, the sun slow to melt the ice crystals that stretched before them in a carpet of glistening white. They had put breakfast on hold to take in the fresh morning air in this oasis of calm, Emma opting to leave her coat behind and wear a short-sleeved cardigan in the belief that a brisk walk would be a corrective measure against the cold. The winter wonderland they found themselves in was, however, an invigorating way to spend time together, despite the absence of birdsong and swans swimming on the lake.

'Look at the benefits,' continued Olly. 'The cold weather strengthens your heart and lungs and reduces the risk of diabetes. Shivering in a cold climate has the same effect as exercising for an hour.'

'A fact disputed by the thousands who've been affected by hypothermia.'

Olly laughed at the preposterousness of the conversation. 'We're strolling in the park, Emma, not snowboarding in the Pyrenees. Those kids over there are happy enough.'

Emma followed his gaze to two girls, aged about six and eight, kicking a ball around on the grass with their father, all suitably attired in puffa jackets, hats, gloves and scarves, having taken the sensible option to ensure they were unburdened by the same survival concerns as the woman who was now watching them with interest. It was a look Olly had not seen on Emma's face before; a dreamy, tender expression of affection that gave him a further glimpse into the enigmatic woman with whom he had, only hours earlier, established a closer bond.

As they rounded a corner by one of the wooded areas, the older girl kicked the ball in their direction and as it bounced into the undergrowth the six-year-old ran after it, unaware of the risk.

Emma held out her hands to stop her. 'Woah, hang on, sweetie, I'll fetch it for you.'

As Emma disappeared into the bushes, the girl gave Olly a puzzled expression as if she was suspicious of the adult's motives. She had clearly been told not to speak to strangers, but being given specific instructions by one had momentarily blindsided her.

After several seconds of grunts and twig-snapping, Emma reappeared covered in scratches, brambles and dead leaves and threw the ball back to her. 'There you go, it's a beautiful ball. Have fun.' With the girl's brief moment of panic that the woman might want to appropriate it for herself dispelled, she ran back to her sibling with a joyous laugh that brought the widest of smiles to Emma's face.

Olly removed the leaves and brambles from her hair, helped brush her down and they walked on, this interesting window into Emma's sensitivities opening up like the rays of light streaming through the breaks in the clouds above. Dismissing the absurd notion that they might somehow be symbolic of hope and optimism for the coming year, he reminded himself how little he knew about Emma and that he could never take anything for granted.

'So, do you have any plans after the summer production?' he asked, risking the possibility that she might think he was probing too much.

'That's months away, Olly. Haven't given it much thought. Why do you ask?'

He shouldn't have asked but it was too late to back out now. 'Well I know you have unfulfilled ambitions. As do I. I just wondered if you had any specific goals you wanted to achieve.'

'I'm career-driven, I won't deny that, but it depends on what opportunities open up. We can't always determine our creative destiny, it's a combination of judgement - and luck.' She took hold of his arm in an immediate display of camaraderie to reassure him that she wasn't about to take off any time soon. 'One step at a time and see where it goes.

Circumstances can change everything. Sometimes we don't have a choice but I'm very happy right now and don't see any reason for that to change.'

He squeezed her arm to acknowledge her show of solidarity. It was a conclusive answer that merited no further discussion because time would tell if any change of circumstance would involve children, marriage, or new career challenges and whether he would have any say, or even be involved.

As they left the park to return to the warmth of the apartment, he reflected on the unassailable fact that although he had been physically close to her on a complete circuit of a park littered with obstacles, both seen and unseen, he had not slipped once on the icy path, skidded into the wildflower garden, or fallen into the duck pond, and that was something to be infinitely grateful for.

OUT OF REACH

The benefits of not producing a traditional Christmas pantomime were evident as soon as the seasonal festivities were dispensed with and *Shadows Never Still* continued its steady production run, thanks to favourable press reviews and word of mouth. The decision to stage a show devoid of giants and talking geese guaranteed its survival as a mystery thriller unhampered by seasonal expectations, with full house bookings providing a welcome incentive for the production team during the traditionally challenging months of January and February.

While Olly was pleased the show was still firing on all cylinders, he had concerns that the upcoming spring play was not as advanced in the planning stage as he would have liked. It was a situation made more difficult by Emma not reappearing at the theatre after the Christmas break to discuss the technical requirements in more detail. When they had parted company on New Year's Day, it was agreed they would meet with Philippa to discuss practical ideas, but she had suddenly gone to ground without explanation and had not reappeared for four days.

'She's sent over a selection of detailed illustrations, Olly, so stop panicking,' Philippa reassured him when they met for a post-Christmas catch-up in her office. 'It'll be fine.'

'But we're tackling a new set of disciplines and creating a unique representation of traditional farce. Your words, Philippa. *Well-choreographed comedic confusion disguised as theatrical mayhem.* At the moment we're on course for unlimited mayhem with no practical game plan.'

Philippa was puzzled by his response. 'We've tackled more complex productions than this. You've seen the ground plans and made detailed script notes and we don't go into rehearsals for at least six weeks, so what is it that's bothering you?'

'I don't have a clear picture of the technical coordination or how the elements create a seamless production.'

'Which is my problem. Emma's seen both our notes so she'll adapt the designs accordingly and then we can have a full production meeting. Meantime, we can communicate with her by text and email. It's all under control.'

What was not under control, and something Olly did not want to disclose, were his concerns that the comments he made to Emma in the park may have spooked her subconscious and resurrected her ambitions to work on bigger productions, resulting in dissatisfaction with their current projects. Although it was too soon for paranoia to set in, he had not met with her in person or even chatted over a video link because she said her camera was malfunctioning.

Although Olly had endured uncertainty and a lack of confidence over the years, he had, for the most part, managed to keep his emotions in check, not outwardly revealing his fears and weaknesses. With constant confusion over Emma's fluctuating emotions and increasing absences, he was finding it difficult to hide his concerns, something that Betty was quick to pick up on during their routine prop check.

'I'm having to repair a rip in Mrs Parson's coat and I'll need to replace the detective's hat because it's gone walkabout. I've got a new one coming this afternoon. In case you were concerned.'

'No, I'm sure you're on the case, Betty. The hat's not essential, he's hardly Sherlock Holmes.'

'No, he's monumentally clueless, nobody would dispute that. Fortunately, his survival instincts guarantee he'll continue solving the case to the end of the run despite the implausibility of the plot. I'm more concerned about you. You're not the usual chirpy Olly we're used to seeing around the place.'

Betty's prognosis on his demeanour was of immediate concern because motivating the stage crew was essential if he was to keep everyone in good spirits. 'I didn't realise it was that obvious. Sorry.'

'No need to apologise. But if you are worried about anything…'

'No, no, the production's going well. Everyone's on form and we have appreciative audiences at every performance. Couldn't be better.'

'Good. So everything's fine.'

Olly's half-hearted smile was met with a raised eyebrow. Betty wasn't stupid. 'Almost fine. Emma and I spent time together over New Year and she seemed, well, keen to move everything to the next level.'

'That's good. It's what you want, isn't it?'

'Of course, yes, but I haven't seen her since and we'd agreed to meet this week. I think she might be having second thoughts about staying with TopLite, maybe considering other career options and unsure whether she should commit to a steady relationship.'

'Jesus, Olly, she wouldn't commit to something that important if she didn't mean it. I've never seen her so devoted to anyone, so stop imagining something's wrong when it isn't. You have spoken to her haven't you?'

'Yes. But something's not right, I know it.'

Betty put Mrs Parson's ripped coat back on her workbench, deciding that the perplexed-looking man standing in front of her needed her undivided attention. 'Olly, we work with actors who spend half their lives being somebody they're not. I spend my days creating fake artefacts for pretend situations, like parchment paper made from wet teabags and ice cream from mashed potato. Both of us spend half our time with one foot in reality and the other half in a fictional, often incomprehensible universe, straddled between the real world and endless months of fabricated fibs.'

The words resonated with Olly, who still harboured dispiriting memories of standing on the stage at Packham Junior holding paper-mâché replicas of bread rolls, biscuits and muffins superglued to a wooden tray in the company of pirates, blacksmiths and serving wenches, compelling him to accept that his sister was right in suggesting that he too may have spent too much time being someone he was not.

'For those of us who keep our feet on the ground, despite the temptation at times to live in a land of make-believe,' continued Betty, warming to the task, 'harsh reality is a gift we need to hold onto with hand and heart, whatever the drawbacks. You have a wonderful imagination but don't allow it to obstruct rational thinking. The two of you have something special and very real. Love is no guarantee you'll enjoy a painless life journey, but it's of no benefit if you create problems where they don't exist.'

Lecture concluded, Olly held up his hands to acknowledge her wise counsel. 'I accept that make-believe can sometimes become a necessary safety valve, and I do realise relationships are never easy at the best of times, so maybe worrying before I've understood the circumstances is a waste of energy and you're right, Betty, I'll let things take their course.'

'Go home and recharge your batteries, Olly. Focus on the fun of discovering everything you can about each other and stop fretting. There's nothing for you to be concerned about.'

Email from Betty to Emma.
Em, Olly knows something's up. You need to come clean for both your sakes because It's not fair keeping him in the dark, which makes him think you don't care for him when we both know that's not true. You have to tell him and you have to do it soon.

Return email from Emma to Betty.
Betty, I feel really bad about this but you know how difficult it's been. I keep meaning to talk to him but I back out at the last minute because I worry he'll have difficulty accepting it. I need some more time, just a few days so I can wait for the right moment.

Two days later, Emma bounded into the theatre at the end of the evening performance with a beaming smile and carrying a presentation box, which she placed on the stage so she could spread her arms and give Olly the warmest of hugs. 'How are you, Scotty? The show's still drawing them in I see.'

'Yes, business is good, so we're getting back on track. I've been trying to give you updates.'

'Yes, sorry to be non-communicado, my cell's been playing up and my parents don't get on with smartphones and computers so it's been tricky keeping in touch.'

'You've been at your parents?' asked a surprised Olly.

'I know, ridiculous, isn't it? I was there all over Christmas, but my mother got herself in a panic because the washing machine and food mixer stopped working at the same time because she'd somehow managed to blow a fuse in the main box and my father is hopeless at fixing things so it was easier for me to drive back and sort her out than call out an electrician which, let's face it, at this time of year would be expensive if not impossible to arrange.'

'And did you? Fix it?'

'I did. And it gave me a chance to tell her all about you, so she made you this.' She broke off to fetch the box, which she handed over with an impish but cautious look.

Olly undid the wrapping and pulled out a colourful, highly decorated but misshapen teapot with 'Olly' painted on the side. 'She's a potter?'

'God no, even she would find that hysterical. It's just a hobby but it keeps her amused, and it's a harmless pursuit unless you happen to spill hot tea over you because the spout points sideways and it takes a while to adjust to the pouring procedure.'

Olly held out the teapot with its right-facing spout and practised a manoeuvre to help him evaluate what his chances might be of not being scalded at his first attempt at making a pot of Earl Grey.

Emma watched him, unsure whether he considered it to be an appropriate gift. 'It's not terribly practical I know, but it's just for fun and you could always take it to the joke shop.'

'I wouldn't dream of it,' said, Olly in defence of the woman who had gone to the trouble of making him such a thoughtful present. 'It has a lot of character.'

'Despite a few imperfections.'

'Which makes it unique but she's bound to improve with practice,'

'I doubt it, it's been an obsession of hers since I was about five. I used to imagine they were magic teapots, a wizard's rejects from an elfin factory after the little guys had been sniffing too much paint and glue.'

'Well it's special to me so please thank her for me.'

'You can do that yourself, she's keen to meet you.'

'She is?'

'Yes, chomping at the bit. I haven't taken a boyfriend home in four years.'

Olly studied Emma's face, brimming with enthusiasm as if she was over-compensating for her disappearing act, going overboard to reassure him that nothing had changed since they were last together, even giving official notification that he was her boyfriend, with an invitation to meet her parents whom she had once disturbingly described as being as mad as a box of frogs.

'We should try it out,' said Emma, giving him another emphatic hug.

He looked confused.

'The teapot. I think we should make a brew and see if it works.'

'You want me to drink tea at ten o'clock at night?'

'No. Magic teapots only work at breakfast. Assuming you've forgiven me.'

Olly was ominously non-commital as he considered her remark. 'Magic's about control and misdirection, a belief that anything's possible in an imperfect world inhabited by imperfect people. You're not five years old anymore.'

Emma was taken aback. Where was this coming from? 'Are you comparing me to a teapot?'

'No, but if you *were* a teapot I wouldn't expect you to be flawless. I'd accept your imperfections as long as I could see them, just like this wonky spout.'

'Oh. You're saying I'm not the person you thought I was?'

'I'm saying that maybe I don't know you as *well* as I thought, because if I did why would I need to forgive you for anything?'

She hesitated, as if about to say something meaningful, but changed her mind. 'You're right, you don't, and I'm sorry if I've seemed distant or made you feel insecure in any way. I don't make a habit of telling someone I love them if I don't mean it. I'm here now and that's all that matters. What more can I do? What more do you want? Tell me.'

CHANGE

The apartment was strangely quiet when Felix walked in. No music playing, no television chuntering away, no leftover takeaway cartons lying around, and there was a dearth of empty beer bottles that habitually littered the coffee table. Socks and shoes no longer lay on the floor where they had been discarded and no T-shirts or jackets had been dumped on the backs of chairs. What had brought about such a change to their beloved man-cave? Felix had only been away a fortnight and the place was hardly recognisable. Had Olly vacated the premises in his absence? Taken on a housekeeper? Had his mother come to stay? Or….

He looked around more meticulously now he was aware that an unseen force of nature had blown in, immediately spotting a woman's handbag lying on the armchair and a winter coat hanging by the kitchen door. Olly had shacked up with someone. Not just for the night as evidenced by the apartment makeover, but possibly for several days, or even weeks.

Not wanting to disturb the slumbering pair, he percolated some coffee, poured himself a bowl of muesli and sat waiting for the first early bird to appear, hoping the mystery guest would be revealed, his expectations dashed when Olly emerged bleary-eyed in his dressing gown and jumped when he realised he was not alone before breaking into the broadest of grins.

'Felix! When did you get in?'

'We drove down last night. Stayed at a hotel near Gatwick so Amelia could catch the early flight to Nice.'

'She got the gig?'

'She did. Six weeks filming in the South of France.'

'Good for her, a rising star discovered at TopLite. Bet she's over the moon.'

'She is.' Felix fingered his coffee cup, his smile betraying a conflict of feelings.

'But not you?'

'Me? It's not about me. Amelia's talented and ambitious and deserves the opportunity. It was just difficult saying goodbye. We'd had a good time.'

'You make it sound like it's over. She'll be back.'

The look on Felix's face suggested otherwise. 'She's twenty-three years old, Olly, beautiful and gifted and working in an environment full of attractive A-listers and bronzed producers holding get-togethers on expensive yachts. You think she'll be falling over herself to get back?'

'It's only for six weeks, Felix. You think she's that shallow? Amelia's the one person I know who has her feet firmly on the ground. Unless she happens to be swaying on a tightrope, six feet in the air, juggling dinner plates.'

Olly's attempt at levity was met with the faintest of smiles. 'She'll have more offers once she's established herself and starts networking, but I've accepted that. I always knew our relationship would be at the mercy of changing circumstances and we all have to move on.

Talking of which…' Felix looked at the handbag lying on the armchair.

Felix's diversion tactic to hide his true feelings did not fool Olly, even though his friend had a perfect right to know what changing circumstances had arisen while he'd been away to affect their domestic arrangement.

'Emma's been staying over,' he responded not bothering to skirt around the issue. 'Not on a permanent basis, just a couple of nights a week.'

Felix nodded approvingly. 'And the other days? Do you stay at her place?'

'No, it's not convenient. She's got the decorators in. Paintpots and wallpaper paste everywhere apparently. Best avoided.'

'Well, I'm pleased you two have got your act together at last, now we can all stop holding our breath. Any other earth-shattering events happened while my back was turned?'

'Apart from sitting on trains, visiting the playgrounds of my wasted youth and being rescued from freezing on my own doorstep, I don't think so.'

'Oh yes, your mystery saviour. When do I get to meet him?

'Not sure. I wanted to invite him over to say a proper thank you. I've called at his house a couple of times to return a box he lent me but he's been away.'

Felix gave Olly his customary quizzical look. 'And you're sure he does exist?'

'Of course he exists. Thanks to him I not only found my keys but had an opportunity to re-evaluate my circumstances, to think how to move forward and not dwell on the past.'

'Sounds like a spiritually uplifting experience. Not dissimilar to the angel who rescues Jimmy Stewart in that Christmas movie.'

'I wasn't suicidal, Felix, just locked out of the apartment. Chris Okoro is as real as you and me.'

'But you haven't seen him since?'

'I haven't but that's not surprising. He's a lawyer, so he's probably abroad helping a global corporation sort out its complex business arrangements. He'll be back. Meantime, anything else I can update you on?'

'Yes. What the fuck is that?' Felix pointed to the teapot sitting on the worktop between them.

'It's exactly what it looks like, a receptacle for making tea.'

'From the circus?'

'No, not the circus.'

'Have you tried it?'

'The need hasn't arisen. I'm more of a coffee person.'

Felix picked up the teapot and inspected it with an amused look. 'Well I'm sure you'll find a use for it somewhere.'

'It doesn't need to have a practical use, Felix. It was a gift from Emma's mother so it's more a token of friendship and love.'

'Not just a teapot then?'

'No, it has more significance.'

'Symbolic of the bond between you and Emma?'

'If you like.'

'Reflecting the imperfections of a relationship that can withstand criticism and accept its fragility?

'You're messing with me.'

'On the contrary. I think it's a concept that could equally be viewed as charmingly optimistic.'

'Well before you say anything else you should know I will treasure it forever.'

'I should hope you would, Olly.'

They turned as Emma approached and gave Felix a welcoming hug.

'How lovely to see you, Felix. Did Amelia get the job?'

'Yes, she's on her way to Nice as we speak.'

'Good for her, it'll be a wonderful experience. We must get together again once she's back.' Emma turned her attention to pouring herself a coffee, dismissing any suggestion that Amelia's good fortune could in any way influence her not returning because of an inability to differentiate between the phoney and the genuine in the madcap world of movie-making.

'So how are the designs coming along for the new play?' enquired Felix, keen to divert the conversation away from Amelia and discuss more immediate pursuits.

'I submitted the final plans a couple of days ago, along with a 3D mock-up for Philippa to play around with. The only sticking point is whether we include a single symbolic carriage set.'

'We think it might help establish the female character's apparent lack of moral conscience,' said Olly, 'after which we use sound and flashing lights moving in different directions across the stage.'

'Which also provides cover for the set changes,' added Emma. 'We don't need to bang on about the train. We know how April travels between locations, we just want to focus on the story, because any normal human being would be exhausted by her travel itinerary, so it's pointless exhausting the audience as well.'

There was a moment's silence in acceptance that Emma was not impressed with the play's lack of moral integrity even though she had, as expected, come up with positive, professional solutions to ensure the sets would work in tandem with the on-stage choreography.

'Sounds terrific,' said Felix, injecting a note of encouragement into their early morning exchange. 'For every problem a solution. TopLite audiences expect nothing less than innovation, even if those of a certain generation may not approve.'

Olly was surprised by the remark. 'Our parents you mean?'

'Not specifically, although they may not find much to laugh about in the play's basic themes of betrayal, deceit and adultery.'

'Sexual philandering's as old as time, Felix,' commented Emma, 'much of it concealed by our parents' generation, and women have been just as much the culprits – or the victims - left alone when men went off to battle and today surviving the pressures of modern living and the sexual freedom they're equally entitled to. Whether we should be promoting questionable values for which countless generations have traditionally paid good money to laugh at is another matter.'

Felix was intrigued by her views. 'So you wouldn't be happy to invite your parents over on the review nights? Might be interesting to hear their opinions.'

Emma paused to reflect on the question. 'I don't think this play would be the most entertaining or appropriate for them to see whether they approve or not. Children view their parents as responsible adults with impeccable morals, and I'm not in any hurry to dash that perception or probe their moral values. I am, however, quite happy to expose them to the wonderfully principled and adorable Olly.' She hugged Olly as verification of her delight in moving the partnership up a notch. 'And they can't wait to meet him.'

Felix looked impressed. 'He's clearly angling for a set of cups and saucers to go with the teapot.'

'He has no such devious intent,' laughed Emma.

'Maybe not, but is he ready for such a historic event?'

'Stop teasing. He's ready, aren't you, Olly?'

'I am. And looking forward to it.'

DISTRACTIONS

'You're not looking forward to this, are you?'

'Why do you say that?'

'Because of the look on your face.'

'I'm apprehensive that's all. I've never met a girlfriend's parents before.'

Emma smiled and turned her attention back to the road ahead. 'It's not because I said they were as crazy as a box of frogs?'

'Everyone thinks their parents are on the dotty spectrum when they're simply out of tune with a generation they don't understand. As long as they give essential guidance it shouldn't be an issue, even if we only appreciate their support when we become adults. I'm assuming your frog reference is meant as a term of endearment?'

'Of course, I love them dearly, but I am concerned the eccentric behaviour that seemed innocuous fun when I was a girl is intensifying and gaining unwanted notoriety as they grow older.'

'Because now they use it as a distraction from the reality of uncertainty?'

'Yes, but maybe it's best that way and I should chill and regard their quirkiness as harmless fun. If they were internet savvy they could be global superstars.'

The car slowed on the gravel leading up to Blackberry Farmhouse, Emma's parents' four-bedroom character detached house fronted by a well-stocked garden and a lawn leading to a converted barn. Quirky they may be, but ownership of this pile suggested that Sylvia and Norman Appleby had not been standing at the back of the queue when it came to making shrewd investments.

Emma's mother waved at them cheerily from the front lawn as they pulled in, abandoning the lawnmower to greet Emma with a hug and a kiss. A rotund woman in her mid-fifties with a warm demeanour and greying hair flecked with pink and purple streaks in defiance of generational expectation, Sylvia looked as incongruous as a snowman in a sauna, dressed as she was in a colourful flowery dress whose fashionable charm had all but been destroyed by the addition of gardening gloves, baseball hat and wellington boots.

'This is Olly,' said Emma, as Olly emerged from the car.

'I should hope it is,' said Sylvia, dispensing with any formalities as she gave him a welcoming hug.

'Why are you mowing the lawn?' asked Emma, puzzled by her mother's involvement in the mechanical rudiments of garden maintenance.

'I wanted the garden to look its best for you. Only the damn thing's stopped working.' Sylvia returned to the mower, looking perplexed.

'Have you plugged it in?'

'Don't be silly, dear, of course I've plugged it in.'

'That's the reason it's stopped working,' said Olly, pointing to the lead that was lying on the lawn, sliced in two.

'Jesus, mum, you must have run the mower over it.'

Sylvia looked horrified. 'Oh heavens. Thank goodness I didn't try out the hedge trimmer first.' She indicated the abandoned trimmer, tied up in a tangle of wires as it lay on the ground next to a stepladder and a large evergreen conifer.

'For heaven's sake, why are you mucking around with electrical appliances anyway? Where's Barry?'

'He's got the day off. Taking his car for a service.'

'Then you should wait until he's back. It's pointless - and dangerous - employing a gardener if you're going to try and do everything yourself.'

'You're right, dear, sorry, I'll put the kettle on.'

Olly stared wide-eyed as he and Emma followed Sylvia into the kitchen. The area resembled a museum of antiquities straight from a spooky children's story, with pottery of all sizes and weird shapes jostling for space on overcrowded shelves and cupboards.

'Tea, Olly?' enquired Sylvia as she picked up a teapot with *Tea-Hee* daubed on the side.

'Thank you, Mrs Appleby,' said Olly, not wanting to complicate the issue by requesting coffee and risking throwing Sylvia's good intent into unnecessary confusion. 'That's a wonderful smell by the way.'

Sylvia waved a hand proudly over a selection of cakes adorning the kitchen table. 'Fresh from the oven this morning. I've been trying out some speciality bakes from around the world for Norman's birthday next week.'

'They look terrific even though I don't recognise any of them.'

'To be honest they didn't quite turn out as planned,' explained Sylvia in defence of her curious-looking gateaux. 'This is Poteca from Slovenia. I had to substitute the walnuts for pecans, cherries for dates and yoghurt for milk and it's a little on the flat side because I forgot to add the flour. Other than that, it is a traditional recipe.'

'And what's this one?' asked Olly, pointing to a circular confection shaped like a bent bicycle wheel.

'Ah, that's a *Galette des Rois*. It's usually made with buttery puff pastry but I had to use short-crust because I was low on butter. And sugar. And I was out of almond cream so I used fromage frais.'

'And what are these square ones?' asked Olly, keen to show his approval for Sylvia's efforts, even if the execution fell short of perfection.

'That's *Revani*, from Greece. It's a moist cake made with semolina, lemon and syrup.'

'Don't tell me,' said Emma with a hint of exasperation. 'You ran out of syrup.'

'No I did not,' said her mother, clearly offended, 'but I did have to substitute rice flour for semolina and an orange for a lemon.'

'And what about…' began Olly.

'Jesus, Olly!' interrupted Emma, 'Do you really want to know what they all are? They're confections masquerading as teatime tarts. Cakes unique to the Appleby household. Experiments in fondant fabrication.'

'There's nothing wrong with experimenting with ingredients,' said Sylvia, put out by Emma's reaction. 'They taste very nice.'

'I'm sure they do, mum, but the kind of smell I was expecting when I walked through the door was chicken roasting gently on a bed of garlic and herbs.'

'Shit! The chicken!' Sylvia hurried over to the oven and pulled out an uncooked chicken.

Olly couldn't help grinning as he turned to Emma. 'Cook's day off?'

Emma poked him in the ribs and walked over to join her distraught mother. 'Don't worry, we all forget to do the obvious when we're distracted. We'll sort something out.' She turned to Olly. 'Why don't you go and see my father, Olly? He'll be in the barn playing with his man toys. He'd love to meet you.'

Olly sensed that he was of no further use in the kitchen so he left mother and daughter to sort out lunch while he walked over to the barn to introduce himself to Norman Appleby.

The sight that greeted Olly as he entered the large converted barn was not, by any sweep of the imagination, what he was expecting. To describe the train set that stretched before him as a mere plaything was to seriously undermine its startling impact, resembling, as it did, an extensive reconstruction of the entire British Rail network, complete with engines and carriages from various eras moving along a complex system of interlinking tracks. These included branch lines that passed over bridges, under tunnels, by the side of lakes and beautifully modelled meadows and beaches containing miniature horses, cattle and people.

It was a scenario that would have given Dr Beeching sleepless nights, such was the detail of this vast construction. Whilst it was a spectacle to behold, it also rang alarm bells, since there was a never-ending collection of spare tracks, carriages, signal boxes and buildings sitting alongside paint pots, gluepots and all manner of plugs and transformers that occupied virtually every foot of shelf and floor space.

Norman looked up as he realised he was no longer alone.'Ah! A foot passenger! Welcome. You must be Olly. Come in, lad.'

'It's okay, Mr Appleby, I can see everything from here.'

'Nonsense. You need to appreciate the detail, lad. Come over and take control of one of these little engineering marvels, you'll enjoy it.'

Olly moved cautiously forward. Enjoyment was not foremost in his mind since he was treading through a minefield of hazards at the behest of a man who wore a stationmaster's hat, a belt with a builder's pouch containing a selection of screwdrivers and a hammer, a red flag sticking out of his pocket, and a train whistle dangling around his neck. Norman Appleby was a tall man of pale complexion, with wavy black hair and a moustache that gave the appearance of someone who had stepped from the nineteen-forties, but he seemed an amiable chap who was unquestionably passionate about his hobby. A railway supervisor who had retired in his late fifties, he reminded Olly of a renowned actor who found difficulty departing the stage when their time came, compelled to take a supporting role because he couldn't bear to let go.

'How long did it take to build all this?' asked Olly as he joined Norman near a section of the track close to a replica of Harrogate Station.

'About twenty years, give or take,' said Norman proudly. 'I started with a couple of Hornby steam locomotives and three carriages running in a loop past some styrofoam hills, then added more tracks until I'd run out of space. I had planned an extension through to the garden, but Emma's mother put her foot down so that idea hit the buffers quite early on I'm afraid.'

'It's certainly impressive, I've never seen anything like it.'

'Didn't you have a train set as a child?' asked Norman.

'I didn't, no,' replied Olly, without elaborating on the reason why moving mechanical objects powered by electricity were banned in the Scott household. 'We did have one at my high school, though on a much smaller scale.'

'In which case you'll be familiar with the standard OO scale of 1-76, with a track gauge of sixteen millimetres, if not the rolling stock you can see. The one puffing its way over the Arnside Viaduct in Cumbria is a Heritage steam locomotive, in contrast to the Class 68 031 Transpennine Express speeding over that hill in the distance, and one of my favourites, just emerging from the tunnel, is the Oxford Rail Class N7 0-6-2T tank locomotive with sprung metal buffers and an eight-pin DCC interface located in the bunker. You will, of course, recognise the most famous locomotive in the world, built in 1923 at the Doncaster Works for the newly formed LNER. It was not only the first to reach a hundred miles per hour, but the first to circumnavigate the globe.'

'The Flying Scotsman.'

Norman smiled broadly. 'The Flying Scotsman, my version being the Hornby R3250, journeying from London to Edinburgh as it first did in May 1928. As you can see, I've reconstructed the London North Eastern track, Kings Cross to Edinburgh Waverley, which uses the same route for passengers wanting to go on to Glasgow.'

'Our next play features a woman travelling on a train to Glasgow.'

'How interesting. Which one?'

'Which one?'

'Yes, which train does she catch?' asked Norman, picking up a train timetable and flicking through it. 'If she catches the 08.10 she'd arrive in Glasgow at 13.04, or if she travels in the evening she'd most likely catch the 18.10, arriving at 23.08. Or is she travelling at the weekend?'

'I've no idea, Mr Appleby, she's going backwards and forwards all the time. It's only a play.'

'Of course, Olly, of course, but the detail's important. It's the kind of question someone in your audience might ask to try and catch you out.'

Olly considered a possibility that had never previously crossed his mind, thankful that he hadn't complicated the issue by telling him that April had to first catch a train from Twickenham, which would involve changing at Vauxhall.

'Here, take the controls, lad, get a feel for it. Have some fun.'

Olly hesitantly took the remote control from Norman, moving his allocated train slowly along the track at first, increasing the speed as he gained in confidence, appreciating the complexity of the set-up. 'How do you keep track of so many trains moving around on so many levels at once?' he ventured to ask.

'There's a master circuit board just here,' said Norman, pointing to a rudimentary block of wood containing numerous switches, dials and wires. 'I can switch the points electronically or manually, but it's easier to switch the tracks from a standard position.'

'That's amazing,' said Olly, clearly enjoying himself. 'How fast can these engines go?'

'There's a limiter on the remote but you can regulate the speed depending on whether you're on the straight or approaching a bend, just as you would if you were in a car or riding a bicycle. Derailments are very rare.'

Olly pushed the dial on his remote to increase the speed of his locomotive, watching it race along a straight section by the side of a field of alpacas, then veering off to the left at a switching point and careering over an embankment. 'Oh! Sorry, I think I've just caused one.'

'No no,' said Norman, fiddling manically with the circuit board. 'The track should have switched you to the right. The engine wasn't supposed to take the bend.' He leaned over the embankment and replaced the stricken locomotive back on the track. 'The points must have got stuck.'

Olly inspected the point where the tracks should have switched, peering closely at the mechanism. 'I think you're right, Mr Appleby, they seem to have jammed halfway.' He clicked the track into position with his fingers but there was a sudden electrical flash accompanied by a sizzling sound and the barn was plunged into darkness.

'Oh bugger!' cried Norman. 'I mean, oh dear! What have I done?'

You haven't done anything, Mr Appleby. I did try to warn you because this is what happens when I'm let anywhere near electrified moving parts, but you did insist.

'I have a torch on my phone, Mr Appleby. If I can find it.'

'Good lad. That might help.'

There was the sound of rustling clothing as Olly fumbled about in the dark trying to extract his phone from his pocket, followed by an ominous clunk.

'What happened?'

'I dropped it.'

'It may still work,' suggested Norman hopefully.

'Yes, but I'll have to move my feet to pick it up, I'll see if I can...'

A sharp crack interrupted the conversation.

'Signal box?'

'I think so.'

'Don't worry, I can make another one.'

'Sorry. Maybe I could check the fuse box.'

'You could, but locating it in the dark will be near to impossible.'

'So what do we do?'

'It's okay, I'll raise the alarm and get the cavalry in.'

Olly stood still, not daring to move, as Norman clicked a switch and a red light glowed in the corner of the barn. Within a matter of minutes the barn door creaked open and Emma stood silhouetted against the frame. 'Oh bloody hell, dad, not again.'

'Good to see you too, Emma.' said Norman as he switched off the alarm and Olly picked up the broken pieces of signal box, helped by the light spilling in from the open door.

'Why didn't you use your torch?'

'It needs new batteries, Em. Didn't think I'd need it.'

'You never do,' replied Emma as she rolled her eyes and looked at Olly. 'Lunch is ready if you two can drag yourselves away.'

Olly followed Emma into the garden, wondering why she was so upset. 'What did you mean by 'not again'? Has this happened before?'

'It happens all the time. He's not safe in there with all those wires hanging loose and dodgy electrical connections everywhere. Why do you think he has an alarm button?'

'So it wasn't my fault?'

'Why would it be your fault?'

'Oh, no reason. It's just that it happened when I switched one of the tracks.'

'Jesus! Why would you do that?'

'I was just trying to be helpful. Didn't think it wasn't safe.'

'Not safe? You're lucky to be alive. So is he. All three of you are lucky to be alive.'

As Emma stormed off towards the kitchen, Olly realised why she was so train-averse. She'd been living with her father and his perilous hobby since she was a child and it was stressing her out, not to mention a mother who was oblivious to the dangers of operating garden machinery without supervision and who indulged in half-baked ideas involving unidentifiable cakes and asymmetrical pottery.

As she reached the kitchen door she stopped and turned to face him, looking tearful and apologetic. 'I'm sorry, Olly, I don't mean to take it out on you, I just don't know how to deal with them. It's not just that they do oddball things, it's more their cavalier attitude, how oblivious they are to the dangers. One day he'll set that bloody barn on fire and they'll lose everything.'

Olly was uncertain how to respond. 'Well your mother's not at any immediate risk from unforeseen hazards - or any of her visitors - unless she poisons them by accident. And I'd be happy to find an electrician to give your dad's train set the once-over and make sure it is safe. Would that put your mind at rest?'

Emma ran a hand affectionately over Olly's face. 'Yes, it would, it's a great idea, thank you. I'll insist he doesn't go back in there until we've arranged something. Meantime, I'll lock the mower and the hedge trimmer in the shed so only Barry knows where the keys are and then we should have lunch and head back. I've exposed you to enough Appleby madness for one day.

By the time they were on the road again, Emma had calmed down, relieved to know that matters were in hand and her parents might survive a few more years before she needed to seriously worry about their welfare.

As for Olly, he reflected on a morning that had taken him on a whirlwind, sometimes scary, roller-coaster ride through a morning in the life of Sylvia and Norman Appleby, an agreeable couple with good intentions that somehow misfired at every turn. They were not old, or disabled, or showing signs of dementia, just preoccupied, a couple in need of distractions; two people doing their best to make the most of life after their only daughter had left to pursue her dreams, a daughter who was possibly unaware that beneath the surface of their happy-go-lucky existence, there may be mitigating factors that forced them to deny the realities of their advancing years, exacerbated, perhaps, by unfulfilled ambition, mental health issues, or money worries. Or maybe it simply was a fear of the future; of growing old together, of knowing friends who had not been as fortunate, constantly reminding them of the fragility of life, of the stumbling blocks that affect all of us in the end and drive us to behave in different and often inexplicable ways as we cope with both the unknown and the inevitable.

Like so many people, Sylvia and Norman were not so much a box of crazy frogs, more a tin of broken biscuits.

ARRIVAL

Despite Emma's reservations about the questionable morals of the lead character and her personal aversion to trains, *One Way Ticket* went full speed into final preparations over the coming weeks, the set designs signed off by Philippa and a rehearsal room booked for read-throughs with the actors. Veronica Stone had been contracted to play the part of April on account of her portrayal of ambitious, powerful women in such plays as *The Matchmaker* and *Barefoot in the Park*. She had also toured with *Shakespeare in Love*, in which her character, Viola de Lesseps, pretends to be a man because women were forbidden from taking part in plays because in Shakespeare's day, only men could be actors. Veronica, it seemed, had taken this particular part to heart, her empathy with Viola as an adulterous woman in a man's world igniting an unexpected passion for the lead character in *One Way Ticket*. This led her to inhabit the role in a frightening tour de force that threatened to upset the balance of the production as she began to request modifications that would effectively reduce the characters of Donald and Duncan to that of bungling buffoons.

'The more inept they are the funnier the situation,' she argued during a heated exchange with an increasingly exasperated Philippa one morning. 'The belief that they're in control is completely delusional and the audience has to see that.'

'No, Veronica, it needs to become apparent to the audience that these men are being exploited because delaying that revelation strengthens the hold April has over them and we realise what a clever, single-minded person she is, with more depth of character than we first realised.'

'But we know that from the moment we meet her.'

'We know she's successful, but if we portray Donald and Duncan as easily manipulated idiots it diminishes her command of the situation. Outwitting two seemingly level-headed intelligent men who believe they could never be taken for a ride is what empowers her and divides audiences and critics when they come to assess her objectives and moral values.'

Whilst it was an argument that persuaded Veronica not to tamper with the basic integrity of the play since she had no desire to inadvertently devalue her own role, she nevertheless made numerous attempts to undermine the competence of the male characters by deploying underhanded tactics such as asking Olly to substitute David's power tools for less manageable screwdrivers and sub-standard hammers with which to construct his furniture, and to loosen the papers in Donald's court brief folders so they spilt onto the floor whenever he was attempting to read them. Olly had never been in a situation when one of the actors was attempting to subvert a production, so each request was referred back to Philippa for approval since these were not decisions he felt comfortable making.

While Olly kept his distance from Veronica as much as he could and busied himself marking up scripts, Emma supervised the set building and prop allocations with Betty, staying with Olly at his apartment only on a random basis since the make-over at her residence was still ongoing, with no early sign of completion.

Felix didn't seem to mind the disruption to their established routine, he was glad of the company and accepted that relationships between friends and lovers advanced over undulating, uncertain ground, and everybody had to accept change and move on at one time or another. He turned his attention to writing more short plays as fillers between the main shows and seeking out new writers and performers in readiness for the spring and summer seasons, his enthusiasm reignited as the ideas began to take shape. Whilst life for all of them progressed uneventfully but with purpose, there were still a few surprises waiting in the wings to destabilise their plans, which none of them saw coming due to being so tied to their schedules.

On the morning of the first rehearsals, Olly emerged from the bedroom, showered and dressed and made his way to the kitchen for a light breakfast, only to be confronted by the familiar sight of a blonde-haired female, slender of age and sleight of frame, raiding the cereal cupboard in her trademark skimpy shorts.

'Amelia! You're back.'

She turned, with a puzzled expression. 'I am, Olly. You sound surprised. Weren't you expecting me back?'

'What? No. I mean, yes, of course, it's always good to see you.'

'But not so soon, once I'd had a taste of the high-life networking with the rich and famous.' She poured herself a bowl of Corn Flakes and stirred in some milk.

'You're far too level-headed to be swayed by that kind of superficial nonsense.'

'Even if it would advance my career and bring me unbridled success?'

'That depends on your definition of success, Amelia. Coffee?'

'Not if it involves you opening a bag of beans. Tea will be fine.'

Olly popped teabags into two cups and refilled the kettle. 'I've never doubted your ambition and tenacity, as long as you stay grounded, which I'm sure you will. Talent like yours always wins through.'

'Not without having to work at it,' she said as she slid the cereal packet over to him. 'It would be naïve of anyone to think otherwise, so what's really bothering you? And don't bullshit me, Olly.'

Olly reminded himself that Amelia was not one to skirt around issues when it was more practical to cut to the chase. 'What makes you think anything's bothering me? I'm concerned for your welfare, that's all.'

'And Felix's welfare. You think I might drop him if better options present themselves.'

'There couldn't be a better option, so why would that even cross your mind?'

'It hadn't, but I suspect it has yours.'

Olly poured water over the teabags and took them back to the table. 'You're right, it's none of my business.'

'Of course it's your business, he's your best friend and you don't want to see him get hurt, I understand that, but you shouldn't underestimate my feelings for him.'

'I don't, I know how much you care for him, but changing circumstances present new choices and dilemmas, which can lead to difficult decisions, something I'm sure you've considered.'

Amelia watched as Olly removed his tea bag with a spoon and stared at it as tea dripped back into his cup, unsure where to place the spent bag. Whilst he appeared to have overcome his basic ineptness with kitchen-related items, his lack of forethought remained a source of amusement. She pushed an empty coffee mug over to him and he dropped the tea bag into it. 'I can't offer any guarantees, Olly, but at the moment I have no reason to doubt my commitment, as much as you wouldn't doubt your commitment to Emma. Felix tells me she's moved in, so her devotion to you doesn't seem to be in any doubt.'

'She hasn't moved in permanently, just a couple of nights a week, but we see each other most days.'

'Then you're lucky. I'm due in Paris for a three-day shoot on a TV pilot this Thursday, but at least Felix is coming with me this time.'

'And what if the show's commissioned? Will you move to Paris?'

'I may have to. And to answer your next question, yes, it's possible that Felix will move there with me.'

Olly could not hide his disappointment. 'But he can't speak French and has plenty of work here at TopLite to keep him busy.'

'Well, nothing's set in stone. The show might not get commissioned for a series and if it did he wouldn't have to move to France immediately. One step at a time. Speaking of which, how's the new play coming along?'

Amelia had neatly side-stepped any further debate about the possibility of Felix relocating to Paris, but since it was only speculative, Olly decided it was best not to pursue it and to discuss more immediate challenges. 'We start rehearsals this morning, so there's the usual buzz of excitement that comes with a new play.'

'Then I'll make sure I catch it during its run, your innovation never fails to surprise.'

'This one could generate debate for some time but then it probably wouldn't be worth the investment if it didn't.' He broke off to check his watch and drank the last of his tea. 'In the absence of a more speedy mode of transport, I'm still cycling to the theatre so I'll need to fly. See you later.'

'Okay, and say hello to Emma. We should get together for a celebratory meal Wednesday night before we leave.'

'I'll let her know, she'd love a catch-up.'

'I thought Geoffrey Key and Takashi Murakami would be appropriate for contemporary paintings in the Twickenham house. David might not appreciate them as works of art but they're colourful and since together they're worth more than his Audi A8 60, he does at least recognise them as a sound investment.'

Emma nodded approvingly as Betty showed her the paintings on her laptop. 'Good choice. We agreed on modern designer furniture with Lucy Fry cushions but with a few of David's mementoes dotted around, maybe a football trophy on the sideboard, a signed cricket bat leaning against the wall and a Manchester City scarf draped over the armchair, to show that April tolerates his chattels as long as they don't make the place look too untidy.'

Emma studied the various artefacts in the prop store designated for the new play, imagining their placement on the sets using her 3D model as a guide. 'At least we've been given a decent budget now our minimalist phase is almost put to bed. Has the shrubbery been ordered for the Hampstead house?'

'Yes, Hemps will deliver plants and bushes for the garden and our in-house construction team will erect the half-complete pergola. Duncan's raised living room will reflect his more conventional taste in art and furnishings and I'll email over some possibilities in a day or two.'

'Brilliant. I've a meeting with Phil in lighting this afternoon to discuss our requirements during the set changeovers. I want to alter the direction of the lights at different times of the day so our imaginary sun is spilling in from different angles and we don't have to stay with a standard set-up for two hours. It'll give you a chance to position Venetian blinds, pictures and ornaments where they would have maximum impact.'

A buzz on Emma's cellphone alerted her to an incoming text from Olly:

Amelia's back to Paris Thursday morning with Felix for a three-day shoot. She suggests a meal Wednesday night. Okay for you to stay over?

She tapped a response confirming the arrangement then stared thoughtfully at the ground.
'You okay?'

'Yes. Olly wants me to stay over Wednesday night.'

Betty sensed her trepidation. 'You still haven't talked to him, have you? You can't put it off forever.'

'It's been tricky with Felix around, but he's off to Paris with Amelia on Thursday so I'll have an opportunity to level with him once they're gone.'

'I don't know why you're so worried, it's not likely to jeopardise your future together. I think you'll find he'll be incredibly supportive.'

'Maybe. The problem is how to explain the unexplainable.'

BOMB PROOF

Grayson's would not have been Olly's first restaurant of choice. He still had uneasy memories from his recent visit, but Amelia had booked a table in advance and he did not want to offend her by suggesting an alternative. The manager, whom he had last seen racing around in a panic spraying extinguisher foam over the tables, greeted them with calm efficiency, signed them in, and directed them to a table by the window overlooking the seafront. As the others perused their menus, Olly risked a glance at the tables where the waiter had flambéed the Steak Diane, the four men had ordered their rounds of drinks, the group in party hats had sung 'Happy Birthday' and the children had sat poised with their spoons ready to attack their cream-filled dessert selection.

Then he relived the moment the little girl gave her TwizzleWheel an over-zealous flick, sending it whirling out of control and over the edge of the table, followed by hysterical shouting and screaming and all hell sliding uncontrollably into his established world. It was an unnerving moment and although he tried not to show his anxiety, the nervous look on his face had not escaped the attention of Emma, who stroked his arm gently. 'Are you okay, Olly?'

'Yes, I'm fine. I just want to be sure everyone enjoys the evening.'

It was a reasonable explanation that needed no elaboration. Olly wanted all their get-togethers to be fun and fulfilling, but since Emma had been alerted to his discomfort, he needed to divert attention away from himself and focus on displaying a less apprehensive disposition. This began with the menu, from which he ordered a prawn cocktail starter in preference to having to negotiate anything in hot liquid form in public.

'So, Paris,' said Emma with a hint of envy.

'Only for three days,' replied Amelia, 'but we might stay on for a while to make the most of being there.'

'Yes, you should take the opportunity. Get to know the place in case it becomes a more long-term backdrop to your life.'

'Or *lives*,' said Amelia, giving Felix a lingering hug. 'No point jumping the gun, but if a series is commissioned I'll find an apartment somewhere and Felix can decide if he wants to move over or just give it a trial run.'

'Good idea. It's only a hop and a jump from here,' said Olly, 'with reliable transport links.'

'Make weekend trips you mean?' said Felix, aware that Olly did not seem particularly keen on him permanently setting up home in a foreign city.

'That could work, why not?'

'It might, if you discount booking taxis, waiting for taxis, queuing at airports, sitting on planes idling up runways and constantly waiting in lines of traffic along the Champs-Élysées.'

Amelia followed the hug with a kiss. 'It doesn't matter whether Felix stays in Brighton or moves to

Paris, we have mutual trust, we're open and honest with each other and we'll always be together in spirit.'

Olly tried not to let his face give the appearance of a man who'd had a sour lemon stuffed into his mouth at Amelia's forthright and assured declaration of love.

'It wouldn't be forever, even if your pilot gets a green light,' said Emma, adding a note of positivity to the conversation.

Olly was desperate for a distraction since he felt his remarks had been misinterpreted. It wasn't that he didn't want Felix to leave Brighton and pursue an unknown future with the woman he loved, just to be sure that their relatively short-term association was a true basis for surrendering all the good work he had produced at TopLite. But however he said it, any further comment risked being construed as negative so he willingly dropped out of the conversation and took in his surroundings, which included an anniversary celebration that was taking place two tables away, a birthday cake that was being delivered to a child at the table beyond, and a waiter setting light to a Crème Brulee with a blowtorch at a table almost within touching distance from his own.

As he broke out in a cold sweat and felt an immediate need to vacate his seat and make for the exit, Amelia's voice jolted him into a teasing reality.

'So this guardian angel just appeared out of nowhere then, Olly?'

'Angel?'

'Yes, the one who took you in when you lost your front door key.'

'The night you staggered back from the mini-mart,' Felix reminded him.

Olly rallied, relieved to discover that their chat had turned to another subject, even though it involved his misfortune in being locked out on his own doorstep.

'Yes, it's true, his name's Chris Okoro, a very helpful neighbour.'

'So tell us what happened,' insisted Amelia, her eyes alight with mischief.

Olly could see there was no backing down since all their faces were wide with expectation, imploring him to tell the story. 'I'd settled in for the night with the TV and a bottle of wine when I realised there was no food in the house and the local shops would start closing down for the holidays so I left the apartment to stock up.'

'Having drunk an entire bottle of wine,' commented Felix.

'Half a bottle. But the minimart's only around the corner so it wasn't a problem.'

'Except you did find yourself locked out when you got back,' said Amelia with a devious smile.

'True, but it could have happened to anyone, drunk or sober. Have you never lost your keys?'

'Not inside a bag of carrots,' countered Amelia, unable to hold back her laughter any longer.

'Yes, very funny, but I didn't know that. I could have dropped them anywhere, on the street, in a shop, anywhere.'

'So by pure coincidence, this neighbour happens by,' said Felix, 'who takes you to his nice, warm, apartment, offers you spiritual guidance and then finds your keys.'

'Well the order of events is correct,' said Olly defensively, 'if not the insinuation that it didn't actually happen, that Chris Okoro was a figment of my imagination.'

'Even though you'd never seen him before and haven't seen him since?'

'Like I said, he's a busy man, he has interests all over the world.'

'Just as any committed angel would,' added Amelia.

Emma leaned forward and gave Olly a conciliatory hug. 'Well I believe him. It's too incredible not to be true.'

As the waiter appeared and distributed their starters, Amelia held out her hand. 'I agree, how could it not be true? But just to be on the safe side, Olly, would you mind handing over your keys?'

Gales of laughter followed, but Olly didn't mind. They were mocking him but it didn't matter because as he looked around he noted approvingly that the anniversary get-together had passed without incident, the children were enjoying their birthday cake without any of their toys rolling onto the floor and the tablecloth on which the waiter had presented the Crème Brulee had not been set alight. Even Olly's wine glass remained in place and the knives and forks had not been inadvertently tossed in the air by a sudden movement of an elbow or wrist.

Olly Scott was positively bomb-proof.

After they had made their way back to the apartment following a cordial evening unhindered by mishaps and said their goodbyes to Felix and Amelia who were making an early start, Emma emerged from the bathroom looking unusually apprehensive.

'You okay?' asked Olly with concern.

'Yes, I'm fine.'

'Only you look like you've something on your mind.'

'Nothing that can't wait.'

'Sounds ominous. Should I be worried?'

'No. I just wanted to discuss our living arrangements.'

'Yes, they are a bit arbitrary,' agreed Olly, climbing into the bed and kissing her. 'No pressure, but it would be good to sort them. We'll talk tomorrow.'

As Olly and Emma lay together reflecting on the evening's conversation at supper, particularly the commitment Amelia had made to trust and honesty in a relationship, each had reason to consider their situations. For Emma, this would involve having to reveal a secret to the man she adored at the risk of losing him, whereas Olly now felt confident he may not need to make any such revelation since he had finally freed himself from the obstacles to happiness and fulfilment that had plagued him throughout his life.

DEPARTURE

In the morning, Olly roused himself from a particularly pleasant night's sleep and wandered into the bathroom, readying himself for another day, buoyed by a new sense of optimism. Staring at his dishevelled face in the mirror, he decided on immediate remedial action by first washing and then spreading a generous helping of shaving foam over his bristles in preparation for his customary shave.

He paused, conscious that the apartment was unusually stuffy and walked promptly through to the living room, where the four-foot-high sash-cord windows required adjustment to allow reasonable airflow through the property. He stepped up onto the adjoining window ledge where he could reach the catch that held the two panels of glass in position but the moment it was released the sash-cord ropes snapped, the downdraught taking his fingers with it and trapping them between the two giant window panes. The pain was intense, his fingers numb and lifeless and possibly damaged beyond repair but no matter how much he wriggled and struggled, he was pinned to the frame without hope of release.

As the shaving foam began to drip down his chin and his pyjama bottoms slid down to his ankles, he was left exposed and naked at the window in the middle of a busy thoroughfare during morning rush hour. Commuters on their way to work and parents and children on their way to school would soon be passing by in a procession of shocked curiosity and Olly could already hear the sound of police sirens wailing in his head long before the first 999 call was about to be made by a traumatised pedestrian. He increased the intensity of his shouts for help, hoping that someone would look beyond the crazed man suspended at the window and realise that he needed immediate help for a predicament that was neither his fault, nor a situation he had put himself in for his general amusement or as a ruse to bring fear and terror onto the streets of Brighton.

He tried turning his head to one side to see if the sound of his cries would carry to the bedroom where Emma was still asleep, but to no avail. With Felix and Amelia halfway to Paris, internal help from a friend was now as illusory as external help from a stranger, along with the false reality that he had conquered his proclivity for terminal clumsiness, a fact that was about to become known to the world at large due to his mug shot being distributed by the police to every media outlet in the UK.

As he was about to give up hope, a familiar face appeared, head down, about to walk by.

'Chris! Chris!'

Chris Okoro stopped and stared at the apparition before him, his face locked in time as if it were a frozen Zoom image. Olly Scott, whom he had last seen at the very same apartment on the outside unable to get in, was now trapped on the inside unable to get out. Was this a kind of cult ritual? Something theatre folk did in their spare time to rekindle their creative juices?

'Chris! I'm stuck and in pain. Need a knife from the kitchen! Please, ring the doorbell.'

Olly hoped to God that Chris Okoro was not a figment of his imagination because if ever he needed a guardian angel in human form it was right now. As if a sudden bolt of electricity had surged through his system, Chris was galvanised into action. He raced up to the front door and rang the bell, not questioning the possibility that there might not be anyone else in the apartment, a fact that might have been completely overlooked by his distraught neighbour, who seemed disoriented at the best of times.

Inside, Emma woke to the sound of frantic doorbell ringing and repeated banging, immediately confused because the space next to her on the bed was empty, which meant that although Olly was up and about, for some reason he was not answering the door. Unless he had opened it to fetch in the milk and locked himself out, which, as she had discovered recently, would not be an uncommon occurrence.

She walked through to the hallway and opened the door, only to find herself pushed aside by a heavily built stranger who ran past her with an alarmed look on his face.

'Hey! What the hell!' She watched in horror as he pulled a large knife from one of the kitchen drawers and, without hesitation, ran forward, picked up the teapot her mother had made for Olly and smashed it over his head.

Chris buckled and slumped to the floor, groaning in pain as he dropped the knife. Emma picked it up and looked around in panic. 'Olly! Olly!'

With no response, she ran through to the living room to find herself confronted by the bizarre sight of the usually calm and dignified Olly Scott attached to the window baring his backside to her and his privates to the Brighton community at large, his pyjama bottoms lying in a crumpled heap around his ankles.
'Jesus! What the..!'

'Emma! Quick! Can't move! Bloody agony!'

She raced up to the window ledge and slid the knife between the two window panes, trying desperately to prise them apart. As Olly squirmed beside her and she struggled to create leverage, images of past incidents raced through her mind. She recalled the moment mayhem had erupted all around her at Grayon's after she had left him alone for a few minutes, and the incident at Chappie's Wine Bar with the cracked glass and wine spilling over his trousers, and the bandaged finger he'd suddenly acquired at supper in the apartment with Felix and Amelia, then fusing her father's train set and plunging the barn into darkness. Was it all just coincidence?

'That's it! It's coming, keep pushing!'

Emma exerted more pressure until Olly was able to slide his fingers free from the frame and move away from the danger zone, nursing his badly swollen, bloodied hands. He sat down for a moment to recover, then remembered his guardian angel. 'Chris! Where's Chris?'

'Chris?'

'Yes, Chris Okoro. He saw me from the street and came to help.'

'Oh shit!' Emma raced back to the kitchen where Chris was sitting in a more upright position uttering less vocal groans, although he had a glazed look as blood streamed from a gash on his head and seeped onto the floor.

'Oh my God! *Olly!*' As Emma stepped forward to administer what assistance she thought might be appropriate, she stepped on some scattered pieces of broken crockery, yelled in pain, and dropped to the floor a few feet from the dazed Okoro.

Olly appeared behind them and looked in horror at the scene of devastation. 'Oh my God! Hold on, I'll call an ambulance!'

He rushed to the wall phone and pulled it from its cradle, forgetting that his numbed fingers were incapable of holding any object, inanimate or otherwise, and it fell and bounced in the space between the two stricken heroes of the hour, cracking in two and spilling the batteries, which rolled under the units. 'Jesus, Olly! Now we *are* screwed!'

The hand beside her pushed a cell phone within reach. Chris Okoro may have been close to passing out but he still wanted to live to see another day and not bleed to death on someone's kitchen floor simply because he had never foreseen that possibility as his exit strategy and was conscious enough to know that the woman beside him whom he had never met was their only hope of release from this moment of unanticipated madness.

As Olly slid down the side of the island nursing his fingers and trying to come to terms with his morning from hell, Emma picked up the cell phone, tapped at the keypad and waited for the inevitable response. *'Hello. Which service?'*

In the hospital waiting area, Emma sat with a bandaged foot propped up on a chair next to a pair of crutches as she reassessed the disturbing events that had occurred less than an hour ago, trying to understand how a normal morning could have turned into the kind of farce that Philippa Chambers would have dismissed as too far-fetched to present at TopLite as a work of fiction. The sash-cords had snapped unexpectedly, which was not Olly's fault, but the whole episode would not have been so ludicrous if he had at least attempted to open the window dressed appropriately and without his face covered in shaving foam. That revealed another side to Olly, the one with a cavalier attitude who didn't take into account the numerous drawbacks that life can throw at you if you don't think your actions through properly.

Her reverie was interrupted as Chris entered the waiting area, his head bandaged, his shirt splattered with blood, and sat next to her. She looked at him, not knowing whether to wince, smile, or cry. 'Please tell me it's not as serious as it looks.'

'It's not. The scan shows there's no internal bleeding or swelling, so no long-term damage, just short-term inconvenience.'

'I'm so sorry. If I'd have known…'

He held up a hand. 'There's no need. I realise how scary that must have been for you. A strange man bursts into your apartment, grabs a knife…'

'Yes, I was terrified, but I could have run into the street for help, not assaulted you with a teapot.'

Chris offered her a sympathetic smile. 'We don't always think rationally in stressful situations. I'm thankful it wasn't the food mixer. I'm Chris by the way.'

'Emma,' she replied, debating whether it was appropriate to smile at his charitable dismissal of her knee-jerk reaction to stop him murdering her in her own kitchen. Olly joined them a few moments later and sat next to Chris with both his hands bandaged and looking suitably contrite. 'Sorry, Chris, I'd forgotten you two hadn't met.'

'Apologies not necessary. I'm just as much to blame for bursting into your apartment without announcing myself. What diagnosis on the hands? You do still have a pair under there I presume?'

'I do. Mangled and unrecognisable at the moment but I'm told they'll heal in about three weeks and the bandages can come off at the weekend.'

'At least it'll stop you engaging in any more perilous stunts.'

'Or anything likely to escalate our notoriety in the neighbourhood,' added Emma.

'I can't guarantee that but I have been advised to avoid cooking meals, fixing electrical installations and playing the violin.'

'Sounds like sensible advice,' observed Chris.

The three of them sat in silence for a few moments, contemplating their next move.

'We should book a taxi,' suggested Emma, 'since it's unlikely they'll lay on an ambulance to take us back.'

'Good idea,' said Olly, fumbling about in his jacket for his cell phone before remembering he needed a pair of functioning hands to complete even the simplest of tasks.

'I have an account,' said Chris, coming to Olly's rescue, not for the first time, as he tapped the number into his cell. 'The sooner the three of us are taken off the streets and into the safety of our own homes the better.'

The apartment had an unfamiliar, disconcerting, presence when Olly and Emma entered. No heartwarming sounds of agreeable chat and laughter; no evidence of panic, shouts, slumped bodies or signs of blood. It was as if the place had never borne witness to such alarming and contrasting events. Evenings spent with friends now seemed a distant memory, even if chaos and confusion lingered still, and there were some questions that needed answering. Olly sensed that Emma had become unsettled by the upheaval before they even arrived at the hospital and she had been unusually quiet in the taxi on the way back. But he knew that from the moment the window pane had crushed his hands the game was up.

'I'll put the kettle on,' he said, hoping to delay the impending inquisition.

'And how do you plan to do that?' she asked, resting the crutches on the coffee table and settling back on the sofa.

Olly held up his bandaged hands and looked at them in quiet anguish. A period of adjustment was going to be needed before he could operate at an acceptable level of functionality and that was not going to be easy. 'I'm not completely incapacitated and it could have been worse. At least you were inside the apartment and we didn't have to call the fire brigade.'

'And the police didn't get involved, so it's unlikely anyone will be filing a complaint, although it would have been interesting to read the eye-witness reports.'

'So, a narrow escape,' he agreed, sitting next to her, abandoning the idea of making tea but remembering that the pieces of pottery that had not been embedded in Emma's foot were still scattered over the kitchen floor.

'How many narrow escapes have you had exactly, Olly?'

'How many?'

'Yes. I mean I know it wasn't your fault that the sash-cord snapped. The windows probably haven't been opened for years so they've just frayed or rotted unless you've been gnawing at the ropes behind my back. But why did it have to be you and not someone else?'

'Just one of those things, Emma. Wrong time, wrong place.'

'Like at Grayson's that first time we met there? I turned my back for five minutes and when I came back it was a scene of total carnage. Are you seriously telling me you had nothing to do with that?'

Olly looked into her eyes. She had seen through him and wanted the truth and he knew that if he sidestepped the issue she would never trust him again and any hope of a long-term relationship would be out of the question. 'I left the table to catch a child's toy. I didn't see the waiter who was carrying the birthday cake but I don't think he could see where he was going with all those candles in the way.'

'But if you'd have stayed in your seat, the pandemonium that followed wouldn't have happened?'

'Probably not. Hard to say.'

'And was the cracked glass in Chappie's just 'one of those things' when I came back from the loo and you'd spilt wine all over your trousers?'

Olly took a breath. The last thing he wanted was for Emma to reel off a list of all the unfortunate incidents that were jockeying for position at the forefront of her mind now she had been alerted to the fact that he'd been covering up his unseen talent for domino calamity since the day they met. 'I do have moments when things don't always go according to plan. Sometimes I can put it down to a lack of concentration, at other times there's no real explanation, accidents just happen.'

Emma looked crestfallen as if this was a revelation she did not want to hear, despite her suspicions. She sat in silence for a disquieting few moments before she retrieved the crutches and stood. 'As you said, it could have been worse, so best to forget it. It's been a hell of a morning and I need a lie-down.'

'But we're okay? You and me?'

'Why wouldn't we be?'

Why wouldn't we be? Olly could think of a multitude of reasons. In a matter of moments, he had single-handedly turned her world upside down, caused her to be in fear for her life, assault a neighbour, slice a gash in her foot which had forced her to dose herself up on painkillers, use crutches that restricted her movements, and now had the possibility of facing the future with a man whose actions were entirely unpredictable. Little wonder she needed a lie-down. He could do with one himself, although a side-by-side arrangement might not be entirely welcomed right now.

He had to hope that the look of despondency on her face as she hobbled off to the bedroom was not a reflection of terminal disappointment in him, nor an indication that she would be reconsidering their planned, more permanent, living-in arrangement at a time when he needed her love and support more than ever.

ABSENCE

It became evident the next morning after Emma had risen early to return to her apartment to oversee the decorators, that without ongoing help, life for Olly could not continue with its previously accepted continuity. Since it was vital he attended all rehearsals for *One Way Ticket*, with its constantly evolving choreography and coordination of lights, sound and performers, Philippa agreed that he should effectively live in, utilising the loo, showers, kitchenette and a prop bed that was earmarked for the Twickenham set. This short-circuited the problem of him having to travel between home and theatre and since he needed someone to be on hand to assist with mundane tasks for the majority of the time, Philippa engaged a trainee theatre assistant along with a deputy stage manager called Clare who worked a staggered schedule to alleviate some of the pressure. With a complicated handover between the two plays imminent, it was a sensible option that Olly was in full agreement with.

For two weeks rehearsals continued with an intensity Olly had not witnessed before due to Philippa constantly changing entrances and exits, upstage positions, downstage positions and even amending some of the actors' lines because she felt they lacked impact or humour. By the end of February, the crew set about dismantling the *Shadows* set on completion of its run and spent three days constructing the four main sets for *Ticket*. To complicate matters, Philippa had decided that David's character should be kept busy during April's trips to Glasgow building a wall of shelves and cupboards to house books and ornaments as a set-up for a pay-off in the final act, an initiative that Clare immediately queried with Olly.

'How are we meant to replace the single living room set during six turnarounds when we're short of storage space?'

'We're not replacing the entire set, just building it up between scenes with interlocking sections. They're small units, all numbered, so we just truck them into position. They'll be marked on the scripts so it won't be a problem.'

'And this is for comic effect, not just to refresh the background?'

'Comic effect, yes. David is inept at constructing anything that isn't prone to fall apart, so as he builds the furniture we build the tension because the audience realises where this is heading even if David and April don't. It's a good idea so it'll be worth the hassle. We can run the transitions through together once the construction team deliver the sections.'

'Then I'll liaise with Betty to make sure the prop table's moved to give us a clearer working space.'

Olly nodded in agreement. Clare was an experienced stage manager who asked sensible, constructive questions, made sure all the angles were covered and had quickly established herself as an essential part of the team. The only noticeable absence from this pre-production period was Emma, whom Olly had not had contact with since the morning after the get-together at Grayson's and she had not made a single appearance to supervise the sets and props due, Philippa informed him, to other commitments. What these could possibly be was a mystery to Olly since she had not given any indication to him that other projects required her attention. He had assumed that she was committed to supervising the handover as a contractual obligation, even though they had never discussed it.

'She was on a rolling contract,' Philippa explained when he questioned her. 'After the initial engagement period, she could leave at short notice if she wanted to.'

'But we haven't even had a technical rehearsal let alone a dress run,' said a mystified Olly. 'How can she abandon the project at such a critical stage?'

Philippa could see he was troubled and not simply at a professional level. 'I'd have thought you could answer that better than me. I agree it's not ideal but we have extensive ground plans and a model set, and Emma did oversee the set construction and liaise with Betty over prop allocation. It would be the same situation if she was taken ill or indisposed in some way.'

Olly couldn't argue with that. Every other department had back-up, the actors had stand-ins, and even he had been assigned an assistant because the unpredictability of reality over make-believe was a determining factor in maintaining stability in what was, at the end of the day, a business venture. Nevertheless, he was concerned that his behaviour had caused Emma to make a radical decision to cut all ties with both him and TopLite, which in his view was an unnecessary knee-jerk reaction that needed remedying as quickly as possible.

He still had limited mobility, which meant attempting any form of contact was difficult, and although Betty was the obvious direct line of communication, he was aware that her loyalty to Emma might prove to be a compromising stumbling block and he had no wish to implicate such a valid colleague in any conflict of interest between business and his personal problems. In desperation, having received no response to his emails, he enlisted Clare's help in making a couple of cursory calls to Emma's phone, the first receiving no reply, the second an unobtainable signal. She clearly did not want to be found.

When he returned to the apartment at the end of the third week, the bandages had been removed, he had feeling back in his fingers, and thankfully Felix had returned from Paris, although Amelia had not come back with him as she had flown on to Bermuda to film a commercial for an exotic Babadoo Cocktail utilising her juggling skills as a mixologist at a beachside bar. There were no signs that Emma had ever been at the apartment, however. No spare clothes, toothbrush or toiletries.

'So she just upped and left?' asked a puzzled Felix.

'It wasn't quite as dramatic as that,' said Olly, playing down her disappearance. 'She was upset after the sash-cord window incident and needed time to think.'

'That was three weeks ago, how much time does she need? It was only an accident, Olly. An accident of some magnitude, I grant you, but I'd have thought she'd be more supportive and understanding.'

Olly thought so too but he wasn't inclined to cast judgement until he'd had an opportunity to confront her and find out why she had reacted so badly.

'Have you been round there?'

'To her apartment?'

'Yes, that's the first place I'd look.'

'With bandaged hands, a frantic rehearsal period and serious lack of mobility I haven't had much of a chance, Felix.'

'But now you don't have any excuses. If you don't want to lose her you need to do something positive.'

Excuses. Is that why he'd been so passive since she left? Was he afraid to face the truth? Was his deception so unforgivable that a trust had been broken that was now irretrievable? Felix was right. He should go and see her, show he cared enough to put up a fight, ask her not to let something so valuable slip from their grasp.

Portland Place was unnaturally quiet when Olly cycled up to Emma's apartment, as if the neighbours had been alerted to his impending arrival and sworn an oath not to reveal Emma Appleby's whereabouts on pain of death. The place was in darkness, with no lights evident, and there was no reply when he rang the doorbell, despite repeated attempts. There was no sign of a builder or a decorator, or any tradesmen's vans parked nearby. Emma's car stood in its usual place, but that was no indication she was at home since when he last saw her it was unlikely she could have driven with one of her feet bandaged, which meant she could be just about anywhere.

He cycled back down to the seafront, stopping outside Jungle Rumble to gather his thoughts, remembering that when he was last here, he had seen Emma with the elusive Finn Pedersen laughing and joking at the Yellowave Beach Café. Is that where she went? To Sweden to take up his offer of working on weird theatrical presentations with upside-down actors and animals wandering willy-nilly about the stage rather than see *One Way Ticket* through to a successful run despite all the obstacles they'd had to overcome? Or did the lure of a West End musical prove too much? Was this one of her 'other commitments' and if so, why had she never told him about it? Then he remembered how hesitant she had been when they went to bed the evening before the sash-cord disaster, as if she had something on her mind but didn't know how to tell him. He could hardly accuse her of keeping important information from him that might affect their relationship when he was just as culpable, so no matter how he looked at it, rough justice had been served despite the unfairness of it all.

But perhaps it wasn't too late. He wondered briefly if he should pay an impromptu visit to Emma's parents. If it was not a professional pursuit that had caused her to take off, the most obvious retreat would be Blackberry Farmhouse despite all the worry and irrationality that it brought to her measured existence; the kind of convenient magnet that draws each of us to the hub of emotional uncertainty when instinct tells us we should exercise caution, whatever affection we might have for those who are closest to us.

At least arrangements had been made for Barry to lock away the lawnmower and hedge-trimmer and an electrician had visited the site to make the barn safe, so there was no longer a serious threat to life, even though Sylvia still had access to knives and an electric cooker and Norman might yet find a way to electrocute himself.

But if a civilised discussion were to suddenly evolve into a battlefield of remorse and accusation, Sylvia and Norman's gentle, dignified haven would not be an appropriate setting for him and Emma to resolve their issues and so he dismissed the idea, committed to letting destiny play its part as it had done since the first day he had met the woman he adored above all others but who was slowly slipping beyond reach.

After *One Way Ticket* had staged its opening night in early April, numerous preview performances followed that allowed Philippa to fine-tune the production in advance of the all-important press night. For both she and Olly, it was a learning experience like no other as they gauged audience reaction during each show which differed depending on the demographic and whether it was a matinee or an evening performance. Timing was paramount, both technically and in the choreography of movement on stage, the most surprising discovery being the difference in reaction when an actor stood in one spot as opposed to another, for some unaccountable reason the line being funnier when their position on stage was a variance sometimes of just a few feet.

The majority of the audiences did not seem bothered by issues of morality, ego, ambition or political correctness, or the narrative being primarily about changing attitudes in the twenty-first century. It was just a bloody good laugh at the expense of characters who were caught in the absurd, implausible world of stereotypes and preposterous misunderstandings. The media was more divided in its opinions, some critics being annoyed at the manipulation of David and Duncan as two supposedly intelligent individuals who were not bright enough to see they were being used, whilst others applauded the unfolding saga as a delightful exercise in a study of modern values entangled in a mix of humour, intrigue and dramatic tension. When would this accelerating train of events slide off the rails? When would April's devious exploitation be found out? What would be the devastating impact on all their lives when it was?

The discovery by April that she is pregnant comes as no surprise and intensifies the dramatic denouement because the big question remained: is it barrister Donald's or the blundering jack-of-all-trades chancer, David, and what genetic influences might determine whether the road ahead is likely to be smooth and rewarding or a nightmare of chaos and disaster?

Whilst audiences and critics differed on this open-ended conclusion, many were pleased that they had been accorded the opportunity to make up their minds as to who the father might be, piecing together possible clues relative to behaviour and geographical possibility as they tracked back through the story. A pointless exercise since it could have been either man, but if the play made people laugh and its ending generated discussion and debate, *One Way Ticket* was guaranteed to run on schedule through the spring season and into the summer. Olly's only disappointment was that Emma had not been able to witness the results of their joint efforts in bringing the play to fruition, even though they had both been sceptical about its staging, convinced that it was a flawed piece of theatre for which an inconclusive ending did not disguise the momentous, life-changing consequences for the characters.

UNEXPECTED

Once the fine-tuning had been completed and the production ran with smooth efficiency, Olly was able to step back to allow Clare to stage-manage many of the performances without him needing to make any input. Leaving her to supervise a matinee performance one Saturday afternoon, he returned to the apartment to find Felix slumped in the sitting room looking uncharacteristically glum.

'Everything okay?' he asked, thinking Felix might be encountering difficulties with his short play programme.

'Not great,' he replied, without elaboration.

'Want to talk about it?'

'Not really, but since it's you.'

Olly sat opposite him, realising that this was more of a personal problem than anything to do with the forthcoming theatre programme. 'Amelia,' he said without wasting time side-stepping the issue.

Felix nodded. 'The agency loved the cocktail ad. They want to film another six while the crew are still at the location.'

'That's good, isn't it?'

'Yes, except the Bermuda tourist board's keen for her to film a promotion for the summer season and the pilot she shot in Paris has been commissioned for a series so she'll have to fly back there for read-throughs.'

'They've developed the scripts already?'

'The pilot was a formality, they've been ready to go into full production for months. Just needed an official green light.'

This was not so good news since Felix now had to choose whether he would stay in Brighton or join Amelia in Paris.

'She'll need time to settle in, Felix. You don't need to make any hasty decisions.'

'I would have to at some point, Olly, whether it's now or next month. It's not a problem that's going away.'

Olly could see the anguish on his face. Amelia would not be coming back to England any time soon, which meant Felix's options were limited. 'Have you thought about what you would do in Paris? Finding work if you don't speak the language will be tricky.'

'It's not practical whichever way you look at it. Even if I learned French there's no guarantee I could develop my career there and I don't want to have to rely on Amelia to keep us in croissants and onion soup forever.'

It seemed that Felix had already come to a decision. 'So you'll stay in the UK?'

'I don't have a choice. She's young and in demand, with the world at her feet. I can't be responsible for standing in her way.'

'So when will you tell her?'

'We've already discussed it, but she insists we can make it work even if it means turning down the series.'

Olly felt sad that two of his dearest friends had arrived at such an impasse. Amelia adored Felix but unless he took the difficult decision to sever the ties, neither could move forward. 'So that's it?'

Felix leaned forward and put his head in his hands. 'I don't see any other way. If I don't put an end to it now we'll just carry on without facing the inevitable.'

It was a heart-wrenching declaration of selflessness that was typical of Felix and his pain was obvious. Here was Olly's closest friend, deeply in love with his woman, yet prepared to sacrifice everything they had so she could move on and not have regrets; a friend who had stood by him since they were boys, pulling him from a river after he had fallen in, replacing his pitiful misshapen poker with his own near-perfect creation, taking the blame for the firework that almost set his dad's study on fire, standing up to the school bullies when he was threatened, and consoling him when the other pupils made fun of his predisposition for creating unprecedented havoc. Felix needed his support and he needed it now.

'I'm sorry, Felix, I know how much she means to you. It may not be as hopeless as it seems but whatever happens, I'll always be here for you and we've enough to keep us occupied down here for the summer.'

Felix forced a smile in acknowledgement of Olly's encouragement for a friendship that would never need validating. It was a bond that had survived endless close calls, based on trust and loyalty in an enduring alliance.

Their reflections on the impact of the emotional upheaval on Felix's life were interrupted by a ring at the doorbell. Visitors were rare in the early evening, so

Olly peeked out of the window, turning to Felix with a confused look.

'It's my parents. What are *they* doing here?'

Felix looked immediately guilty. 'Ah. Yes. Your mum rang this morning to ask if everything was okay, how the play was going, and how you were. I told her your hands were healing nicely, not realising you hadn't told her about the accident.'

'Oh, shit.' Olly walked to the front door, hesitated for a moment and then opened it, knowing he had no option but to face the predictable inquisition.

'Hello, Olly. Sorry to call by unannounced,' said Helen apologetically.

'Don't tell me - you were just passing.'

'Don't be silly. All the way from Romford? We decided it was time to pay you a visit.'

'You don't need a reason to be here,' said Olly, standing back and waving a hand to welcome them inside. 'It's good to see you.'

As they entered the living room, Helen looked around approvingly. With Emma only having recently vacated the apartment, the boys had not had time to re-trash the place, with socks, T-shirts, jackets and takeaway cartons not currently on display to offend the casual visitor. Felix stood, ready to extend a hand that was trumped by Helen descending on him with the warmest of hugs. 'Felix, how are you?'

'Very well, Mrs Scott. I wasn't expecting to see you so soon.'

'We've been thinking about coming to Brighton for a while. For a short break. And I did promise Olly we would see one of his plays.'

'You've booked seats?' enquired Olly, hopeful they hadn't yet made a commitment to any of the performances.

'For tonight, yes. I enjoy a good comedy. Your father not so much.'

'Takes a lot to make me laugh,' said Martin, 'especially with these alternative comics rubbishing everything, taking the piss out of all the things we used to appreciate and value.'

Olly could only concur with his father's enduring sense of humour failures. These days Martin rarely smiled, chuckled or guffawed, usually being on high alert if someone was about to make a conversational faux pas in mixed company, be prone to errors of judgement - mainly political - or if an apostrophe had been placed somewhere in a sentence when it wasn't needed. In many ways Olly blamed himself for his father's insecurity on his own erratic behaviour since his antics as a child must have put a strain on both of them.

'And we were looking forward to meeting Emma,' said Helen, steering the conversation in a direction that caused Olly to instantly panic, since he had not had time to think up a credible excuse for Emma not being there.

'She's away at the moment,' was all he could offer. 'A work thing.'

'Well that's a disappointment,' said Helen, studying Olly's face for any clues as to whether 'a work thing' was a reasonable explanation for her absence. It seemed so vague when what Helen really wanted was detail. 'I was keen to have a chat, to get to know her.'

'You will,' said Olly, desperate to placate her suspicions and move the pleasantries along. 'We've all been busy during the transition between the two plays and we don't live in each other's pockets. I'll let her know that you're down for a few days.'

Helen removed her coat and lay it on the sofa arm, content to accept the explanation and deciding not to turn her questions into an interrogation about Olly's private life. 'So. Show me.'

'Show you?'

'Your hands. Show me your hands.'

Olly held out his hands.

'Well they look okay, I was expecting worse.'

'Bloody dangerous those sash-cords, you could have lost them both,' added Martin.

Helen cast him a look that suggested he wasn't being helpful and looked back at Olly. 'Wiggle your fingers.'

Olly obliged by wiggling his fingers.

'And you're not in any pain?'

'No. I was when it happened but not now.'

'So why didn't you tell me?'

'I didn't want to worry you.'

'I wouldn't have worried if you'd told me. These things happen. It's not always necessary for me to have a knee-jerk reaction.'

'Seriously? You found out this morning – and yet here you are.'

'As I said, we needed a break and we wanted to see your play. Well *I* did.'

'I think that's a terrific idea,' said Felix, deciding it was time to lighten the mood. 'Tea or coffee, Mrs Scott?'

'Tea, thank you, Felix.'

'Coffee for me,' said Martin, walking over to the window and giving it the once-over.

'It's been repaired with new rope,' Olly assured him. 'Cotton braided apparently.'

'It should last your tenure if you don't fiddle with it.'

'No, we'll try not to open and close it,' countered Olly, with uncharacteristic sarcasm. Martin ignored the remark, inspecting the rest of the room with a critical eye. 'First chance I've had to see the apartment. I was only able to view it online but it looks in excellent decorative order.'

'Yes,' agreed Olly, 'it was a good choice. The window was just an unfortunate incident. Everywhere else is safe enough.'

Martin almost broke into a smile as he punched Olly playfully on the shoulder. 'Nowhere's safe with you around, Olly.'

'Martin!' Helen gave Martin another reproachful look.

'He knows I'm only kidding, Helen. Lad can take a bit of ribbing.'

Olly smiled to reassure Helen that he was neither offended nor upset, because he recognised that Martin's remark was borne of years of frustration living on a knife edge of uncertainty. He had anticipated that the following years might relieve the anxiety for both of them and although this recent event proved that he could still be exposed to unforeseen calamities, he hoped that while they were on a flying visit he would not have to worry them with any more surprises.

'We're staying at the Queensbury by the way,' said Helen as they joined Felix in the kitchen to help organise the refreshments, 'so no need to concern yourselves about sleeping arrangements or us getting under your feet.'

'I'm just pleased to see you, Mrs Scott, and you really should make the most of being here. Do you have any plans other than seeing the show?'

'Take in the sights, walk along the beach, sample the seafood, and we thought we might have dinner together one evening. Maybe invite Emma and her parents. They live locally, don't they?'

'They do, yes, Polegate.'

'I think they're away,' said Olly in an attempt to quash such a possibility whilst trying to conceal the alarm in his voice. The thought of both sets of parents sitting together in a restaurant lamenting how times had changed and trading stories of how they have adapted to life now their children had left home sent warning bells ringing in every fibre of his body. Helen's preoccupation with making costumes for parties and school plays, Martin's obsession with global threats to our security, Sylvia's misplaced talent for producing inedible cakes and wonky teapots and Norman's passion for model railways and all the pointless trivia that accompanied it were the stuff of nightmares. That and the risk of them divulging too much information about Emma and Olly's childhood peculiarities that were best left unsaid and laid to rest. 'Another time. I'll set something up for you to meet when you're next down. I'm sure there'll be some fun events taking place during the summer.'

Helen acknowledged Olly's offer with a smile and turned her attention to pouring the tea. She thought it odd that neither Emma nor her parents were around even though they lived in the area but accepted that it was early days and Olly probably needed more time to get to know them before arranging get-togethers. 'We should come down more often. It seems a very vibrant and interesting place. You must be pleased you made this decision.'

'We are,' agreed Felix, dismissing any notion of revealing how unfulfilling his life was now that Amelia was in Paris, whilst Olly concurred with Helen's brief assessment of Brighton life with an enthusiastic nod, hoping his misfortune at being locked out on a cold winter's night, creating an inferno at Grayson's, cracking a wineglass in Chappie's, cutting his finger at supper, or anything else that might cause her to bundle him into the car and whisk him back to Romford on a critical rescue mission could be put on hold until after she had said her goodbyes and was safely on her way on the other side of the M25.

'In the meantime, we have a play to see,' she added enthusiastically, 'and if the reviews are anything to go by, we're in for a real treat.'

'That's one way of looking at it,' said Olly, conceding that aside from an earthquake or a tsunami unexpectedly hitting the south coast, there was no way of stopping them from attending that evening's performance.

The usual pre-show audience buzz was made all the tenser with Helen and Martin seated in the auditorium, particularly with his mother's expectations being so high, but Olly reasoned that every TopLite production brought with it an element of surprise, often breaking new ground, and it was pointless trying to shield them from the more controversial content. They were grown-ups, the play represented their son's passion and commitment to the performing arts, of which accolades and criticism were an accepted part, and it was unlikely there was much that could upset or shock them unless it posed any personal threat.

He risked the occasional glance at them from his position backstage, pleased to see that Helen was lapping it up and laughing at the appropriate moments, whilst Martin sat poker-faced throughout, doubtless formulating a protest letter in his head to rattle off to Philippa once he had access to his laptop.

In the interval he caught up with them in the foyer to ask if the play was meeting their expectations.

'Technically excellent,' said Martin as he sipped his coffee. 'Co-ordination of lights and set changes very impressive.'

No mention of the storyline itself or the performances, although Helen had some observations to make. 'The mother and father are a bit over the top, but they are funny and it is a comedy so I suppose we have to suspend our disbelief. On the other hand, I love the way Veronica handles the two men. Classic male egotism put to the sword.'

'You don't find that deceitful or immoral?'

'Of course, but I suppose it has to be that way to emphasise how weak they are. Veronica has complete command of the situation, although we all know there will be consequences at the end.'

'There will – but it's the character of April who'll have to face the result of her actions, not Veronica. She's an actress who happens to be playing her part.'

'Yes, of course, but she's so *good* at it. So believable.'

Olly left them to finish their coffee, relieved that neither were offended by the play's darker undertones that were gaining momentum, but interested to discover that his mother's instincts had led her to confuse fiction with reality in respect of the female lead. Viola de Lesseps, it seemed, was exacting fitting revenge on her male counterparts for being banned from playing strong female characters unless she could find a way to outwit the men, and Veronica Stone had managed to fast-track her personal brand of twenty-first-century girl power to make sure the message struck home.

As Olly was about to return to his post backstage he passed a familiar face.

'Chris! How are you doing?'

Chris Okoro stopped as soon as he recognised Olly's voice. 'I'm fine, Olly. And thanks for the invite. Very enjoyable. Lovely venue.'

'Then I hope to see you here more often. I wanted to apologise for that unfortunate incident but I've been a bit tied up - and incapacitated.' He held up his restored hands. 'I really am sorry though. Emma was mortified.'

'Forget it. I saw her this morning and told her not to worry, so she knows I won't be suing her for aggravated assault since that charge could equally be levelled at me.'

'You spoke to her? Where was this?'

'I bumped into her on the promenade. She's walking normally again so it looks as if we're all on the mend.'

Olly gave him a half smile. They weren't all on the mend just yet. There was still some serious patching up to do. 'That's good to hear. Enjoy the rest of the show.'

He hurried backstage to where the prop table was set up to find Clare replenishing it for the second act. 'Clare, where's Betty?'

'She had to leave, some kind of emergency. She made sure everything was ready to go, so no panic.'

'Right. Good.' He ran through his options, deciding that the rest of the play would be in safe hands if he left the theatre. 'Can you stage-manage the second half? I know it's asking a lot since you supervised the matinee and I appreciate that, but I need to go somewhere.'

Clare looked mystified. 'Okay. Not a problem, but is there something I should know? No mass evacuation imminent?'

'No, it's personal, loose ends I need to sort before it's too late.'

'If it's that important you should go, Olly. It's never good to leave loose ends.'

SHOWDOWN

The cycle ride to Portland Place took an eternity, everything on the roads and pavements passing by in a blur. Olly's focus was to speak with Emma before she disappeared again since she may only have returned to her apartment to pack up essentials and vacate, having found somewhere else to live. She had not been in contact since they had returned from the hospital together, had not answered any of his voice messages and texts, and although he had an overwhelming sense of guilt about leaving Clare to stage-manage, it was vital he did not allow Emma to slip through his fingers again.

He dumped the bike against the railings, aware that there were several tradesmen's vans parked along the road, and peered in through the windows. The place was in darkness as it was before, but he could hear various clanks, bangs and unidentifiable sounds coming from inside, so he rang the doorbell. When the door finally opened he was greeted by someone he had not expected, carrying a pair of large bath towels and wearing a head torch.

'Betty! What are *you* doing here?'

Betty stared at him as if she had been caught red-handed committing a misdemeanour for which she had no explanation, the torch lighting up his face to give him a scary appearance that was compounded by the anxious look on his face.

'Emma had an emergency. She needed some help.'

'What kind of an emergency?'

The banging and clanking emanating from the kitchen answered his question, along with a thin trickle of water that he could see seeping into the hallway.

'Jesus, Betty, what happened?'

He followed the undesirable riverlet into the kitchen, where a pair of legs could be seen sticking out from under the sink, illuminated by a camping lamp and two candles. 'Be finished in a jiffy,' said a voice from under the sink, followed by two more bangs and the rotation of a spanner.

'That's Jason. Came at short notice. Not sure what we would have done without him,' said Betty, throwing the bath towels over the floor to soak up the water.

'But why did he need to be here in the first place? Did the pipe burst?'

'Not exactly. The tap started dripping so Emma tried to fix it with a wrench.'

'That doesn't sound sensible. Has she used a wrench before?'

'It would appear not. She didn't want to call a plumber unless it was necessary.'

Olly ignored the illogicality of the remark. He clicked the wall light switch a couple of times but to no avail and looked questioningly at Betty.

'The circuit's fused. She had an accident putting up a painting.'

Olly had no words, so he waited for Betty to turn and lead him to the problem. They squelched together into the living room, where an electrician was rewiring a damaged cable in the wall behind a large crack.

'This is Bernie. Luckily he was doing some work in a house across the street.'

Olly looked aghast at the crack and the severed cable. 'She didn't try to repair this herself, did she?'

'No, Olly, she's accident-prone, not someone with a death wish.'

'Are these isolated incidents? Are the other rooms okay?' Without waiting for a reply, he walked down the hallway and peered into the toilet, stopping to inspect three large cracks in the ceiling.

'Spider. Enormous one she said. Chased it over the ceiling and squashed it with a broom handle.'

He moved on to the study, where rows of shelves had collapsed onto the floor, the books and ornaments scattered over the carpet.

'I told her she should have used plasterboard wall plugs, not the regular ones.'

Olly looked at the mess in disbelief. Emma Appleby could design a theatre set but hadn't the foggiest idea how to put up a painting or a row of shelves. 'That's ridiculous, she's been supervising huge set builds at TopLite for weeks without any mishaps.'

Betty sat down in the study chair, accepting that her friend had been rumbled. 'Yes, but she always supervises the installations from the stalls. Emma never goes anywhere near the backdrops, or any areas where there are paint pots, nail guns or spray pumps.'

Olly was dumbfounded. This was the last thing he expected to find inside Emma's apartment. No wonder she had never invited him in. 'Where is she now, in the bedroom assembling a set of wardrobes?'

'No, she'd forgotten to stock up on supplies while she was away so she's made a trip to the mini-mart.'

He glanced at the notice board which was lit by a single flickering candle on the desk, his eyes alighting on a photograph of Betty and Emma smiling at the camera, Emma sporting a red rash all over her face. 'Why is her face all red?'

'Nettle rash. New Year's Day. You went for a walk together in the park and she went into some bushes to retrieve a child's ball.'

He studied the picture in suppressed horror. 'And that's the reason she didn't turn up for work for five days?'

'Yes,' said a dispirited Betty.

'What about the day she missed the first tech rehearsal for Shadows? I was told that was the result of a domestic situation.'

'The bathroom handle fell off when she tried to get out and she found herself locked in.'

'All day?'

'Most of it. She forced the window open eventually and managed to call out to a neighbour when she went into the garden to hang out her washing. The neighbour called the fire brigade.'

'And this old school photo,' said Olly, running his finger over the image of happy smiling pupils. 'Connington High. Isn't that where the art department burned down some years back?

Betty stared back at him, not sure how to respond.

'Oh, please tell me it wasn't her.'

'It was an accident, an unfortunate incident.'

'One they blamed on a bunch of unruly pupils indulging in an act of premeditated vandalism.'

'Emma's no more a vandal than you or I, Olly. She'd been cleaning a piece of stained glass for a set she'd designed for the school play but left it propped up on a piece of fabric underneath a fanlight window during the lunch break. When it was exposed to the sun's rays the fabric must have caught fire.'

'Didn't she explain that to anyone?'

'No, and she's lived with the guilt ever since. I'm the only one she's told.'

Olly was rendered momentarily speechless but as someone who had gained notoriety as an arsonist at the age of five, he was hardly in a position to pass judgement. It explained why she was so uneasy when the table caught fire at Grayson's and was so opposed to creating a fire on the set of *One Way Ticket*, and so concerned that her father's barn was in danger of being burnt down through his carelessness.

His mind flashed back to other incidents that put Emma's problem into perspective, the significance of which he had been blissfully unaware. The heel of her shoe coming off after they had left Grayson's, forcing her to walk back home in stockinged feet; the frightening moment she veered into the road on her bicycle into the path of an oncoming car. And could she say in all honesty it was not her fault when they chinked glasses at Chappie's and he was drenched in wine?

'I had no idea, Betty. Never understood why she kept disappearing. I thought she was unsure about the two of us being together.'

'I don't think that's ever been in question, Olly, but maybe it's best she doesn't know you came round. Give her time to sort this mess out.'

'But is she planning to stay or move on?'

'She's made an expensive commitment to the place so as far as I know she's staying here until she's had a chance to assess the situation, so there's no need for either of you to decide what to do until you've talked.'

'But she has to know that *I* know, Betty. We have to face up to this at some point.'

'Of course. But do you want to do that right now?'

A key turning in the lock decided for them, as Emma entered the hallway wearing an oversized shabby jumper and threadbare jeans and carrying a large brown paper bag. Her eyes had lost their sparkle and she wore no makeup but to Olly, she was the same vision of loveliness that had left a gaping hole in his life and he had missed more than words could ever convey. She glanced along the hallway and saw him framed against the study door, backlit by the flickering candle. 'Olly!'

The bottom of the bag collapsed, spilling the contents onto the floor, including a carton of cream and a box of eggs. 'Shit, the cream must have leaked.'

'Don't worry about it,' said Olly, scooping up the three unbroken eggs and dropping them back into their box, 'it can happen to anyone.'

While Betty dashed off to fetch a sponge and bucket, Emma looked in dismay down the hallway at the water-soaked carpet. 'I was hoping they would have sorted everything by now.'

'They're nearly done,' said Olly to reassure her as he picked up a bunch of bananas, some cheese and a tin of beans, 'Jason and Bernie have it under control.'

'My God, it sounds as if you've been project managing.'

'Not quite, but I would have made them a cup of tea if the kettle had been working.'

Emma sighed and walked through to the kitchen with Olly following at a discreet distance, aware that she may not be in the best of moods for any discussion about how each of them had not been entirely honest with the other.

'Shouldn't you be at the theatre?' she asked, dumping the soggy brown bag despairingly into the bin.

'I should, yes, but I thought it more important I should be here.'

'How did you know I was back?'

'I ran into Chris Okoro. He said he'd seen you. I'm glad your foot's healed.'

'Yes, I can walk into all kinds of disasters now,' she replied without a trace of humour.

'These aren't disasters, Emma, they're the occasional accidents that everyone has.'

'Some more than most.'

'Of course, but maybe some people experience a more concentrated intrusion of them in their lives, their mishaps spread over a longer period.'

Emma's face morphed into a look of disbelief. 'How long have you been dreaming up that excuse? It doesn't even *sound* plausible.'

'It's perfectly plausible if you don't let being clumsy dictate your life - and I should know. Most things are under your control. I've seen how you can organise the most complex projects and supervise set builds.' He broke off when he noticed a large ground plan for *One Way Ticket* pinned to the kitchen wall. 'Look at the research you do, the lengths you go to, the attention to detail.' He walked over to the plan for a closer look but noticed that alongside illustrations of the sets themselves were photographs of the actors with other photographs stuck randomly over the top of them. Over April's stage mother was a photograph of Sylvia, her own mother. Over April's stage father, a photograph of Norman with his train set. And, more disturbingly, over a photograph of David the bungling partner, was a photograph from the theatre programme of Olly himself. He turned to face Emma, his face filled with confusion. And he looked hurt.

'Is that how you see us, Emma? Is that the reason you dislike this play so much? Because everything in it is too close to the truth? People that perplex you, behave erratically, let you down because you don't understand what motivates them or because they don't live up to expectation?'

Emma seemed lost for words. She was not prepared for him to appear out of the blue with this line of questioning when her spirits were down and she was struggling to find answers.

'I'm going back to the theatre,' interrupted Betty, as she emptied the dirty water into the sink. 'I'm more use there than I am here now. Will you be okay, Em?'

'Yes, you go. And thanks, Betty.' She turned back to Olly as Betty left. 'I'm surprised you think I might not be committed to those close to me. They mean everything.'

'I'm not doubting your commitment to those you care about, Emma. Your compassion's obvious whenever we're in the company of friends and family, as is your passion and dedication to every show we've worked on.' He indicated a scan pinned next to the other photographs. 'Even to the point of mocking up a scan of April's pregnancy, which is beyond most people's devotion to a production.'

'The work we do can often move us too close to our personal truths, Olly.'

'Then we have to find a way to detach ourselves. Life doesn't necessarily mirror art, Emma.'

Emma did not respond. She stood in silence, hardly daring to speak.

He turned to face her and he saw the look. 'What?'

She opened her mouth but the words wouldn't come and he became instantly aware of her distress.

'What? What is it?'

'It's not April's scan, Olly. It's mine. Ours.'

'Ours?'

'Yes. Yours and mine. Two boys and a girl. I'm sorry.'

Olly wasn't sure whether to laugh or cry. It had been one revelation after another, culminating in a disclosure that now knocked him sideways and he could only stand motionless before the woman he loved and try to understand how his life, the one that he thought could not become more complicated or challenging, had blown up in his face in the space of just a few minutes. The room was unnervingly silent, save for the banging coming from the kitchen as Jason the plumber knocked the cupboard under the sink back into place.

Two miles away, on the stage at TopLite, April asks David to stop hammering the final section of his shelving, and as he stands and looks at it admiringly, she informs him that she is pregnant. Even though she cannot confirm that he is the father, the news comes as such a shock that he faints and falls backwards onto the rows of cabinets and cupboards that he has been painstakingly constructing throughout the play, resulting in the set collapsing into a pile of rubble. Philippa's visual metaphor for his familiar world falling apart is a concept the audience immediately acknowledges as the theatre vibrates to raucous laughter - a reaction, perhaps, that human beings engage in as a protection mechanism when the pitfalls of life are happening, by the grace of God, to someone else and not to them.

The lights are snapped off and as the stage area is plunged into darkness, a train crash is heard somewhere in the distance.

The lights click into life in Emma's apartment as the electricity is turned back on to reveal an equally shocked Olly easing himself onto a stool as he absorbs the news. While for him this is no laughing matter, he would doubtless appreciate the dramatic irony of how two identical situations can be funny in one place but not so funny in another.

'You're sure about this?'

'You mean are they yours? Yes. There hasn't been anyone else.'

'But why do you say you're sorry?'

'Because I wasn't sure if it's what you'd want. It's a serious commitment.'

'I don't think there's anything I'd want more. I want us to commit.'

'Despite the obvious drawbacks?'

'Drawbacks?'

'The fact that we're both prodigiously accident-prone. You don't see that as a potential stumbling block?'

'In us raising three children?'

'That, yes. And the possibility of one or two hereditary complications.'

Olly had an immediate vision of the two boys spilling milk and custard over their sister's head and running over her dolls with their tricycles. 'It doesn't necessarily follow, Emma. I don't recall my parents or any other family member being involved in regular catastrophes.'

'But it is possible.'

'Is that why you went away? Because you didn't think we could share a future if they had our genes?'

'I stayed with Betty for a few days and then went out to find work that I could do from home because it would be impossible to carry on doing what I'm doing with three children to look after.'

'But that assumes I wouldn't be there to help.'

'You have your own career, Olly. I couldn't ask you to sacrifice that.'

'We all have to make sacrifices,' he said, thinking of Felix cutting his ties with Amelia so she could be a free agent and pursue her dreams. 'You have unfulfilled ambitions. That West End musical is still a possibility.'

Emma could see that his commitment to her was genuine and she took his hand to reaffirm her loyalty in case he thought for a single moment that she might sideline him and bring up their children without the need for his support. 'Not for now, Olly. Maybe not ever. A publisher is contracting me to write an illustrated book on theatre design, and another has asked for contributions for a planned part-work for amateur theatre.'

'But that's not what you do. You need to exercise your talents *inside* the theatre, that's the buzz, not sitting at a computer.'

She smiled. 'It doesn't matter how I'm involved – how *we* are involved - as long as one of us is actively taking part because we have to accept that we're not normal and compromise is going to be necessary.'

Not normal? Surely Emma didn't believe that. He thought of Felix's dad's dubious appearances on social media with his failed magical illusions, a man not certifiable but certainly delusional, and Mr Bradshaw at Packham Junior waving handkerchiefs and prodding sticks in the air, a perfectly respectable part of history dating back to the fifteenth century, even though its traditions mystified many, and Mr Sparks with his fixation for creating an epidemic of origami animals at Chase Hill and Finn Pedersen with his actors suspended from ceiling flats while hedgehogs roamed the stage beneath. Not to mention the several million eccentrics whose weird and wonderful obsessions are accorded courteous acceptance because which of us can honestly say we are not saddled with the odd quirk or two? Crazy or genius, it was the familiar, invisible line that runs between an immeasurable number of the world's population.

'There's no such species as normal, Emma. You and I are as well balanced as anyone and nobody has the right to challenge that or to categorise us in any way. We'll guide our children through every adventure and misadventure they experience as they make their way through life, doing our best to ensure they're never inhibited by the judgement of others.'

'They'll have minds of their own, Olly, influenced by all kinds of situations and all kinds of people. We can't always control the outcome.'

'As long as they show respect and compassion towards the less fortunate and those who suffer discrimination through no fault of their own, they won't go far wrong. It's a shared responsibility and it won't be easy, but it's a journey I want us to take together.'

Olly was moved by the tears that streamed down Emma's face and he held her in his arms and gripped her tightly to reassure her that nothing would ever come between them in a madcap world occupied by human beings who each carry their personal subtext of ambition and anxiety, because life is fragile, whoever you are.

He stared at the scan pinned to the ground plans with a mixture of trepidation and optimism for future generations, hopeful that they might have the resourcefulness and capacity to overcome the stumbling blocks that can derail all of us and drive us to behave in different and often inexplicable ways as we cope with both the unknown and the inevitable, whether by design or by accident.

For Olly Scott, the children he was yet to meet were the most terrifying and most beautiful accident of them all and he knew he would do everything in his power to make them proud of what they do and to ensure they would never feel disadvantaged in any way.

THE AUTHOR

Bob Harvey has worked on a diverse range of television programmes, from *The World at War* to *Horizon* and *The Spice of Life*. As a Writer/Director, his career has encompassed documentary, drama, children's, light entertainment and current affairs and includes *The Animal Magic Show, Olympic Hall of Fame, Timebusters* and *The Six O'Clock Show.* He wrote and directed *Stagestruck*, a series of workshops on the art and craft of theatre for the Discovery Channel, followed by a selection of network television commercials. His book *How to Make Your Own Video Or Short Film* was published in 2008, followed by *Falling Through Trapdoors, A Television Adventure*, published in 2020. In between broadcast assignments, he tutored film-making courses at Ravensbourne Media College and the Met Film School at Ealing Studios and in 2004 received a BAFTA for his directing work on BBC TV's *Raven* series.

Printed in Great Britain
by Amazon